VAPOR

Also By Amanda Filipacchi

Nude Men

VAPOR

a novel

Amanda Filipacchi

CARROLL & GRAF PUBLISHERS, INC.
NEW YORK

For their advice and encouragement, I am very grateful to Sondra Peterson, Melanie Jackson, Martine Bellen, Randy Dwenger, Andy Rasmussen, and Giulia Melucci. I would also like to thank Yaddo, where part of this book was written.

First Carroll & Graf edition 1999

Carroll & Graf Publishers, Inc.
19 West 21st Street
New York, NY 10010-6805

Library of Congress Cataloging-in-Publication Data is available.
ISBN: 0-7867-0617-1

Manufactured in the United States of America

For my parents, Sondra and Daniel
and in memory of my teacher and friend Ed Levy

Chapter One

For months I had been trying to be less myself. This effort extended to every aspect of my life, including my personal tastes and opinions. I wanted to be pliable like warm wax. I began to admire vague people, even weak and spineless ones, and ones who could be easily influenced, or better yet, who had not much of an opinion to start with, on anything.

My acting professor, Aaron Smith, had repeated to me many times that my problem with acting was that my personality was too strong, and that therefore I was unable to adopt a different one, or even a variety of emotions.

I took his words seriously. I believe the reason I followed Aaron Smith's advice with so much tenacity was partly out of stubbornness. He had provoked me, in a sense, and it was a challenge I was determined to meet, even though I had almost lost sight of the original and ultimate goal: it just so happened the only thing I cared about in life was becoming a great actress. Let me say right off that it was not necessarily for the fame and the glamour, but for more noble and worthwhile reasons that had to do with art and a fascination with, and love of, human behavior.

Today, like every month, I was having a meeting with this same professor in his office in school. But this time he was crushing me to bits. I listened to him, shocked.

"Anna," he was saying, "I advise you to switch career goals, and I'll be very blunt as to why. You're twenty-seven years old, you have a cute face, but it's by no means ravishing, and let's just say that the rest of your body does not make up for it. You could not be a leading lady."

I needed a cigarette, but the large No Smoking sign behind his desk stopped me from reaching into my bag for one.

Aaron then reiterated his usual criticism of me: I was myself too much. Or: I was too much myself. Same thing, but he always varied the wording a little, as if it would help me understand his concept better and I would do something about it.

As he continued talking, he got harsher and blunter. He went to the extreme this time. No ambiguity. It was a nightmare. He then made a strange request that was so unexpected and stupid, yet so humiliating despite its stupidity, that I tried to forget about it as soon as I left his office.

Chiara Mastroianni was standing outside the door, waiting to see him. I briefly said hi to her and hurried off. This particular student was a very good actor, which might have been partly due to the fact that she happened to be the daughter of Catherine Deneuve and Marcello Mastroianni, and therefore had acting in her genes. And it probably also helped to have been raised in that kind of actor's atmosphere.

I was not fortunate that way. My parents were fencers. My mother was a champion fencer and gave lessons. My father fenced well too, but he wasn't a champion, he was the super of an apartment building. My brother and I had been subjected to fencing since we were born, so we had no choice but to end up quite good at it. To my annoyance, communication in our family was achieved principally through this medium. We fenced to express anger, to play pranks, to tease, to irritate, to persuade, and even, in the most convoluted way, to express inexpressible love. (In addition, it was pretty obvious my parents had their own, private uses for fencing, not shared by the rest of the family: seduction and foreplay.) But I don't think it could be said, by any stretch of the imagination, that fencing was helpful to my acting. Except, I could play Zorro.

I walked in the street feeling annihilated and powerless. I bought myself a pair of sunglasses from a street vendor, to hide my crying.

Chiara was probably enjoying a splendid conference with Aaron Smith at this very moment. As for me, I never imagined conferences could get as bad as mine had.

Evidently my efforts at erasing my personality hadn't been successful. I hadn't tried hard enough. But how was that possible? I recalled numerous attempts at self-erasement, many of which occurred at my job at the Xerox shop, and also in my uncle's jewelry store, where I pierced ears part-time to help him out. My natural tendency was to have a rather bad temper when I was even just slightly provoked, and in my six years of ear piercing,

I had endured many dramas, many scenes, many fights. Ear piercing is a field rich in possible conflicts; there are an infinite number of potential causes for problems, and I had experienced a large number of them, ranging from clients hesitating, asking infinite questions, fainting, wanting to do it themselves, to the ear stapler breaking, puncturing the ear at the wrong place, holes being not even, holes getting infected, clients hitting you when you pierce them.

But in the last few months I had restrained my temper remarkably, including the time when a rude and pretentious young woman entered the store and hit me, before I even pierced her, simply because she felt the cold of the stapler on her ear. I did not hit her back. All I did was pretend the stapler slipped, and I pierced her high up on the ear, far, far from the dot.

And that was just one of many little efforts, in everyday life, at being as bland as possible. I also made these efforts with my family. For instance, it was ages since I had reprimanded my parents for fencing in the lobby of the building they lived in and of which my father was supposed to be the superintendent, or gotten mad at him (he's a hemophiliac) for not wearing his protective gear, or screamed at either of them for saying *"En garde!"* and drawing their swords every time I attempted to have a meaningful exchange with them.

It was clear that I had tried hard. Yet, I blamed myself, suspected that part of me had been too proud or stubborn to become warm wax. I had a sudden desire to punish that side of me, teach it a lesson, bring it to its knees, subject it to humiliation so that it would be stripped of its pride and stubbornness, and would obey my desire that it should fade.

All at once, I knew how to accomplish this; I knew how I would discipline and break myself like one broke a wild horse. I went to a costume store and rented the largest, most cumbersome and embarrassing costume they had. It was the Good Fairy Queen Costume. It consisted of a long crinoline dress (like in *Gone With the Wind*), made of lavender satin. That was one step in the right direction; one large step toward being not myself. When I put on the dress, it dragged on the ground a bit; it must have been made for a tall woman, which I was not. I was average.

The salesman forced on me the crown, the wand, and the wig that came with the dress. I forced myself to accept them. I placed the wig on my head. The long straight blond synthetic hair was quite a change from my own, shoulder-length, strawberry-blond, slightly curly hair. I stood in front of the mirror, holding the wand, as he stuck pins into my head to hold the wig. I felt like a martyr. He then placed the crown on my head.

I left the costume store walking stiffly, staring at the people who stared at me, hoping my acute embarrassment would traumatize me somehow, causing some sort of transformation within me, a transformation for the better; a beautiful metamorphosis, such as becoming a creature of talent.

I walked the streets all evening, thinking, and not thinking. I tried not to replay too often in my mind Aaron's words, but I failed. I tried to come up with a new philosophy of life, or at least a new frame of mind, a new way of looking at things, a solution, *anything* that might make me a little more optimistic about my future in acting. I failed. No solutions, no revelations. I went into a church to get inspired by the interior architecture and the atmosphere. It didn't work.

At 3:30 in the morning, after walking for hours, I went down into a subway station and sat on a bench on the deserted platform. I was not waiting for a train. My mind was blank, which had never happened to me before. I was actually having no thoughts. It was a little frightening. I was floating, completely lost, completely unattached to any belief, to any hope. Perhaps I had finally achieved the state of warm wax. Though somehow I doubted it. I lit a cigarette.

Three young businessmen walked in. As they passed my bench, they informed me that it was illegal to smoke in the subway. I ignored them. They inquired whether I was deaf. I ignored them. They proceeded to utter certain words such as *bitch* and *suck*. I felt at peace. I stared into space, wondering if they meant *suck* in a literal sense (as in "suck me") or in a slang sense (as in "life sucks"). As they walked away I picked up bits of their musings: "Costume . . . insane asylum . . . Halloween . . . play . . . actress . . ."

That last word sharpened my despair. I uttered the word *help* in my head. I looked at the columns, at the ceiling, at my cigarette.

Suddenly, as if echoing my thought, a man screamed "Help!" at the other end of the platform. I looked.

"Help!" he screamed again, and I saw him, being attacked by two men who were pulling him down onto the tracks. He was trying to free himself, but they dragged him into the tunnel.

The three businessmen leaned over the edge of the platform and looked on.

"Should we call the cops?" asked one of them.

"You're right. Go call," said another.

"Yeah, but hang on a sec. I wanna see what's going on."

In my bag I had Red Pepper Spray that my mother had given me in case I was ever attacked. I took it out, walked to the edge of the platform, and jumped down onto the tracks.

It was as if I was responding to my own cry for help. Or, who knows, perhaps it was simply a convenient excuse for, and roundabout attempt at, suicide.

The businessmen exhibited curious indignation at my behavior, as if they had been personally, and terribly, insulted. They asked what I was doing, what the *fuck* was I doing, and who the hell did I think I was, Super Cinderella or something?

I can't blame them for their harshness; after all, what must I have looked like, waddling down the train tracks, cigarette in my left hand, pepper spray in my right, wand tucked under my arm, dress dragging over the garbage, sunglasses on, wig and crown still in place.

I had trouble walking because I kept tripping over the front of my dress, which my hands were too encumbered to hold up. I therefore resorted to kicking the gown forward at every step to free my feet.

My emotional state seemed to have desensitized me. I approached the danger with strange indifference and detachment, something like lassitude. The sensation of fear was present, but only vaguely, like a faint pulse in someone dying. Even though I knew it was far from true, I almost imagined that if I were to be shot or stabbed, it would not significantly add to my pain.

The inside of the tunnel was so dark that I could barely make out the three vague human shapes, and at first it didn't occur to me to take off my sunglasses, which I hadn't realized I was still wearing. But even when I finally did realize it, I did not take them off, because I preferred not to see my opponents' faces; I feared that if I saw what was before me I might suddenly lose my indifference and become terrified.

The attackers stopped moving and stared as I approached. They began to threaten me. I replied something along the line of, "Please release him or I will spray you."

Then they made fun of my spray. They were under the mistaken impression that it was Mace, so I informed them that it was worse, that it was Red Pepper Spray.

The conversation started to flag, and I unconsciously took a drag on my cigarette, which, like the sunglasses, I hadn't realized I was still holding.

Not knowing what else to do, and feeling it was too soon to spray them without having first tried a peaceful alternative, I pulled out of my bag the literature on the red pepper spray and read to them the scariest parts regarding the effects of being sprayed.

By that time I had taken off my sunglasses and had flung them aside, to be able to see the print on the instruction sheet, and when I was done reading and looked up at the men, I was less frightened by the attackers' faces, than strangely annoyed by the victim's sex appeal.

He was being held by one of the men. His nose and lip were bleeding.

A physical struggle began between me and the other man, during which my wig came off in his hand. I was still not shooting my pepper spray, I don't know why; I felt okay just holding it. I cannot wholly attribute my lack of concentration to the victim's charisma, but it probably played a part. Thankfully though, I did have enough presence of mind to use my cigarette, extinguishing it on my assailant's bare arm.

Before things got worse, they got better for a moment. The feel of the wand in my hand must have triggered old fencing habits, because when the attacker pulled out his switchblade, my arm lashed out in a familiar, oft-repeated motion, and with a quick flick of the wand, the knife leaped from his hand, rather theatrically, and went flying a few feet away.

Things quickly degenerated to the point where I had somehow been flung over the man's shoulder and was beating his back with the wand, from which sparkles were flying off, attesting to my energy. But the blows were useless.

In the end, however, I did manage to use my spray. The bright orange pepper juice was more effective than I had anticipated, and it quickly put an end to the whole affair, not unlike the way I imagine a machine gun might have. The men fell to their knees, screaming and throwing up, their faces against the floor. The victim had been sprayed a bit too, which was unfortunate but inevitable, since he had been held closely by one of the assailants.

I picked up my wig, grabbed the victim's arm, and helped him climb onto the platform. I led him up the long stairway, hugging my wig to my chest, perhaps for comfort. My legs were nervously springing me up, and I was dragging the man with more energy than I knew was polite. Who knew how quickly they would recover from the spray? Judging from my companion's agony, however, they were probably not recovering too quickly.

I informed the subway teller that we were attacked and asked him if there was a bathroom we could use to rinse the pepper spray off of my friend's face. He said no.

We hurried out of the station.

In the street, I looked around. All the stores were closed. An all-night supermarket shone in the distance. The man's eyes were shut, and his head was bent as I guided him, telling him when to step up or down a curb. I also asked him if he knew the attackers. He shook his head.

In front of the supermarket there was a bench on which I helped him sit. I rushed into the store and looked for the bottled water section. I ran through the aisles like a swift bulldozer, my wide skirts mopping the floor as I went. My quest was slightly delayed when I slipped on a piece of lettuce while turning a corner. I collapsed on my side, but luckily didn't get hurt because my dress cushioned the fall.

I finally found the bottled water section, and wondered if I should get an American or a European brand. The latter might lend a desirable air of sophistication to my person. Unfortunately the European brands only came in little bottles, and it would not have been reasonable to choose little bottles to rinse off a man in agony. But when have attempts at being attractive ever been reasonable? I picked up as many little bottles of Evian as my arms would hold and paid for them.

He was still sitting on the bench, his head in his hands, when I returned.

"I'm back," I said, and helped him lie down on the bench. His eyes were closed. I kneeled next to him and opened a bottle. "Okay, I'm going to pour water on your face now, so hold your breath."

As soon as the water hit his face he groaned. The wetness must have revived the sting of the pepper spray. He wriggled his body with discomfort as I kept on pouring, and suddenly, out of the corner of my eye I perceived something that was arresting: a unique, rubbery, loose and rapid jiggle, that, as far as I knew, could only be produced by one thing. I believed that, for an instant, through the fabric of his pants, I had seen his penis.

His singular outfit, which I had hitherto been aware of only vaguely and subconsciously, had now abruptly jumped to the forefront of my consciousness: his loose-fitting pants and shirt were made of cloth that was thin, white, and extraordinarily transparent. I looked again at his crotch, but without much luck this time, because the angle had changed; he kept shifting in discomfort.

I was tempted to ask him why he was wearing transparent clothes, and why in this cold weather.

He suddenly sat up, groaning again, this time not so much with pain as exasperation, which I was afraid was because he caught me looking.

"Enough," he said.

I leaned back on my heels. His legs were open in front of me, but I didn't dare look. My eyes were fixed on his chest, a neutral point. His reproachful silence became unbearable, so I slowly raised my eyes to his face, only to discover that my fears were unfounded; his eyes were still closed.

"What's wrong?" I asked.

"The pH is very uncomfortable."

"The pH?"

"Yes," he said, and asked: "Isn't this Evian water?"

"Yes."

"I would be so grateful if you could get me water with a lower pH, like Volvic."

I tried to register his words, but I couldn't believe my ears.

"Are you still there?" he asked, like a blind person.

"Yes," I replied. "You're saying the pH level is uncomfortable? Don't you think it's maybe just the wetness that has revived the stinging of the spray?"

"Yes, but the alkalinity of this water is also the cause. I'm in no condition to have to endure a gap."

"What gap?"

"From seven, neutral pH. Please get me Volvic water."

"Okay," I said, and went and got him Volvic water.

He was lying on the bench again when I returned. I kneeled next to him, opened a bottle, and started pouring it on his face.

He sighed, and said, "Yes, that's better. Thank you."

I opened a second bottle and emptied it on his face as well. It drenched his collar.

"Now open your eyes so I can rinse them," I told him.

"I can't," he said, so I held his eyes open with my fingers, one at a time, and poured a third bottle into them. My fingers on his eyelids started to feel a little nervous as I noticed, once again, his attractiveness. His face was sinuous and his features aquiline, with no sharp edges. His hair was blonde, shoulder length and slightly wavy. He seemed to be in his early thirties.

By the fourth bottle, my eyes had started wandering down his body again, and I had all but forgotten the matter of the pH, because, to be frank, the matter of his humanness interested me more than that of his super humanness. Accordingly, I tried to get a glimpse of his penis again. But maybe I had hallucinated.

I leaned toward his crotch slightly to get a closer look. I hadn't hallucinated. It was really there.

The man suddenly grabbed my wrist. Straightaway, I imagined the worst: that he caught me looking. But no, he was simply readjusting my aim, repositioning my arm over his face, because I had begun pouring the water on the sidewalk.

"You seem distracted," he said, keeping a hold of my wrist. "What were you looking at?"

They say that when you lie you should try to stay close to the truth: "I thought I saw a policeman for a second, but I wasn't sure if I had hallucinated."

"You weren't hallucinating. But ignore him, because he won't make any difference."

I suddenly realized with discomfort that he knew perfectly well I was looking at his penis, and that it was the subject of our conversation. That being the case, I wondered what he meant by telling me that his penis wouldn't make any difference.

"Then why is he there?" I ventured.

"It'll emerge in time."

I wondered if the "it" referred to the answer to my question, or what. I decided it was probably to the answer, but possibly to what.

I started to rinse his hands and asked, "Do you know why these men attacked you?"

He shook his head.

"Do you think we should report it to the police?"

He shook his head again.

"Do you want to go to an emergency room?"

"I don't think so," he said. "I'd like to go home. If you could just hail me a cab, I'd be grateful. And would you mind also giving me your phone number so that I can thank you properly?"

I took out a piece of paper on which I wrote Anna Graham, and my phone number. I handed it to him, and he squinted at it, still unable to open his eyes completely.

"Thank you," he said, shoving it in his pocket. "I'm Damon Wetly. I won't shake your hand in case I'm still contaminated with your spray. How far do you live?"

I told him, and since we didn't live in the same direction, we decided each to take our own cab. I hailed two and before Damon climbed into his, he gave my cabdriver a twenty-dollar bill. I told him it wasn't necessary.

"It's the least I can do," he said. "It was a relief to meet you, and almost a pleasure, which is saying a lot under the circumstances. And again, thank you."

It was only once I was in the taxi going home that it occurred to me we could have asked to use the supermarket bathroom. But then I recalled the pH problem: the tap water's pH level might not have been to his liking. This seemed preposterous to me. I didn't know what to make of it.

When I got home I sat on my couch for an hour, wondering why in the world I had put my life at risk to save this man. Was I a courageous person and just hadn't known it? Was I noble, deep down? I wasn't sure, but these possibilities made me feel good.

Or maybe my risk-taking had simply been caused by the frustration of having tried so hard to succeed at something and failed. And I certainly had tried hard to improve my acting. . . . In addition to striving to erase myself, I did all sorts of other acting exercises. Among those, of course, was the standard practice of performing scenes in front of the class. But apart from that, I had my own strange little activity that I performed exclusively at my other job, at Copies Always, the Xerox shop. I was supposed to copy documents, but actually, I also copied people. When customers came in, I immediately copied their mannerisms, behavior, and tone of voice. Since the customers didn't know my true self, they had no idea I was imitating them. One day, however, I think a client did notice it because as he was paying the bill he said, "Your prices are quite reasonable here. And you didn't even charge me for your Xerox of me."

I think the sound of the copiers triggered off this need and ability within me to become a copier myself. It wasn't unlike singing along with a song on the radio: I felt quite competent as long as the real singer's voice was there to support, guide, and slightly drown out mine, but as soon as I tried to sing that same song alone, the result was usually less gratifying.

I knew I had tried hard at my acting. Yet perhaps I had to try still harder. But what did trying harder consist of? What more could I do? I mean, should I just abandon acting?

No. That, I would never do. I would rather spend the rest of my life trying without success than succeed at anything else.

Chapter Two

I spent the following day doing my acting exercises. I was still quite depressed about my meeting with Aaron, but in the midst of this sadness, I experienced little sparks of joy whenever I happened to think about the subway incident and, more particularly, about Damon. Unfortunately, these thoughts interfered with my acting and spoiled my concentration. So I tried to push them from my mind, but to no avail; they were too pleasant.

I wondered if Damon would call to thank me, and if so, how he would thank me. I wished I knew more about him. Out of curiosity, I even looked in the phone book to see if he was listed. He was. I wanted to see him again. It was practically all I could think about. I felt so lacking in willpower that I almost regretted having saved the man. I finally decided to put an end to these thoughts by promising myself that if he were to call me and ask to see me, I would refuse. This decision put me in a grim mood, but at least I felt virtuous and dedicated to my craft.

My concentration improved, and I was able to work on my acting more productively. At least for a day or two. But the problem was that my virtue was unearned, and my sacrifice soon started to feel like a fraud. My mind began drifting again, because after all, Damon had not called yet, and I had not rejected him yet, which meant that the potential for happiness was still present, floating around in the air. I started doubting whether I'd have the strength to stick by my decision, were he to call. And why wasn't he calling, anyway?

The situation finally came to a standstill one morning, when I was on the roof of my building, with my scene book, and realized I had reread the same simple line five times without grasping its meaning. I stood there, feeling powerless, not knowing what to do. Suddenly, the sky became very dark and rain started pouring. And the solution came to me.

I realized sadly that if I were to have any chance of regaining my concentration, I had to extinguish the sparks of joy completely. I had to speed up the rejection process. Since Damon had not called me yet, I had to call him. I would do it under the guise of a courtesy call, as if to find out how he was doing, which I was genuinely curious about anyway, naturally. After some small talk, if he asked to see me again, I would refuse, claiming that it was impossible, that I had no time, that I was swamped with work, and then the whole business would be over with, once and for all.

I felt strangely invigorated by this sad scenario. I was back in control. A flash of lightning suddenly lit the sky, which had become almost as dark as night. The rain was pouring over my scene book, and I quickly ducked indoors

and ran down the stairs. When I entered my apartment it
was dark, lit only by occasional lightning. I did not turn
on the lights. I stripped down to my T-shirt and underwear, leaving my wet clothes strewn across the place. I sat
on the floor with the phone between my knees. I felt that
I was about to commit a very significant and symbolic act,
not entirely unlike black magic that could very well turn
my life around. I was, after all, going to perform a sacrifice. This instrument, this phone, resting between my
knees was the key. It was the weapon with which I would
sacrifice not life, but love.

The storm outside was undoubtedly adding importance
and mystery to the occasion. I liked this atmosphere and
desired to push it even further, to make the whole procedure even more formal and solemn, so I lit some candles
and sat back down. The lightning lit up my phone and
legs. This should be an hour of celebration, I told myself.
Don't be sad. Rejoice!

I dialed the number I got from the phone book, which
I hoped was Damon's number.

"Hello," he answered, on the second ring.

"Hi," I said. "Is this Damon?"

"Yes."

"It's Anna." I paused for a second and added, "We met
in the subway the other night."

I think I heard a faint intake of breath. And then
nothing.

"Hello?" I said.

"Yes," he answered very softly, very seriously, with
more surrender this time, and a hint of sadness.

"I'm sorry, you probably don't remember—"

"Anna Graham, my savior. Please don't think such a thing. Of *course* I remember."

"Oh. Well, I'm just calling to find out if you recovered from the attack, and from the spray."

"Yes. Thanks to you. I was going to call you. I was wondering if you'd be willing to have dinner with me sometime."

"No, it's really not necessary."

"Why don't we, for a moment, ignore the fact that that statement, other than being completely beside the point, is wrong. Having dinner with you would mean a lot to me. I would very much . . . enjoy it. That's if you're not too busy, of course."

"Actually, I am very busy."

He paused. "You don't have any time?"

"I really don't have much free time."

He paused longer. "Can't I persuade you?"

"I'm sorry, it's just that I'm so busy."

"Oh. How disappointing. I wish I could change your mind, but not at the risk of being a pest. Hopefully another time then."

"What other time?"

"Whenever you want. Like in a month, or whenever you're less busy."

"Hmm. Well, I don't know, because unfortunately I'll be even more busy in a month."

"Oh. Well then, in six months, or whatever. No big deal."

"Okay. Though in six months I will be even more busy."

"Ah. I see. Well, it doesn't matter then, don't worry

about it. If you want, give me a call whenever it's practical for you."

"Okay. Though since I *will* be increasingly busy, from now on, then, logically speaking, the most practical time for me would be this evening. But I don't know if that's convenient for you."

There was a long silence.

Finally, he answered, "Yes, it is."

We settled on a time and place.

When we hung up, I sat motionless, staring at the phone for a while before getting up. I left my apartment and climbed the stairs back to the roof, oblivious to the possibility that someone might catch me in my T-shirt and panties.

I walked out into the rain and sat on the ground, cross-legged, unblinking. My hair and T-shirt were quickly drenched. I was cold, but I did not allow myself to shiver. I forced my muscles to relax and let the cold enter me, hoping it would numb my body as well as my anger.

Maybe I could hang off my balcony by my hair. Or I could dump garbage all over myself. Or perhaps I should step in front of moving vehicles. No. Dying was not the point. Punishment was.

There would be a steep price to pay for that little number I pulled. If I thought I was going to let myself get away with it, I was wrong. I didn't know what the price was yet, but I sure would think of it. And it wouldn't be merely to be sitting out in the rain.

Strangely, my anger infused me with strength, making me feel invulnerable, invincible, even against the elements. The thunder and lightning seemed like a breeze. I felt in complete control. All I had to do was think of a bad enough punishment, and everything would be fine. I set my mind to work immediately.

I could fast for three days. I could deprive myself of sleep for four days. I could stop talking for a week. I could whip myself, slap myself. I could not blink.

These weren't great; I was just warming up.

I could streak naked around my block. I could be a prostitute for one night. I could sleep out on the streets for a few evenings or spend an afternoon begging on the subway. I could shoplift and get arrested.

I was not satisfied with any of these ideas. They were not quite on target and seemed slightly irrelevant to the crime.

Torture. I could do something with bugs. I could try to get my hands on a cockroach and eat it. I could breed cockroaches in my apartment and set them loose. I could eat worms. I could do something horrible with my own excrement. I could sneak into a lion's cage.

These were not much better. My difficulty in coming up with a suitable sentence made my crime seem all the more serious. The rain was beating down on me, wearing me down. I began feeling fragile in the middle of the lightning.

I could cut myself.

I could bruise myself, break a finger. Punch my fist through a glass window.

Enema.

I could stare at the sun.

Raindrops were running into my eyes as tears were running out. I had a block. I could not think of any more punishments.

Self-criticisms and reproaches, however, I had not run out of, so I indulged in throwing them at myself: How could I have been so pathetically weak? And deceitful? How could I have betrayed myself this way? Part of me suspected that I knew from the start that I was calling him to get invited out. I bet I knew all along I was going to accept. I even bet that if he hadn't asked me out I would have asked him myself. In fact, that was pretty much what happened. And all that for a pretty face whom I didn't even know. I was willing to jeopardize my future, my dream, for a pretty face. How shallow could I get? How superficial? While I was at it, why didn't I just walk up to a total stranger in the street and tell him I wanted to sleep with him, right then and there? That wouldn't be much worse than what I did. It would have saved time, been easier, more true to my lazy, undisciplined nature. I forced my mind to visualize myself accosting a man in this way. I made myself endure the distress of picturing the man's reaction, the shock, the embarrassment.

I continued pondering with disgust this hateful little drama, when suddenly, to my horror, I recognized it for what it was: my Punishment. It loomed large and obvious in my mind. I had finally found it.

I immediately tried to reject it. I could never perform such an act. It was impossible, too hard, too awful and sinister.

Which, of course, was why I had to do it. Why I *would* do it. I already knew it was inevitable, that it was the only solution. And once my initial horror passed, I was awed by the perfection of it and relieved by the dreadfulness of it.

I would do it now.

I got up. The sky had cleared and the rain was letting up, as if handing me the reins of discipline.

I went down to my apartment, got dressed, and went out into the street.

Before I fulfilled my sentence there were a few factors that needed to be determined, a few rules that had to be set. Rules were necessary, or I'd try to get off easy. So as I walked down the street, I established in my mind all the rules of my punishment.

For instance, how, exactly, would I accost the man?

Well, for starters, I would approach him and say something along the line of, "Excuse me. I want you. Badly. Here and now or as soon as possible. I can't wait." I would then make an assertive physical pass, such as placing my hand on his backside and squeezing it. I would keep up this act, not forgetting to include some variations, like hugging and sighing.

The next very important point that had to be determined was: How long did this have to go on before I allowed myself to stop? I thought about that for a while and finally came up with: until he started running away. Yes. I would not allow myself to stop harassing him and pressuring him, verbally as well as physically, until he ran away. In fact, I would even begin taking off his clothes, if necessary, to make him run.

We'd see how good an actress I was, how much of a fool I was willing to make of myself. Great actors had to be willing to go to extremes.

But what if—oh horror of horrors—he were to reciprocate or take me up on my offer? Then *I'd* have to start running. Anyway, whatever trouble it got me into, I deserved.

All that was left for me to do now was to choose a man.

The streets were wet and not very crowded. I gazed at every man that crossed my path. I wanted to check out a few before making my selection. There was no point in rushing things. I walked three of four blocks, occasionally stopping in stores along the way to see if I could find some good ones lurking around.

I finally entered a store selling musical instruments and saw a man who was quite appealing, more so than I deserved for my punishment. But after all, I had not specified in the rules that the man had to repel me. And anyway, an attractive victim did not really make the task any easier. On the contrary, in a way—it created its own challenges and barriers.

I had decided not to bother trying to not be myself during my punishment. The act I was about to perform was so unlike anything I would normally do, that I would automatically be acting unlike myself, without even trying.

I stood behind a harp and stared at my prey through the strings of the instrument. He was checking out a piano. While I contemplated him, I was absently plucking at a chord from the harp to seem busy.

"May I help you," asked a salesman, coming up behind me.

"No, thank you. I was just looking," I said, leaving the harp and checking out a cello (my favorite instrument) before moving on to the synthesizers.

I pressed a key and it made the sound of thunder. I punched a few buttons and made the sound of a lashing whip.

My prey was still at the piano. I did not want to accost him inside the store, as it might make a scene. So I would have to appear busy until he left.

I continued to mess around with the buttons, and by accident I pressed a key that made loud, consecutive kissing sounds that did not stop. I tried punching various buttons to make them stop. I even tried taking a step back from the instrument, but it didn't help. My prey glanced at me with an amused expression, so I quickly moved away to another synthesizer and tried to look absorbed.

The kissing sounds went on, embarrassingly loud and persistent. I pressed a key on my new synth, hoping to camouflage them with a more neutral, less suggestive sound.

To my regret, the key I pressed produced a panting sound. It was real, quick, earnest, human panting. And to my horror, it did not stop either. The store was now filled with kissing and panting noises and no one came to stop the racket because the salesmen were all busy.

I looked at my prey. He was smiling, and called out, "You have a way with those!"

I nodded and chuckled politely and edged my way out of the store. I could not accost him now. He practically knew me.

I walked a few blocks, breathing deeply, and entered a sporting goods store. I soon spotted a possible prey. I followed him discreetly. He stopped in the water sports section and examined a floating mattress. I stood a little ways off, and tried to look interested in the diving masks. He poked at the mattress and squeezed it, testing its firmness. I placed a mask on my face, pretending to be testing its suction power, while through the mask I watched him tentatively sit on the mattress. As soon as his whole weight was on it the air plug popped out and the mattress went limp, expiring with a wheezing sound. The man got up and glanced around to see if he had been observed. Since no one was nearby except me, his gaze lingered in my direction. So I made sharp jerking motions with my head, to seem utterly engrossed in the suction power of my mask. He relaxed and walked away, believing his dignity to be intact. I followed him.

He went to a corner of the store and wandered behind a display case. I couldn't follow him there because the space was too tight and he would have seen me. He stayed there awhile, and I wondered what he was doing. By some unexpected stroke of luck, there happened to be, on the other side of the display case, a minitrampoline, on which I climbed after slight hesitation. I bounced, tentatively at first, and tried to look innocent. I was not bouncing high enough to see over the display case, so I bounced higher and caught glimpses of him examining a jump rope. He unraveled it and began jumping rope in that tight corner, the fool. Over the display case, in midair, our eyes met. And then there was a crash, on his side. He must have knocked some things off a shelf.

I decided that he would not do. He was awkward and clumsy to a degree that made him worrisomely unpredictable.

I spotted the next potential victim in a mirror store. We strolled among the mirrors before he stopped to examine one that was full-length and three-way. Being able to see him from three sides simultaneously was wonderful; it gave me a more complete, well-rounded perception of my prey. What ruined it for me was a subtle movement he made, a mere brush of the hand against the back of his pants, but performed in a manner that did not please me. There was nothing horrendously vulgar about the gesture, but it was enough to make me decide he would not do.

I don't believe I was being picky or trying to get out of my obligation. These last two specimens were clearly not possible, by any standard. I mean, if I had accosted the jump rope one, he probably would have said something like, "Am I on *Candid Camera?*" And this mirror guy's response to my statement "I want you now," might have been something like, "Why? Is it my appearance or my personality that attracts you?"

I had to find better. I wandered into a florist and spotted a man who struck me favorably. I stood behind a high-perched pot of daisies and observed him through the stems and petals. Now *this* guy was not like the last two. He looked sane and well-balanced, simple and straightforward, sensible, alert, confident, possibly intelligent. He did not hide in a corner of the store and knock pots over. His movements were efficient and coordinated, economical. No frills. He did not touch his own body appreciatively. Though he did have a rather nice body. He was tall, solidly built, with an okay face. When accosted, he was not likely to complicate the situation in some tiresome or whiny way. All in all, he seemed like a real "no-nonsense" type of guy. It was refreshing. I watched him for a while and he did nothing to disappoint me.

He left the store without buying anything, which was just as well since I preferred not to make advances on a man encumbered with a bouquet. I followed him down the street, suddenly nervous because I realized the time had come. I was not likely to find a more perfect accessory for my punishment, a more appropriate recipient for my offensive, than this man.

I trotted up behind him. My tongue stung and my heart was pounding. I was four feet away, my hand was extended toward him. I had to do it now. I cleared my throat and was about to touch his arm when he turned and entered a deli. I followed him in, hurried to the back of the store, and stood behind some jars of mustard. I would accost him as soon as he exited. My mouth and tongue were stinging more than ever, which was something that always happened when I was nervous, particularly before I got on stage.

He paid for his purchase and left. I hurried after him. This time I did not stall. I firmly placed my hand on his arm and said, "Excuse me."

He turned and looked at me politely, considerately, and said, "Yes?"

Suddenly I wanted to chicken out by only asking him what time it was. No, not allowed.

Then I wondered if I could cut a deal with myself by toning down the punishment to asking him merely if he wanted to have coffee one day. I could then combine this semi-punishment with one of the others, like dumping garbage all over myself.

No. I had to do it: out of respect for my acting. And it couldn't be a half-hearted attempt either; it had to be convincing. So I dived. I dived into his eyes and said, "I want you. Now or somewhere close. I can't wait."

He looked at me, almost with pity, I think, though this might be my imagination.

I placed my hand on his backside, squeezed it, and began to repeat "I want you," when he slapped my face with the back of his hand.

I felt swatted. Like a mosquito. Or, to be fair, perhaps

like something a bit worse: a wasp, or a flying cockroach. But swatted, definitely. It wasn't a particularly hard slap. I don't think it was meant to knock me out or anything, but he was wearing a rather sharp ring that cut my upper lip. When I touched my mouth there was blood. I looked up at him, stunned, but he was already walking away.

My lip hurt, and the blood was running into my mouth and down my chin. I pressed my fingers on the cut to stop the flow, but it simply ran down my wrist as well. Dammit. I couldn't afford to have a scar on my face. My non-existent acting career would be ruined. I probably should get stitches. It was a drag, but I had to be conscientious, to minimize the wreckage.

Perhaps I should go home first and see how bad the damage really was. I hesitated. I was quite far from my apartment, and the hospital was in the opposite direction. I looked at the faces of people who passed me, trying to read from their expressions how serious my cut was. Was it really as bad as all the blood on my hands led me to believe?

Their gaits slowed, but steered clear. In their faces I detected shock, curiosity, and, to my surprise, fear. Why fear? Did they think I was dangerous, that I would attack them, that I had murdered someone? And yet there was no question that they were afraid of me, which was puzzling, until I remembered why and felt like an idiot: the fear of modern blood.

I finally just walked up to a parked car and craned my neck to catch a glimpse of my face in the side-view mirror. I was horrified.

I tried to hail a cab, but none stopped until I wrapped my scarf around my face and hid the blood. All I could think about in the taxi was that I would have a huge, disfiguring scar that would annihilate my chances at acting. A scar could never attain the same caliber, glamour, and cachet as a mole, even if situated in approximately the same place. Come to think of it, even a facial tattoo didn't seem as tragic as a scar.

I went to the emergency room, and after examining me, the doctor said I didn't need stitches, that in fact it was generally preferable not to stitch that area of the face. He said it was unlikely that I would get a scar, but that to play it extra safe I should avoid smiling or laughing for a couple of days. Talking and eating, however, were okay, he said.

He then went on to explain the situation in more detail. "Cuts on the mouth are a delicate case. One cannot completely rule out the possibility of scarring, because the mouth is an area that normally moves and stretches a lot, which can cause delays in healing. As we know, delays in healing can mean the formation of unsightly scar tissue, especially when the cut extends beyond the lip's outer limit, as yours does, slightly. That is why I advise you to avoid all social contact during the next two days. If that's not possible, then you should restrict your contact to people who are not likely to make you laugh or smile. I do realize that this may be impractical. If it can't be managed, you have only one other alternative, and it is of utmost importance: you have to perform the MMO procedure."

"What is MMO?" I asked.

"It's an abbreviation for Manual Merriment-Obstruction. It consists in pressing the tips of your hands on either side of your mouth, like so, to obstruct the formation of a smile."

He demonstrated the procedure on himself, which was very unflattering to his appearance.

He continued: "The MMO procedure must be performed each and every time anyone in your proximity says, or does, anything funny, and every time you sense you're about to smile or to—God forbid—laugh. Obviously, alertness is of vital importance, because smiles can be diabolically quick. And be warned: you have to press hard—smiles have tremendous muscle, more than anyone ever imagines until they actually wrestle with one."

I left the hospital feeling unnerved. There was no way in hell I would not go to that dinner. After everything I had gone through to pay for my sin, I had a right to enjoy it. The doctor had no conception of how dearly I had earned this dinner. Not only would I go, but I would relish every moment of it, absorb it with all my senses, enjoy it to the fullest.

At home, I stood in front of the mirror and practiced the MMO procedure. It looked awful. Something like a cruelly designed cartoon of something that held a vague resemblance to a chipmunk. I would not do it. I would just have to have enough self-control not to laugh or smile. But what if I did not, actually, have enough self-control, and ended up having unprotected laughter? I could just imagine my cut stretching and opening, and the little scar tissue cells getting to work, multiplying. I tried not to think about it. I'd simply have to muster the necessary self-control, period.

Chapter Three

I arrived five minutes early at the restaurant. It was rather small, intimate, and quiet, save for the murmur of a water fountain next to which the headwaiter seated me. Two long candlesticks were burning on the table. I was facing the front door; I would be able to see Damon when he arrived.

I had decided not to diminish the pleasure of this dinner by using it as an exercise in not being myself. I *would* be myself. As much as I felt like it.

At exactly eight o'clock, Damon entered the restaurant like a body of water. His movements were strikingly fluid, and he was dressed the same way as the first time I met him: his white clothes were made of such thin material that they seemed to float around him, follow his movements in slow motion. He was chewing gum.

Soon after he sat down, I asked him to please not make me laugh this evening or I'd have to do something very unattractive.

"Oh? Really?"

"Yes, I just had an accident, this cut on my lip, and if you make me even just smile I'll have to perform the MMO procedure, which is an ugly thing."

"You had an accident?" he said.

"Yes, it was just a fencing accident, I lied."

"Oh, you fence. Actually, I noticed you were very limber with your wand."

When he asked what I did in life, I told him I was a Xeroxer and an ear piercer.

"And an aspiring what?"

"Does one need to aspire to anything else?" I retorted.

He shrugged and smiled and said no.

"An aspiring actor," I said.

He looked struck, even somewhat ill. I asked what was wrong. He shook his head. I asked whether he disliked acting, but he assured me that, quite the contrary, he liked it very much. He said it was a beautiful art form, and he then tried to change the subject by asking if I pierced ears independently or in a store, and where, exactly, was the store located, in case he might have passed by it sometime. I answered his questions.

When I inquired what he did, he replied: "In the past few days? Not much."

"No, in general," I said. "In life."

"This and that."

"Meaning?"

He said he should warn me that he didn't like talking about himself, but that he would answer that one question: he was a scientist.

That was the last thing I had expected him to be. "May I ask what area of science?"

"Later, perhaps."

This time it was my turn to change the subject, and I did so by returning to the subject he had previously changed: "Why did you look upset when I said I was an aspiring actor?"

"You're persistent."

"In this case, hardly. I only asked you once before."

"All right, I'll tell you. When you said you were an actor, it brought back a bad memory of someone you've been reminding me of, painfully, who also happens to be an actor."

"Someone you hate?"

"No." He paused. "Just the opposite."

"A girlfriend?"

"No. A man."

"A lover?"

He smiled. "No . . . I'm not . . . "

"Well, then who?"

"I'm sorry, I can't talk about it further."

We read the menu and ordered. His manner of ordering was surprising. When the waiter asked him a multitude of standard questions, such as, How did he want his meat cooked, What kind of dressing did he want on his salad, and Did he want potatoes or rice with his meal, Damon answered one of two things: either that it didn't matter, or that he didn't care (also stated as, "I have no particular preference").

However, when the subject came 'round to that of the water, yes, the table water, he was not satisfied with merely choosing bottled over tap, or plain over sparkling; he demanded to know every brand of plain bottled water the restaurant carried. He requested to be shown each brand (there were two), and he spent at least a minute comparing their labels, as if they were wine, before he made up his mind.

We then chatted, only touching on light topics for a while. The food was good, I could see his nipples through his shirt, and halfway through the meal, as he was pouring me more wine (which he had picked with less concern than the water), he said, out of the blue, "Have you ever felt ceaseless torment?"

I was startled and answered hesitantly. "Perhaps of a kind, I suppose. Depending on how you would define 'ceaseless' and 'torment.' "

"Why did you do it?"

"Do what?"

"Have you ever wronged someone terribly?"

"I don't think so. At least no one other than myself."

"Save me."

"Excuse me?"

"Save me, Anna. Why did you save me?"

"I don't know."

"You must know. I must know."

I could have answered "You looked like you could have used some help," but decided to be more honest. I said, "I felt like it."

He didn't look happy with my response. It seemed to perturb him. "I don't understand what you mean," he said.

"Well, I was . . . in the mood, I guess."

He gazed at me for a while, mulling this over, and finally said, "Why?"

I wasn't sure I wanted to tell him about my meeting with my acting professor, which had been responsible for my dark mood, so I said, "Oh, it was just one of those days, you know."

"No, I haven't the faintest notion what you mean. One of what days? I've never known of a day that could put someone in the mood to perform such an act."

"I think I would prefer not to talk about it. It was an unpleasant day."

It seemed my fears about Damon making me laugh had been unfounded. So far this conversation was very safe for my cut.

"I see," he said. "All of my days are unpleasant. Particularly the ones since you saved me. Your act has propelled me into a state of such unpleasantness, it is hard to describe. I have hardly been functional. I've done little but pace the streets and sit in my apartment in the dark, barely breathing, rarely blinking, having forgotten how to eat. The methods I had perfected, over the years, to soothe my pain, don't work anymore: being cruel; destroying things; causing fear; taking baths of various liquids such as milk, citrus juice, and wine; burying myself in grass, leaves, or pebbles; subjecting myself to deafening music and noise; riding on roller coasters; watching documentaries on animals eating each other and on concentration camps."

He paused dramatically, and added, "I, too, you see, have had unpleasant days. I, too, have had days during which I have been disconcerted. All because of how rare, how unsettling it is to find anyone (let alone a young woman), so extraordinarily selfless as to willingly risk her life to save a complete stranger."

I was so stunned by his mention of the roller coasters and documentaries that it took me a moment to answer. "You give me too much credit. I wasn't myself that day.

And to be honest, I'm not sure I would have done it if I had been."

"How were you not yourself? And why?"

At that point it seemed I had no choice but to tell him about my depressing meeting with my acting professor. So I gave him a summarized version of it (including Aaron's weird request). But in doing so, I had to relive in my mind the painful, unabridged version of that meeting, which was:

After telling me I should switch career goals, and that neither my body nor my face were that impressive, and after I had an urge to smoke but was stopped by the No Smoking sign behind his desk, Aaron Smith said, "If your acting were exceptional you could be a character actress, but it isn't. The reason I'm telling you this is that I feel you could be very successful at something else. You're motivated and persistent, and you have so much potential, but I just don't think you're going to make it as an actress. I'm sure you'll be able to get little acting jobs, here and there, but they'll be mediocre. Your career will be mediocre and unsatisfying and, ultimately, disappointing to you. You will be moderately happy, at best. I've seen people like you, and they all end up the same way."

I reached inside my bag for a cigarette, but was again stopped midway by the sight of the No Smoking sign.

"I think you should drop my class," he said. "If you want to finish the semester, that's fine. But in any case, I strongly urge you not to take it again next semester, because I can't bear to see you wasting your time in this field, which will have no rewards for you. You are a strong woman, Anna. I've observed you now, over the months, and I've noticed the power you hold over people.

In a way it's surprising that you don't hold this same power on the stage or in front of the camera, but you don't. And it's precisely this strength of yours that works against you in acting. As I've been telling you for months, your identity is too strong for you to be able to become someone else convincingly. You are too much yourself. I think you are caged within yourself. You are incapable of being affected, much less of becoming someone else. You are genuine and true to a fault."

He really loved to hear himself talk, it seemed. As for me, I think I was in some sort of denial of the pain I was in.

"Now, not to seem insensitive," Aaron said, "but there is a pressing matter that I would like to discuss with you." (Here it came, the request.) "One of the students in the class has an ugly name. It's Esmeralda. I was wondering if you would mind if I told her to change her name to yours, for career purposes. I feel she has great promise. I think she's the next Meryl Streep. Or a mixture of Meryl Streep, Glenn Close, Jodie Foster, and/or Michelle Pfeiffer."

I took a cigarette out of my bag and lit it.

Aaron continued: "Your name would be an amazing screen name for an actress, so if you decide to follow my advice and change careers, would you mind it if a very promising actress wore your name?"

After taking a few drags, I took the cigarette out of my mouth, and a long string of mucus hung between my upper lip and the filter. I looked at it with puzzlement, and touched my face. My cheeks were wet.

Aaron continued: "You do understand that names are not copyrighted property, and she could take it if she wanted to, but I thought as a courtesy I would ask you first, before I suggest the idea to her."

I was carefully wiping my face with my sleeve.

"Come now, no need for tears," he said. "To be frank, Esmeralda will succeed no matter what name she has, because remember, as Shakespeare said, 'A rose, by any other name, would smell as sweet.' But then again, Gertrude Stein was also right when she said 'A rose is a rose is a rose.' That word certainly is beautiful and pleasant to repeat. So is Anna Graham. An anagram is the actor of words."

And that was the end of my meeting with Aaron.

Damon's first reaction was: "He thinks you should give up acting because *you are yourself too much?* What utter nonsense! How amusing. I hope you're not telling me you listened to a word of it."

"He's well respected."

Damon thoughtfully peeled wax from the candlestick and kneaded it between his fingers. "Influence. You have allowed yourself to be influenced. All good things have the capacity to be influenced. Evil things and dead things do not. But influence is strange and complex. One must know which kind to accept."

He played with the wax as he continued speaking of influence.

When the check arrived, he paid it. He asked if I wanted to go to the park by the river for a few minutes. I agreed.

When we got up from the table, I noticed again the fluid manner in which he moved. As we left the restaurant I couldn't resist asking him if he did any sports.

"No," he replied. "I stretch, but I'm not sure that counts."

The air outside was cold. This was a perfect opportunity for me to pierce the mystery of his transparent clothes.

I shivered and said, "It's so cold out. How come you wear clothes made of such thin material?"

He didn't answer immediately, so I looked at him, and he replied softly, without looking at me, "It is punishing."

We walked to the river, and stood at the railing, looking down at the water in silence.

He spoke first. "The greatest actor is right here in front of us."

"What do you mean?"

"Water. You should study it. You might learn a lot about your craft."

"How is water the greatest actor?"

"If you observe it and search through it, you'll see."

"Okay, I'll do that, but in the meantime you could also just tell me?"

His eyelids fluttered wearily, and he said, "It has the capacity, through influence, for pronounced reversible change, without ever ceasing to be itself."

For some reason, this reminded me of my previous curiosity. "Can you tell me, now, what kind of scientist you are?"

"A meteorologist."

"As in the weather?"

"Yes."

"In what capacity?"

"I'm sorry, but that's too personal."

How personal could anything involving the weather be? I was annoyed. So then I asked him why my act of saving him had disturbed him so much.

He answered, "It revived my past. In addition, it destroyed a convenient lie I had erected for myself during the last few years."

"What kind of lie?"

He hesitated. "The kind that allowed me to hate myself less than I should."

"What was the lie?"

"A simple process, really, merely consisting in readjusting my view of the entire human race, lowering my opinion of it until it reached my shameful level, and thereby increased my sense of belonging, decreased my sense of guilt, and enabled me to spread my contempt over us all, instead of just over myself as I deserved."

He turned away and slowly started walking along the river. I walked at his side.

After a while, he said, "I was on the verge of calling you, countless times this week, before you called. But I was afraid of contacting you, afraid of knowing you, afraid of who you might or might not be. Also, I was afraid of the risk, and I still am, for you and for myself. Part of me wants to have no part of you."

I didn't know what to say. I could have said, "I see," or something of the sort, but I didn't say it because I didn't see. And even though I didn't see, I was still okay, basking in a cloud of confusion, not unpleasant confusion. But then, he said something clear, something that woke me like a cold shower.

"Did you enjoy yourself this evening?"

"Yes," I replied.

"Good. Our dinner was just a small sample of my gratitude. All that matters to me now is to find a worthwhile way of paying you back for saving me. That's all I care about, all I want. Nothing else. We should arrange to see each other again. Once I know you a little better, I'll know how to thank you most meaningfully and usefully. For starters, of course, I could give you money. But aside from that, I want to bestow on you a favor, any favor, that is worthy of the one you bestowed on me. Though that may be impossible, because your act is a tough one to follow."

I made up my mind at that moment not to see him again. I was not interested in being thanked. I was hurt. I had hoped that his interest in me went a little beyond gratitude, but obviously it didn't.

"It's all right," I said, stiffly. "You've thanked me more than enough already." I tried to think of another platitude. "I'm glad I was able to be of service, but it was really just a matter of being at the right place at the right time."

I was a little too moved by my own words for my own good. I was afraid tears would start welling in my eyes. I looked at my watch, claimed another engagement, and rushed out of the park before he had a chance to react. He didn't try to stop me.

Two hours later he called me at home and asked if something was the matter. I said no. He asked if we could have dinner again. I said no. He asked why. I was cold: I said I'd rather not, that I didn't feel like it.

Just because I felt like saving him didn't mean I felt like having dinner with him. I felt like saying that, but didn't. He was silent. I said good-bye, and "Thanks again, by the way," and hung up.

He didn't call back. Good.

I cried.

*   *   *

The next day, as I was working in the jewelry store, Damon walked in and stood in front of me.

"Hello Anna," he said.

"What are you doing here?"

"I'm very grateful."

"I see. But isn't this a little more than gratitude?"

"You're right. I was putting it mildly."

"No, I mean . . . Never mind. What is it that you want? Again to have dinner?"

"No. I want a hole."

"Excuse me?"

"I want you to pierce my ear. It's obvious you're upset about something. You ran off last night, and you refuse to see me again. I must have done something terribly wrong, and I must be punished."

Strangely, instead of being struck by the fact that he was talking of being punished, when I myself had recently gone through my need to be punished (which I had assumed was very unique to my person), I said with a touch of disdain, "By getting your ear pierced?" This punishment seemed so insignificant compared to the one I had inflicted on myself.

"Is it reversible?" he asked.

"Not completely. If you take the stud out right away, the hole will close and heal, but there will always be a visible dot; a small scar." I wasn't sure this was true, but I wanted to discourage him.

"Well then, there you have it," he said. "From my point of view, getting my ear pierced would be quite a substantial punishment, for there are few things in life I loathe more than irreversibility."

I hoped he wasn't serious. I had no desire to pierce his

ear. "You're a really nice guy, but I can't have dinner with you because I don't have time for your gratitude and appreciation."

"I'm not gay. Despite what you thought at dinner. And I don't want to appear gay, since that's not what I am. So, do straight men get holes on the left or on the right? I can't remember. And what kind of maintenance do holes require, and for how long? Do I get a choice of studs or is there only one kind used for piercing?"

I felt he was bluffing, so I bluffed too and answered his questions. However, he didn't seem to be backing down, and he even made the choice of a stud, a silver one, so I finally said, "Listen, I'm not upset with you. You did nothing wrong. I had a lovely time last night. I just don't want to see you again. So why don't you leave now. Please just leave me alone."

"I'm not leaving until I get pierced. I must pay for my crime, whatever it was," he said, and sat down on the chair provided for people who got their ears pierced. "I'm getting a hole, no matter what. You can't persuade me not to. It's obvious I deserve it."

His attempt at levity (if that's what it was) irritated me. I grabbed the ear stapler and positioned myself. He had a big head, and very high, chiseled cheekbones. I couldn't help being flustered by his beauty, up close. This was a problem. Any state short of perfect *sang-froid* is not advisable in the art of ear piercing. I was about to go ahead anyway, but at the last second, I paused and said, "I'm trembling. Are you sure you want this? It might not be centered."

"Do it," he said.

I did.

Right afterward, we looked at each other, both a bit stunned, I think. He averted his eyes and stared straight ahead. To my surprise, he was blushing. He finally broke the silence with a cracked voice: "Now will you have dinner with me?"

"No, I told you I wouldn't. You've thanked me more than enough. You don't need to thank me again. I don't want to be a burden. I don't want to be seen out of obligation."

"So *that's* what this is about?" he nearly shouted. "Then I've been unjustly punished! You falsely accuse me of generosity, which is a crime I didn't commit, nor intend to commit, at least not in inviting you to dinner." He turned to the mirror, and added crossly, "It's unfortunate about the ear. I resent that. When in fact I was operating out of purely selfish motives."

I made no response.

"I very selfishly want to have dinner with you again. Unless, of course, you just . . . don't like me, which I could understand. I would perfectly understand if, for example, you didn't like the way I dressed, or if you thought I was too discriminating about pH levels, or if you disliked any number of other little deviations of mine. But even if that were the case, I would not care, because you see, your inclinations don't matter very much to me, nor your desires. I am being very selfish, I hope you notice. Please Anna, accept my invitation. I promise you I'm thinking only of myself. I'm being a selfish bastard."

"Well, if you put it that way, I can't refuse."

That evening, we met at a restaurant near the one we had been to the night before. Damon was already sitting down when I arrived. I was stunned when I saw him. Over his ear, he was wearing what looked like a diaper. It was actually a big white bandage, which covered almost half of his head. I thought he must have had an accident. But he explained that he had taken the stud out of his ear, wanting the hole to close and heal, and was simply being cautious, trying to minimize the chances of infection and maximize the chances of complete reversal.

He then added: "But I want you to know that I'm only getting rid of the hole because I didn't deserve it. If I had, I would leave it open forever."

During the meal he asked me a lot of questions about my life and about my past. I felt he was fishing for something, but it took me a while to figure out what it was. He was fishing for a pattern; some pattern of self-sacrifice. He wanted to know if selflessness and heroism (his words) were recurring traits of mine. He asked me how many instances, comparable to the subway incident, there had been in my life. At the risk of disappointing him, I had to answer: none. In my own defense, I pointed out that opportunities for heroics of that type don't often arise in the average life.

Then we talked about my love of acting.

After dinner we went to the same park we had gone to the night before, and walked along the river, and talked. Eventually, we stopped talking and stood side by side, looking at the water.

He asked, "After that meeting with your professor, did you consider giving up acting?"

"No. I realized I'd rather spend the rest of my life trying

to become a successful actor, even if it meant failing, than succeed at anything else."

We glanced at each other. Struck once again by the absurdity of his bandage, I almost burst out laughing, but thankfully restrained myself just in time and avoided having to do the MMO procedure. His bandage looked as though it were hiding some huge protrusion, some horrible deformity. But I was not disgusted, as he smiled softly, and leaned his head toward mine, clearly to kiss me. I could not imagine, at that moment, anything he could put on his head that would disgust me. I closed my eyes.

But the kiss never came.

When I opened my eyes, his face was transformed; frozen in an expression of pain. His eyes were vacant.

With the movements of an old person, he turned away and went to sit on a bench nearby. I sat next to him and asked him if something was wrong.

His voice was faint. "I was almost happy with you this evening," he said. "Normally, I am never happy. I sometimes try to be; I often seem to be, but I never am, and probably never will be, and undoubtedly never should be."

"And now, you are no longer almost happy?"

He chuckled sadly and said, "No, not almost at all."

"Are you merely not almost happy or are you actually almost not happy?"

"Neither. I am way past 'almost.' I'm downright unhappy."

"Why are you suddenly not almost happy anymore?"

"Because, I just realized how to make you happy. And

the thought of it makes me shudder." He paused. "I will do it, though. Not right away, mind you. I'm not ready yet. But before long. And our relationship will change."

"For the worse?" I asked, choosing to ignore the more obvious questions.

"I can't say." He got up and faced the river.

To his back, I nagged: "Would you mind clarifying why you're not almost happy anymore? It didn't come through clearly."

He looked at me, seeming slightly hurt, and finally answered: "Because I will be sacrificing my happiness for yours."

He turned away again, but before I had a chance to come up with an appropriate response, he spun back, and, with forced cheerfulness, said, "Hey, do you want to go dancing?"

"Right now? Where?"

"At a nightclub, for instance."

I agreed. He took me to a nightclub that he said he went to—sometimes frequently. He danced. I didn't. I suppose I shouldn't have agreed to go if I wasn't in the mood to dance, but I didn't know I wasn't until I got there.

He knew a few people, some of whom danced with him. The fluidity of his movements, which I had noticed before, was even more apparent in his dancing. I watched him for a long time. I overheard people talking about him. They referred to him as the Liquid Angel. Suddenly, a woman he was dancing with tried to kiss him and he slapped her. I think I was more shocked than she was. She merely shrugged, rolled her eyes, and danced off, apparently unfazed. He continued dancing as if nothing had happened, while I delicately touched my cut, remembering the man who had slapped me in the street.

After a while, I started feeling neglected, even though Damon did not seem to be enjoying himself a great deal dancing. The expression on his face was very intense. He sometimes closed his eyes and shook his head in a way that resembled someone trying to forget something. Eventually, I no longer wanted to be there, but I couldn't get myself to interrupt him, so I decided to just leave; he had been rude anyway, by ignoring me, so I tried not to feel guilty about not saying good-bye. Looking at him one last time, I saw him for what he really was: a stranger, to whom I meant nothing, and who should mean nothing to me.

I left the nightclub and stopped at a pay phone in the street. I left a message on his machine saying I was sorry I left without saying good-bye, but that I had suddenly felt very tired and dizzy and hadn't wanted to disturb him.

I went to the park by the river, to think and try to relax before going home. After the subway incident, one might have expected me to be weary of dark and deserted city places. If I hadn't been so preoccupied by my own thoughts, I might have actually noticed that the park was dark and deserted. I might even have cared. And perhaps been reluctant to wander there alone at such a late hour.

It wasn't until two young men were blocking my path, clearly menacing me, that I realized my mistake. I, who had never before in my life been mugged or bothered violently by strangers, was greatly surprised to find myself involved in such situations twice in one week. Tonight I learned that it was much worse to be the victim than the rescuer.

My attempt to use my pepper spray was awe-inspiringly brief this time: I reached into my bag for it, but one of the men, as if reading my mind, plunged his hand into my bag as well, grabbed the spray, and flung it aside. It was at that moment that I felt myself slipping into a strange state of shock. I made only one more attempt at saving myself, by darting between the men and heading for the park's exit. This didn't work, of course, and that's when my state of shock became full-fledged: my brain started forming strange expectations as to what would happen to me.

In retrospect, I realize that the men were about to rape me, but at the time, when they pulled off my pants and unzipped their flies, it seemed unquestionable that they were going to pee on me. For some reason, I was convinced, right then, that all vicious attacks began by getting peed on. I could almost recall hearing evening TV newscasts, frequently reporting stories such as, "After getting viciously urinated on by the five assailants, the tourist was robbed, and then stabbed to death." Of course, I can only relate this painlessly (even, somewhat, lightheartedly), now that it's in the past.

I wasn't sure what would happen after the initial peeing process. Perhaps the robbing and stabbing processes. Thankfully, I never got to find out, because a stranger came to my rescue. It is probably distasteful of me to mention that he was very handsome; or to have even noticed it, I'm sure; and for it to be the first thing I mention. But he was. In a TV actor sort of way. And as he was wrestling with my attackers, a commercial of sorts ran through my head: the new way for young singles to meet! Rescue someone, or get attacked and be rescued yourself!

The struggle lasted a long time. I was of no help, having lost all my strength and presence of mind early on. Finally, the attackers gave up and ran away, and the stranger was left with barely a scratch. He did, actually, have a scratch, on his hand, which he was looking at. He touched it and groaned and said "Ow."

"Is it broken?" I asked.

"Yes, the skin is almost broken."

"No, I meant the hand."

He looked at me with mild shock, and said, "No. But the skin is scratched, chafed, almost bleeding. And how are you? I trust I interrupted the ceremonies in time?"

Not believing my ears, and still without my full mental faculties, I said "Hello?" Although I did not like his last comment, I did not want to dislike him. He had possibly just saved my life.

"I hope they did not get very far with you?" he said.

Instinctively, I looked down at myself, and, seeing no trace of urine, replied, "No, I don't think they did."

"Fine. Do you need help with your pants?"

"No," I said. Sitting in the cold dirt, I kept turning my pants over and over in my hands, having apparently forgotten how to put them on. In truth, I felt as if I had never known, never owned that piece of information. The man was standing near me, and I wanted to fool him, make him think I knew very well what I was doing. I maintained a frown of know-how and determination on my face for as long as I could, until I no longer could, and then broke down in tears. He squatted next to me and gently, effectively, helped me into my pants without uttering the slightest wise-ass comment. I felt a surge of gratitude and was restrained from expressing it only by my embarrassment.

He dropped me home by cab. Before we parted, he handed me his card, and said, "If you wouldn't mind, I would be grateful if you could phone me tomorrow to tell me if you're all right. It would ease my conscience."

"Okay," I said, and looked at his card. The name on it was Nathaniel Powers and underneath were the words: Etiquette Expert.

"What's your name, by the way?" he asked.

"Anna Graham," I replied, and tried to think of some suitable parting words. "Thank you" came to mind, but felt strange, inappropriate somehow. It struck me as something one said regarding a nice experience. One could, of course, argue that his rescue of me was a nice experience, especially for me. But still.

So, as I stood in front of my building, watching him get back in the cab, all I said was good-bye.

Chapter Four

The next day, I just wanted to sleep, I just wanted to stay unconscious. The phone rang twice, and I let my machine answer. The first call was from a friend; the second was from my boss at Copies Always, wondering where I was.

The phone woke me up a third time, a few hours later. When I heard Damon leaving a message, I picked up. I was barely awake, and he asked why I sounded so strange.

"I was sleeping," I said.

"In the middle of the day?"

"Yeah."

"Is something wrong? You don't sound well. I'm sure it's my fault. I feel terrible about last night. I was rude. I abandoned you at the nightclub."

"Yeah, but it doesn't matter. It's nothing, compared to . . ."

"Compared to what?"

"Compared to other things that can happen in life."

"Like what? What happened?"

"Nothing. Nothing special. Just . . . nothing."

"Tell me. What happened? I can tell something did."

"Oh, I was just . . . slightly . . . attacked. Last night."

"Attacked!"

He made me tell him the story, which I did as briefly as possible, so I could go back to sleep.

Then he said, "I wish I could have saved you myself. Why was I not there for you? I should have been there for you. Can you imagine if something had happened to you? Can you imagine the guilt you would have left me with?"

Once again I found myself subtly hurt by what he said, but I ignored it, out of exhaustion.

"Is there anything I can do for you?" he asked.

"No, it's okay, I'm very well."

"All right, I'll let you get some rest. But I do want to see you again. Is that okay with you?"

At the mention of "rest," I dozed off and missed what came after.

He shouted "Anna!" in my ear.

I asked him to repeat his question.

"Is it okay with you if we see each other again?" he said.

His syntax was too complex for me, at that moment. "Can you repeat that, more simply?" I asked.

He was silent, and then said, "I want to see you. Do you want to see me again?"

"I can't remember," I mumbled. "But tomorrow I'll remember if I wanted to. Okay?"

"Okay. Sleep well," he said, and hung up.

I fell asleep so quickly that I almost missed noticing how

wonderful it was to be too tired to care about something one cared about too much.

When I woke up later, it was too late to call Nathaniel, as I had promised him. I felt guilty. I would call him tomorrow and amply make up for the oversight. I took a sleeping pill and went back to bed.

The next morning I was extremely awake and alert, unpleasantly so, in fact; painfully aware of everything that had happened to me, down to the last, horrid detail. I stayed in bed for forty-five minutes to straighten out my thoughts and figure out how I felt about things. I *would* see Damon again, since he wanted to, but things would have to change. He'd have to open up a bit. I would see Nathaniel too, if he wanted to. I'd thank him, and, who knew, in addition to saving me, he might succeed in distracting me, which, in the state I was in, was not necessarily the easier task.

I went to work at Copies Always and called Nathaniel during my lunch break. We had dinner that evening. He was fun to be with, much more straightforward than Damon. He told me about his etiquette expertise. People call him when they are in a crisis and urgently need to know about some rule or other. His etiquette hot line is a 900 number that costs $3.95 per minute, the average length of a call being six minutes. I asked him if that was all he did in life. No, he said; he also played the cello. I was thrilled: my favorite instrument. After dinner, we walked over to his place so that he could play it for me. When we arrived at his building, instead of following him up to his apartment, I sighed and said it was such a beautiful evening, and asked him if he would mind bringing his cello down instead, so that he could play some for me outside.

"You're cautious and wise," he said. "I'll bring it down."

We sat on a bench under some trees. He played me his own compositions. They were unusual, very beautiful and strange; sometimes even sinister.

When he had finished, I said, "An etiquette expert who's an expert cellist. Funny combination."

"You think so?"

"I think so. Is this all you do in life?"

He shook his head and said "No," suddenly serious, almost gloomy. He took a ticket out of his coat pocket and handed it to me. "Tomorrow night, if you're free, and interested."

"What is this?"

"Why spoil the surprise? Although honestly, I doubt anything could spoil the surprise."

The following night I went to the address on the ticket. To my astonishment, the ticket I was holding was my admission to a show of male strippers. Perhaps Nathaniel was just going to *watch* the show with me. Perhaps this was the third thing he liked to do in life: watch men strip. I held on to this hypothesis until I no longer could: there were no men in the audience.

From a purely objective point of view, he was very good. He had everything those men are supposed to have. He was one of the best. He went about it professionally, the audience seemed very pleased with him, and yet, I— who knew him a little better than the rest of the women— suspected, even sensed, that his heart wasn't in it. But he put on a good act. There was a radiant smile on his face, much of the time. He rolled his hips energetically and strutted around the stage in apparent good fun.

Afterward, we went to a bar. I told him I had enjoyed the show, that I thought he was good. My critique was limited to remarking, "You dance well." I did not feel comfortable expressing any of my other opinions, such as, "You rolled your hips wonderfully. You are very sensual." Probably the most coveted compliment would have been, "You turned me on." Although, on second thought, I didn't get the impression this was the type of thing he was breathlessly waiting to hear. At least not in connection to his stripping. With regard to his cello playing, it would have gone over better, I think.

Later, I said to him, "Etiquette expert, expert cellist, male stripper. Are you hiding any more professions up your sleeve?"

A cloud swept over his face. "Yes. There is something else." He slid a hand up his sleeve and took out a piece of paper. He held it up between his index and middle fingers, and said, "I always hide a profession up my sleeve." He flipped the paper over. It was blank on both sides. He took out a pen, scribbled something on it, and handed it to me.

On the paper was an address, specifying the third floor, and underneath he had written "My guest," and had signed his name at the bottom.

He then said, "If you're interested and free. Tomorrow evening. At seven."

The next day, at seven, I went to the address on the paper. To my great surprise, what I found on the third floor of

that address was a Weight Watchers meeting. I didn't
know what to make of it. I showed the paper to the receptionist, and she told me to go in. I sat in the audience
and waited. A few people were already there, and more
were coming in. And then Nathaniel came in. He didn't
look at me. He walked to the front of the class and started
talking. Apparently, he was a Weight Watchers counselor.
He talked about his experience, about how fat he had been.
Supposedly 375 pounds. (Hard to believe.) Following a
tragedy in his life. A tragedy that led him to overeat. I
wondered what the tragedy had been, but he did not
mention it. He spoke with intelligence and sensitivity. He
was appealing. It occurred to me he might have made a
good actor. And perhaps he was that, too.

After the meeting, I had dinner with him. It was strange,
sitting in front of him, watching him eat, after knowing
the problems he had with food. He must have sensed my
discomfort, because early on in the meal he told me he no
longer had much of an eating disorder. I asked him what
the tragedy had been.

"It's nothing like what you're thinking," he replied.
"It's not romance or family-related. It was business-
related."

"Business-related," I mused. "I can't imagine which of
your four businesses it could be related to. Unless these
are still not your only businesses."

"Yes, well, I don't feel comfortable discussing it further."

We finished the meal talking of other things.

The next day, Damon and I were walking in a park, by
the river, a few blocks away from the one in which I had
been attacked.

Hanging out with Nathaniel had reminded me what a normal person should be like: open. (Not that Nathaniel was terribly normal, but still.) I was fed up with Damon's secrecy and mystery. It offended me. And I was telling him exactly that, as we strolled among the benches and trees. I told him I had trouble accepting his "private ways" and that as much as I enjoyed his company, I did not see the point of continuing to see him if he was not going to open up to me at least a little.

"You won't tell me anything about your family or your past," I argued. "It's too bad, but I can take it. At least for now. What I can't take is that you don't even want to talk about your job. That's going too far, don't you think? You can't be secretive about *everything!* You told me you work with the weather. So maybe you're a weatherman or something. What's the big deal? I mean, I could understand your secrecy if you were a stripper, or a weight-loss counselor, or even, I don't know, an etiquette expert. But the weather? There is no reason, no reason on earth, why you should be reluctant to talk about that profession. Which is why I am losing patience." I huffed and looked away.

He reached inside the bag he was carrying and took out a present, which he handed to me. It was a box, about four inches long, gift-wrapped in blue paper, with a pink ribbon.

"What is this?" I asked.

"It's for you. Open it."

"No," I said, "I want to know about *you*, not get some material gift as a substitute."

"It's not material."

Although I barely paid attention to this response, I did

wonder if the present might be a poem. Was a poem material? "But still, Damon," I said. "I want to know about what you do, exactly."

"Then open the present," he repeated.

Exasperated, I opened it and looked inside. At first I thought there was nothing. But after a moment I saw that there was *nothing;* so much so, in fact, that there was not even the bottom of the box. Or at least, I could not see it. It was blurry, foggy.

I looked at Damon.

"Take it out," he said.

"Take what out? There's nothing."

"Come, now."

I snapped at him: "I don't see anything inside the box. Not even its bottom."

"Take out that which prevents you from seeing."

I stared at him.

"Just scoop it out with your fingers," he said.

I felt foolish, but obeyed him, and the fog came out in my hand. It was denser than fog, and did not disperse. What it looked like, actually, to a tee, was a small white cloud. It sat there on my hand, but I did not feel it; it was not concrete enough, not material enough. I lowered my hand, and the cloud just hung there, in the air, like a week-old birthday balloon that had lost the energy to soar, but was not yet dead enough to sink to the ground.

I looked inside the box, to see if there was anything even more incredible. There wasn't. Inside the box, this time, was the bottom of the box.

I looked again at the cloud, which had floated two or

three inches away, due to the slight breeze coming in from the river.

My first concern was whether other people were close enough to notice this thing, hanging out in the park's air. I looked around, but there was no one near us.

"What is this?" I finally asked.

"It's my career."

Ah, yes, that had been my question, which, in retrospect, seemed rather petty and stubborn. And yet I did not regret having asked it.

"You wanted to know about my profession," he said. "So now you know. As I told you, I'm a scientist, and I work with the weather . . . but more specifically, with water." He cleared his throat. "I discovered a way to make small clouds. Bonsai clouds, you could call them. I've been working on developing different varieties, different strains, and I'm now focusing on one area of development. But I don't want to bore you with that."

"I'm not bored. What area?"

"Giving them more substance."

"It's incredible," I said.

"What part? Giving them more substance, or—?"

"No, I mean the cloud. But everything else too, actually."

"Oh, thank you! I'm glad you like it."

I nodded, feeling extremely self-conscious, I don't know why. "Can I touch it again?" I asked.

"Of course. Fondle it as much as you want. Though you won't feel much. Actually, I'd be interested to know how much you do feel, since you're the only person so far I've shown one of my clouds to."

I stared at him in disbelief.

He went on: "I've often wondered if one's sensory perception of such an insubstantial thing differs from person to person. My guess is no, but let's see."

I touched the cloud, and slowly pushed my fingertips against it. My fingers did not enter the cloud more than half an inch or so. Instead, the cloud was being pushed by my fingers. I then grabbed it with both hands, and my fingers sank into it without any perceptible resistance. Yet it did not quite feel like air. The difference was very subtle, and I wasn't yet sure how to describe it.

Then, like an ax, I sliced my hand through the cloud, and it remained whole, barely disturbed. I joined my palms together and sliced both of my hands through the cloud, halting in the middle and parting my hands. The cloud separated into two halves, which I then pushed back together.

"It's dense," I said. "More dense than real clouds in the sky, I imagine. It does not disperse. It tends to remain whole."

"I'm pleased you noticed. I'm striving for yet greater density."

It was only then that a question popped into my head; a question it was odd of me not to have asked sooner and that it was irrelevant to ask now because the answer was obvious. But I decided to ask it anyway: "Are you putting me on? Is this some kind of trick?"

"No, I'm not a magician," he said.

Damon left for his country house the next day. He said he had some work to do, but that he would be back in a week. He let me keep the cloud.

I missed him while he was away. I was truly enamored, and I decided that the next time I saw him I would make a move on him.

I cherished the cloud that whole week. It was almost like a pet. It even peed in the pocket of my windbreaker once. Or rather, "rained" in my pocket.

I saw Nathaniel a few times. He was charming, and interesting, and interested in me, romantically, even, I believe. But my thoughts were too full of Damon for me to be able to return his interest. That did not prevent us from spending time together, however. He played his cello again, and when I remarked that I had never known anyone as multitalented, he scoffed and said, "You don't even know the half of it."

"What's the other half?" I asked.

"You might never know."

I did not persist, but instead thought to myself, dreamily and snobbishly: Well, whatever it is, I'm sure it doesn't compare to making clouds.

Suddenly, his buzzer rang. He ignored it.

"Aren't you going to answer it?"

"No."

His tone was a little gruff, so I didn't probe further.

The buzzer rang again and kept ringing for about a minute, and then stopped. A moment later, something struck his window. And then again. Pebbles. I looked down at the street, which was not far below, his apartment being on the second floor. I saw a man, a Hasidic Jew, with a black hat and ringlets, looking up at me and throwing pebbles at the window. It was a very beautiful man, who looked strangely familiar.

"There's a Hasidic Jew throwing things at your window."

He sighed. "It's not a man, it's a woman in disguise."

"Why is she in disguise?"

"So that people won't recognize her. She's famous."

I looked down again at the person, who did indeed look like a woman, now that I was aware of it. A very beautiful woman. But I still couldn't place her.

"She looks familiar," I said. "Who is she?"

"Chriskate Turschicraw."

"The model?"

"Yes."

I looked again and it did look like her exactly. But how was it possible?

I had read articles about Chriskate Turschicraw. She was the most famous, the most highly paid model in the world. During the past few months, a series of strange events had occurred surrounding her. There was a cult, growing larger, who had decided that she was God. They worshipped her, collected her magazine interviews and modeling photos, killed the paparazzi who annoyed her, and then went to jail for life for the murders (this happened on two occasions). They sacrificed themselves for her, and killed their own members if one of them didn't treat her well or displeased her. One member killed himself because he was following her down the street, asking her if she needed help carrying her shopping bag, and she said, "You're bugging me." He then said, "I'm sorry," and shot himself right in front of her. I remember being astonished, when I heard that story on the news, at how sensitive and offended the man must have been, and thinking that he should have had thicker skin.

"Why is Chriskate Turschicraw trying to get your attention? And why are you ignoring her?" I asked Nathaniel.

"I've known her for a long time, since before she became a model. She's been in love with me for years. Or infatuated. Or obsessed—whatever you want to call it. Sometimes we're friends, but sometimes her infatuation makes it hard for us to be friends, and we go through periods of tension, like now, when I need space, need to be alone, and she doesn't let me, and she gets upset. I have to warn you she's very jealous."

"And you have no interest in her beyond friendship?"

"I'm not in love with her. I've tried, I can't be; she's not to my taste."

"In what way is she not to your taste?"

"She's not beautiful enough."

"What!"

"It's as simple as that. I'm being frank."

"But she's considered the most beautiful woman in the world. I mean, she's *gorgeous.*"

"But not enough."

"Are there women you find more beautiful?"

"No."

"Men?"

"No."

"Then I'm confused. Is beauty the only thing that can make you interested in someone romantically?"

"I thought so all my life. But I'm not sure anymore. I may have encountered an exception," he said, looking at me meaningfully.

I chose not to ask him what that exception was.

When I left his apartment, after talking about Chriskate

another half hour, the model had apparently given up and left, but I was wrong, for she accosted me as soon as I walked into the street. Up close she was breathtakingly beautiful.

"You're the woman who was just now with Nathaniel, right?" she asked.

"Yes," I answered, intimidated.

"He seems very interested in you. You must be interesting. Would you mind if we had coffee?"

"Oh, I don't know. Why do you want to?" I asked, as casually as possible.

"I think he's in love with you. You must be an extraordinary person. I very much want to know you. Please, there's a coffee shop right there. Just for ten minutes. I'd like to talk to you."

So we went. Soon after we sat down, she asked, "Are you in love with him?"

"Not at the moment."

"That's a relief. I'm in love with him, and he's not in love with me, and I don't know why. But he is in love with you. Isn't he?"

"I don't know," I said, even though I thought he seemed to be.

"Do you know what it is about you that he . . . appreciates so much?"

"No."

"That's too bad. I would like to know. I would like to be friends with you for a while. Can you help me? I would like to study you," she said, as I studied her face.

There was something vulnerable, innocent, and pure about her. Magazines had often remarked on the fact that she was beautiful in a way that made you like her. When you saw her face, you felt warmly toward her, you wished her the best, even though you'd never met her.

She had wispy blond hair, and her features were of the most extraordinary delicacy and exquisiteness. She was twenty-three years old. The media had nicknamed her "the Shell," partly because of her reclusiveness and lack of cooperation with them and partly because her complexion and coloring resembled the subtle pink and white tones inside a conch. It was a well-known fact that people got the urge to stare at photos of her for longer than at other models. It was even considered therapeutic: it filled the viewer with pleasure, and it relieved pain. There was a new form of therapy in which patients were made to focus on different parts of her face in a photograph. They had to stare at her left eye, then her right, then a nostril, then parts of her mouth. Staring at her eyebrows had been found to be particularly soothing.

"I can take you to great parties if you're interested," she said to me. "Really fun parties. I think you'll enjoy yourself, and you'll meet a lot of interesting people. This way I can be around you and get to know you, and hopefully understand."

I felt sorry for her. "I'm not sure that it would do much good. There's nothing unusual about me that you'll pick up and that will be of any help to you."

"There must be. I may not figure out what it is, but I'm sure it's there. Nathaniel would not be with you so much if there wasn't something about you that made a very strong impression on him. He's never been with anybody very much, except a bit for me, at one point, because he found me pretty. But he seems more into you than he ever was into me. Have you two slept together?"

"You know, I don't know if this is such a good idea. I'm very sorry that the situation is not how you would like it to be, but I'm not sure we should get our lives mixed up together."

"But you said you're not in love with him. Wouldn't you like to be friends with me as well as with him? I'm an interesting person too, you know. Maybe even more than him."

She did indeed seem rather interesting, even if it was just her naive boldness.

Perhaps in an effort to get me to know her, she sped me through her childhood, her background, her life. She tried to be charming, and was. She asked me some questions about my life, which I answered reluctantly and without revealing much, and she responded with interest, insight, and even wit. When she asked me what my occupation was, I did mention that I was trying to be an actress.

She said there was a movie party the following night, and asked if I would please go with her. It was going to be a small, private party for a big movie that was about to be released, and the cast would be there. She said it might be a good opportunity for me.

I had to admit it sounded very exciting, more exciting than any party I had ever gone to. It seemed like an opening into a world that I had never expected to get a glimpse of before I got at least my first movie role. Nevertheless, I felt guilty for accepting, since I knew I wouldn't be able to help her, that there'd be nothing she'd be able to detect about me that could explain Nathaniel's interest in me.

I told her these thoughts, and she said it didn't matter, that she would still be very grateful if I'd go to the party with her. So I accepted, feeling uneasy.

At the party, men flocked to her while she flocked to me.

She told me about her feelings for Nathaniel. She told me how incredible she thought he was, how he wasn't only incredibly good-looking and charming, but so intelligent: he was the most intelligent person she knew, by far, and so independent in his thoughts, and so caring. And his *cello compositions!* They were amazing. They were confessions, and reproaches, and expressions of anger, she said. Personally, I had never thought of them that way, but now that she mentioned it, hers was not the most unsuitable way to describe his music.

"And what do you think of the fact that he strips at Chippendales and works at Weight Watchers?" I asked.

"That makes him even more perfect, because it contrasts so mysteriously with his deep personality and genius."

I had a good time at the party. Chriskate was charming and tried to please me, and almost wooed me like a lover would, just because she wanted to study, scrutinize, and examine me. She hung around me "to learn," she said. She interrogated me. I found it grotesque: this gorgeous creature, sitting there in front of me, wondering how she was inadequate. All the men buzzed around her, and yet she was observing *me*, the fool, the poor girl.

I felt ugly and inadequate next to her, yet tried to be strong and unbothered. Not a single man paid any attention to me, and yet I felt sorry for Chriskate. The world wasn't fair: that this most beautiful of creatures couldn't get the one she loved, and that plain old me was the one he loved. Then I realized that this reasoning was ridiculous and that what would be unfair was if only beautiful people got love (which was actually often the case).

I finally decided I could be more useful to Chriskate by trying to crush her obsession with Nathaniel. I tried to make her see that there were plenty of other men out there, even better men. I told her she should forget about him, have no more contact with him.

"So that you can have him?" she asked, uncharacteristically suspicious.

"No. I'm in love with someone else anyway. And speaking of men who are more impressive than Nathaniel, this man I'm in love with is a hundred times more impressive."

"You're deluded. I'm sure he doesn't have the talent and genius that Nathaniel has."

"Oh yeah?" I took Chriskate into the bathroom with me and locked the door. I took the cloud out of my handbag and showed it to her. "You don't call *this* talent?"

She was suitably amazed.

I had intended to keep the cloud a secret, even though Damon hadn't asked me to. But I had been unable to resist showing Chriskate. I put the cloud back in my bag, and as we exited the bathroom, I asked, "Did that impress you enough?"

Three men swarmed around her, smiling, kissing her on the cheeks, offering to get her drinks. "It's incredible," she answered me, shooing them away.

I went on: "The man I'm in love with invented a way to make small clouds. I'd say that rates at least as high as Nathaniel's cello compositions, wouldn't you say?"

"No, it doesn't even come close," she said. "It's a beautiful thing, this little cloud; a beautiful little scientific concoction, but it doesn't move me. It doesn't speak to me. It's not art."

"*I* think it's art."

"Science cannot be art. It's a contradiction in terms." Two new men accosted her, one of whom was the star of the movie this party was for.

I felt strange hearing a model talk that way, undoubtedly due to the stereotypes about models.

"Perhaps," I said. "But then if science isn't art, it's greater than art."

We talked of other things for a few minutes, while Chriskate resumed studying me. Suddenly, she looked depressed and edgy, and said to me, "Come." She quickly walked toward the front door with her face in her hands, and I followed her. People watched her leave the apartment.

We were alone in the hallway. She was crying.

"They all look dumb to me, compared to Nathaniel," she said, pacing. "I often flip through magazines looking for male models, and they all look dumb."

"Why would you look to male models as a source of high intelligence? You should go to bookstores and look at author photographs."

"I do. It's the same thing. They look dumb. I walk down the street and no one I pass looks as smart as him. His expression is very intelligent. You can immediately see that he must have a really interesting way of looking at life, that he must have really interesting and original thoughts. Don't you think so?"

"Not particularly. Your perception is skewed by your

love for him. That's what love does. Or infatuation. You're not objective. If you were to let a year pass without having any contact with him, I think you would be cured. You would see him for what he is: not exceptional. You think there is no one else like him, and you're right. Even though there may not be any man who has the same specific qualities he has—because no two men are alike—there are many men who have different qualities, more extraordinary qualities."

Even though I had had a good time with Chriskate, I felt a bit overwhelmed by her obsession, and I needed to take a break from her. So I turned her down when she suggested that we have dinner the following night, and instead I had dinner with my family, at their apartment.

The cloud had rained in my bag at the party, after it had been shown off in the bathroom. When I got home after the party I decided to do an experiment and freeze the water, to prevent it from turning back into a cloud right away, just to see what would happen, if anything. By morning, the water had turned into an ice cube, which I brought to my parents' apartment when I went for dinner, because I couldn't bear to be parted from Damon's gift for very long. Damon had been gone for a week, and I missed him.

I placed the ice cube in their freezer. There were no other ice cubes there, which was good; there would be no risk of my not recognizing it when time came to go home.

My parents and my brother and I sat in the living room and chatted before dinner, catching up on things. My brother and I hadn't seen each other in a while, and I asked him how school was. He was feeling down, felt uninterested in anything, didn't know what he was going to do in life, had low self-esteem. We were drinking soft drinks as we talked, and when I asked him about his grades, he seemed reluctant to answer. He took a gulp of his Coke and chewed on the ice while mumbling his response, making it conveniently impossible to understand, which annoyed me. Suddenly, my annoyance changed into horror, and I got up and screamed, "Spit that out! Stop chewing! Don't swallow the ice!"

"Why?" he asked.

"Spit it out! Just do it! It's bad, it's not ice, it's not water, it's *dangerous!*"

"I can't, I swallowed it already. What do you mean it's dangerous?"

"Nothing."

I was upset that my little cloud had been eaten alive, while it was in a paralyzed, helpless state.

My brother looked at me angrily, as if expecting an explanation.

So I gave one: "It's just that it was my ice cube, which I brought from home, and I didn't want you to eat it. It was *my* ice cube."

I hung my head low and mourned my cloud melting in his stomach. I wondered if it would harm him. I was nervous about that, actually. More nervous about it than about the fate of my cloud. But maybe it wouldn't harm him. Maybe it would become part of his person in a helpful way.

The following night I had dinner with my family again, still needing a break from Chriskate and even from Nathaniel, and feeling too lonely to have dinner alone. Suddenly, in the middle of dinner, my brother let out a big fart, and my little cloud came out intact and rose above his head. Not having yet seen the cloud, my brother looked at us sheepishly and said, "I'm sorry, it had a mind of its own."

Seeing the direction of our gazes, he looked up and saw the cloud. I jumped to my feet, overjoyed, and grabbed the cloud and put it in my handbag.

"Hey, do you *mind!*" said my brother. "Give that back."

"No."

"*Yes*. It's *my* fart."

"No, it's mine."

"Oh really? How do you figure that?"

"Someone gave it to me as a present."

He looked at our parents. "Everyone at this table knows that this is my fart. They heard me make it and they saw it come out of my body."

"That's enough now. Calm down," said our father.

"But she stole my fart!" My brother stomped his foot and looked as if he were on the verge of tears. "I produced something extraordinary for the first time in my life, so I should have a right to keep it. Or at least *examine* it, for God's sake!"

I quickly left the apartment, apologizing to my parents and telling them I'd call them later. My brother didn't try to wrestle his fart from me, which was a relief.

The following day I did agree to see Chriskate again. We had lunch, but this time our encounter was not pleasant. She asked too many questions. She looked at me too intently, studied me too studiously. She even took notes. And she asked the same questions again and again. She didn't believe my answers.

"What is it about you that Nathaniel likes so much?"

"I don't know."

"You must know. He must have told you."

"No."

"Why don't you want to tell me? Because you think it's pointless? Why don't you let *me* be the judge of that?"

"No, I wouldn't mind telling you if there was something, but I don't think he said anything."

"You don't *think?* That means he might have. That means you're not sure. Can you please think about it harder?"

"I have, I think. I swear, I can't remember. I'm pretty sure he never told me what he liked about me."

"Do you think it's your looks or your personality? Is it mental? Does he think you're smart?"

"I don't know."

"Please, Anna, think."

I sighed and mumbled, "I am thinking. But why do you want to know this?"

Her eyes opened wide. "Oh, so you don't want to tell me, is that it? Cause you don't *approve.* You think it would do *no good.* But you said you would tell me. You assured me you would tell me if you knew."

"Yes, I would tell you if I knew, even though I also think it would do no good. But I would tell you."

"Well then *guess.* Why do *you* think he likes you?"

"I don't know. I'm hideous compared to you. I'm not successful. I'm an aspiring actress who's not even a waitress in her free time: I'm a Xeroxer and an ear piercer. I'm not strikingly witty or gentle or even fun. I may be a little strange, but he didn't see that side of me. Take your pick."

"I'm sure you have some assets you're hiding."

"I wish."

"No, no, you must have. Either you're not telling me on purpose, or you're just not trying hard enough to think of them." She then added musingly, "Or maybe you take them so much for granted that you don't realize they're there and remarkable."

I couldn't wait for the lunch to be over. She insisted that we go get a drink somewhere, to continue the search for my hidden assets, but I declined and said good-bye. She would not accept that. She would not say good-bye. So I started walking away, and she followed me, begging me to tell her my secret. Then some photographers recognized her and started taking her picture. She was loudly asking me, "Why are you special? How are you remarkable? What is it that you *do?*" Embarrassed, I started running away, and she ran after me, and the photographers ran after her.

"Just tell me, what is it that you *do?*" she repeated.

I shouted back: "I don't do anything! Leave me alone! I just am."

I finally ditched her and went home, panting.

I was not special and I was not remarkable. Anybody who thought so was deluded.

I took a hot bath when I got home and relished the silence. I had never relished silence as much as then.

All I cared about was for Damon to come back. I

wanted to see him again. I wanted him to take me away from this insanity, into a world of fantasy.

As I was getting out of my bath, he called. A perfect ending to a perfect bath.

"I'm back," he said.

"Great!"

"But I have to leave again."

"When?"

"In an hour or two."

"For where?"

"The same place."

"Why?"

"Same reason. Work."

"Oh. When will you be back?"

"Not for a while. Two or three weeks, perhaps."

"Oh." I was crushed and disillusioned. I said nothing.

"But would you like to join me for dinner this evening in the country?" he said. "We could drive out together. Although I realize it's short notice."

I accepted without hesitation. He asked me if two hours was enough time to get ready. He added that I might want to bring an overnight bag in case I felt like extending my stay a little.

While I was packing, I could not help thinking about my plan to take the initiative romantically next time I saw him. I decided that the plan would remain in effect. After our dinner, I would try to kiss him, and if he responded by either (a) slapping me, like he did to the woman in the nightclub, or even just (b) gently rejecting me, I would leave. I would take the train home. Or a taxi, if I had to. But—clouds or no clouds—it would be over.

I called the train station to find out at what time the last train left for the city, from the station near his house: 12:40 A.M., they said. This meant a move would have to be made by midnight. If not by Damon, then by me.

Chapter Five

The drive out was pleasant and uneventful. Damon asked about my social life, my friends. I didn't tell him about Chriskate Turschicraw, or about my lunch with her. I only said I had had a miserable day, and that I didn't want to think about it. In a little over an hour we arrived at his driveway, a long dirt road winding into the woods. The house was large and slightly elevated. A dozen steps led to the front door.

He grabbed my bag and his, and asked if I could get a small bag out of the trunk. I sensed that this request was intended to postpone me, to allow him to get to the house first, because as soon as I went for the small bag, he sprinted up the steps and disappeared inside the house, leaving the front door open. Maybe he wanted to make sure the place was presentable, turn the lights on, or whatever.

A few moments later I slowly followed him and found myself standing alone in a small entrance hall. Extremely small, for such a big house. It was in fact a little room, completely enclosed, with a door straight ahead. There was a chair against one wall, and I was trying to decide if I should sit or knock on the door, or just open it. I felt like a frustrated Alice in Wonderland, because the signs were missing; it seemed to me that if the chair were not going to wear a sign that said "Sit on me," then the door should have one that said "Knock on me." Or vice versa. I was about to knock on the door, when Damon opened it and stood in the doorway, against a background that was astonishing.

He was looking at me very intently, scrutinizing my reaction, while smiling in a shy, sheepish way. He seemed happy and alive, brimming with vitality. I, on the other hand, turned white; inwardly at least, and I'm pretty sure outwardly too.

Behind Damon was a huge room with not much furniture, and the little of it I could see seemed to be made of marble and glass. But what was noticeable about the room, and let me stress that this was very noticeable, very visually striking, was that there were clouds in the air of it. Big clouds. About seven of them. There was one just to the left of Damon, shoulder level. And another, further back, was bigger than me.

Damon stepped aside to let me in, but I didn't budge.

"This is a bit unsettling," I explained. "You didn't warn me."

"Oh, I'm sorry. Are you uncomfortable? I didn't anticipate this reaction," he said, shooing away the closest cloud with a few waves, like a smoker realizing his smoke is disturbing another person. "The reason I didn't warn you was that I wanted to surprise you. In a pleasant way. But come in. Don't be afraid."

My footsteps echoed on the marble floor. "Is this what you've been working on this week?" I asked.

"Is what?"

"Making these big clouds?"

"No. I've had clouds like these for a long time. Size was the first thing I figured out; it was the core of my invention. This week I was taking care of other matters."

I looked around, still nervous. There was a blue vinyl couch on the right, which I hadn't seen from the doorway, and there was a glass clock against a wall. The room looked to be straight out of a Magritte painting. There was a staircase at one end, with a cloud halfway up the stairs, or halfway down; I couldn't tell where it was going, if anywhere. There was another close to the window, as if looking out nostalgically. Another one's top was popping out from behind the couch. Two floated near the ceiling. Some were very white and dense, like cotton; others were more loosely knit and see-through. They were all relatively motionless at this moment. I didn't know names of various clouds, but one of them was sort of stringy and fibrous; sickly looking (the kind that looks majestically feathery in the sky, but obviously less so in a house). Most of the others looked plump, like well-fed sharks.

I became aware of a strange sound, music actually, coming from a large object, or sculpture, standing in a corner. On closer look it seemed like a fountain, dripping drops on various surfaces, each one producing a different note, and each note sounding ethereal. The notes were not random; there was a definite melody. It was probably pre-programmed, like a mechanical piano.

Before I had a chance to ask him about this musical

fountain, Damon said he wanted to take me for a row in the boat on his pond while it was still light out. We went.

He was beautiful, rowing in the late afternoon light. And he was calm. Not at all nervous, for someone who was hopefully on the verge of making a move on me. His shirt was transparent, like a sweating man's shirt, except he was not sweating. His chest was heaving from the effort of rowing, and yet there wasn't the slightest sound of breath. His full lips were slightly parted. He looked at me, looking at him, and I looked away. At least I *think* he was looking at me, with his white-blue eyes, but it was hard to be sure because of the hair hanging in front of them.

He raised his face to the breeze and closed his eyes. The wind swept his hair aside. He then looked straight at me. I looked at the oar.

I wished I, too, had hair hanging in front of my face, to hide me. As I contemplated the oar traveling through the murky transparency, something suddenly struck me as odd, as not quite . . . realistic, about Damon's rowing: There was no sound to it. Not even the sound of a ripple when the paddles entered the water. Yet I was not hard of hearing; from this boat, I could hear the birds in the forest. If Damon had been rowing slowly, the silence would have been somewhat more conceivable, but we were advancing swiftly, and his movements were powerful. I don't mean to sound corny, but it was as if he and the water were one, as if he knew it as well as himself, knew how to touch it without disturbing it, without clashing with it.

He was still looking at me, and instead of allowing myself to wallow in self-consciousness, I decided to be courageous. I looked back at him and did not look away. After a moment, he smiled slightly. I reciprocated, almost imperceptibly, and I felt myself relaxing. It wasn't so hard.

I hated the idea of destroying this thrilling, loaded silence, but I couldn't resist venting my new boldness.

"You look like a ghost," I said.

"How?"

"Your rowing is so quiet. You make no sound with the water."

"If you ever, one day, know something well, it won't make any sound either."

I chuckled, a bit disappointed by the silliness of that statement.

"Don't laugh," he said. "It's true. What you know well grows silent."

"True of everything?"

"Yes."

"Even of people?"

"Most obviously of people."

"How sad."

"No. But what's more interesting for you is that it is also true of art."

"Even of music?" I asked, wanting to trap him.

"Yes. Great composers make very little sound with their music."

"You mean good music is minimalist?"

"No. I mean good music is silent."

"No notes?"

"Yes, it has notes."

"So you mean metaphorically silent."

"And also literally."

"How?"

"Oh, come now, Anna, you know what I mean. No matter how loud a piece is, no matter how many *notes* it contains, it is silent if it is great: it is pure, it is essential, it is wholly itself, and it makes no sound."

At the risk of irritating him, I said, "I take it you don't like music."

He stopped rowing and came toward me, crouching low, like a lion stalking its prey, which may not have been an intended effect; I think he was just trying to avoid rocking the boat. He sat down next to me, straddling the bench. "I like music fine," he said softly, so close to my face that I could feel his breath on my cheek. We stared at each other for a while. He said, "Look up."

I looked up, while his eyes remained glued to me.

"Are there any clouds?" he asked.

"A few."

"Do they please you?"

"Yes," I said, looking back at him, wondering if this meant he had made those too.

"More than mine?"

I looked back at the sky and said no.

"Why not?"

"Yours are inside a house."

His face became cold, as if disappointed. He looked away.

I quickly added, "*And,* your clouds are also more substantial, more dense, some of them, and more . . . puffy-like." I made some gestures to illustrate just how puffy and cottony his clouds had struck me. "And their color, also, is more beautiful, more bright, more sharply white."

He laughed, affectionately I believe, even gratefully.

"Thanks," he said.

He rowed us back to shore, and we went for a walk in the woods.

We treaded over slightly rough terrain. He led the way, parting the branches, and was considerate about not letting them whip back in my face. A couple of times, his flimsy shirt and pants got caught on some thorns and I helped deliver him. I could see he was not in his element here, like he had been on the pond. But soon we arrived at his element. A river. Along the edge of which we sat.

First moves are an interesting subject. A male friend of mine once told me that the first move between himself and his girlfriend was made when they were sitting on a bench and it became more awkward to not make a move than to make one. Damon and I were sitting on a rock and I waited for the move that would make the situation less awkward rather than more. He must not have shared my outlook, however, because no move was made. I could have done it myself, of course, but wanted to give him a chance to do it first. The evening was still young and I was still optimistic.

"Dinner must have arrived by now," he said, after a while.

We walked back to the house and went in through the living room's sliding glass doors. Damon walked straight through to the front door. He unlocked it and entered that horrid, instructionless entrance hall I had waited in earlier. Now waiting for us on the chair and on the floor was what, in a moment, was revealed to me as our dinner, in large paper bags that Damon took to the kitchen, saying he'd be back soon.

I didn't mind being left to myself, to relax and feel unself-conscious, after a whole afternoon of his intense presence.

Few activities in life are as tiring as that of hoping to be liked. I felt like a smile, frozen for hours by politeness until it twitched from exhaustion. My charm muscles, wherever they were located, were aching.

After impersonating a jewel all afternoon and aiming my sparks of brilliance at Damon's heart, mind, and groin, I was dying to stop.

In case it isn't clear what sparks of brilliance I'm referring to, I must explain that some people's attempts at being charming consist in *not* doing many of the things they would normally do; in other words, repressing large portions of their personality. I was such a person. Taking this route to charm, I realize, is misguided. At least in my case I think it is. I hope it is. But it's also instinctive. So when I refer to my sparks, I largely mean my few repressed words and gestures. If such a phenomenon were to exist in physics or cosmology—and maybe it does—I imagine it might be called something like: positive absences.

I paced the living room, itching to vent my lack of inhibition before Damon came back. First off, I hummed "The Hills Are Alive with the Sound of Music," to draw pleasure from the room's reverberation, followed by a tune from "The Double Life of Véronique"—always my favorites when it came to testing the resonance of a hard, bare, and promisingly resonant room. As I walked around, I kicked my heels on the marble parquet and increased the loudness of my humming. I was surprised at how good it was, the reverberation; I had almost expected the clouds to act like carpet, absorbing and ruining the echo.

Still wound up, I ran my fingers along the back of the couch to make sure it was as awfully vinyl as it looked. It was. The kind that likes to stick to your skin. I opened my mouth a little, and my eyes a lot, to give the couch the gaping treatment such an unworthy fabric in such a beautiful living room deserved. At least it was a rough, textured vinyl, so it did not shine. I scraped my fingernails across it, producing a menacing, grating sound. I kept this up a little longer than one would expect.

Having entertained myself sufficiently for now with the couch, I directed my attention to my next object of fascination (other than the clouds, which I didn't want to harm or dishevel): the musical fountain. I stuck my finger under one of the drops to block its fall. As expected, I pierced a hole in the melody. I watched the drop tremble on my fingertip, fragile and vulnerable, like a tear, crushed it against my neck like perfume.

"A poetic end for a musical drop," said Damon, watching me from the doorway. "Dinner's outside."

I followed him onto the terrace, trying to console myself with the thought: better to have been caught catching one of his drops than using his couch as an emery board.

Outside, a table was set for two. The food had been ordered from a nearby restaurant; a practice he often indulged in, he informed me. A very good restaurant, I decided, after my first bite.

I didn't like how much I liked him. It frightened me. I didn't want to be in such a vulnerable position. I was in no mood to suffer over love; that most frivolous yet most potent source of suffering.

I stared at Damon and tried to find defects. I looked for a flaw in his face. The problem was, he looked like a model. I tried to find that unattractive. Some women did. I didn't see why I couldn't: that typical charming smile. So . . . typical of gorgeous men.

The physical plane wasn't working. Perhaps I'd have more luck on the intellectual one.

For example: Good music makes no sound. What rubbish. Unfortunately, it was not entirely uninteresting rubbish.

Why not then try coming down on his mannerisms. Yes, mannerisms are a good thing to pick on. I searched. His were so . . . They were perfect, actually.

No. Don't give up. There had to be a flaw. Try harder. I held my breath and clenched many muscles and stared at him hard, until I felt my eyes bulging.

"Is something wrong?" he asked, just as I found what I was looking for.

"No."

"You look a little flushed."

"I don't feel flushed."

What I had found was a slight popping out of the jawline on both sides when he chewed. I latched on to that for dear life, as onto a life buoy. But it was a very flimsy buoy that could only keep me afloat while he was chewing; as soon as the slightest wave came along, such as one of Damon's ordinary charming or surprising comments, the buoy and I would sink. And there were other waves as well, such as the fact that everybody's jaw does that when they chew. I fought the wave: just because everybody's jaw does that doesn't mean it's not unattractive. I held on to the buoy.

But it and I were no match for him. He was simply so prodigious, in every way. At least in my eyes.

Before dessert, I grew cold.

We moved indoors and sat at the end of a long glass table and ate a floating island. A dessert I had never heard of or seen before, it consisted of a large bowl of warm liquid custard, with whipped egg whites floating in it. After serving me and himself, he pushed the large bowl to the side.

We ate slowly and talked, and I was smoking, and I noticed absentmindedly that my cigarette had never produced so much smoke. So absorbed was I by our conversation that it took me a while to notice that I could barely see Damon's face behind the smoke. This phenomenon was gradually becoming more pronounced, which I found extremely strange, and I wondered what could be wrong with my cigarette. I was about to remark on it when I realized my cigarette contributed only slightly to the effect. We were not sitting in a cloud of smoke, but in a cloud, period. It must have drifted onto us. I interrupted our conversation to briefly express my delight.

Damon nodded slowly, smiling, and we continued talking, bathed in this mysterious foggy atmosphere that endowed our every word with depth and perfection. Or so it seemed.

I was suddenly distracted by a pitter-patter coming from the dessert bowl. Drops of God knows what, from God knows where, were splattering onto the liquid custard. The floating island was sinking under the weight of what I soon realized were raindrops. This foundering made me nervous.

"I don't mean to interrupt you," I finally said, "but the cloud is raining on the dessert. And sinking it."

Damon leaned toward the bowl and looked. "So it is," he said. He covered the bowl with a plate.

Raindrops started falling on me as well.

"It seems the rain likes desserts," he remarked. "Shall I

cover you with a plate too? Or should we just get out of the rain and take a walk in the woods? The weather to-night is worse indoors than out. There's a section of the woods you haven't seen. I saved it for after dinner because it's particularly pretty at night. I have a warm coat you can wear."

He opened a closet and took out a large down coat. "I haven't worn this in years. I no longer wear opaque clothing." He said this with the same finality, with the same entirely justified self-righteousness as the people who say, "I no longer wear fur."

We entered the woods from another side of the house, but this time we did not walk randomly through uncleared foliage; we followed a beautifully manicured path made of stones, grass, and moss, with flowers along the edge. Lamps were hanging from tree branches at regular inter-vals, lighting the way. We passed iron benches, some black, some white.

We arrived at a small clearing and sat on a white bench. We listened to the crickets and the rustling leaves. I wrapped the coat more tightly around me. And I waited. I leaned my head back. He did too. We couldn't see the stars because a lamp was shining near us. Damon got up and turned off the lamp. We were now in the dark, and the stars were bright. I was a little nervous, and optimistic, expecting him to turn toward me and make his move at any moment. He sort of had to. It would be just too silly of him not to.

Time passed. For the life of me I couldn't figure out what he was up to just sitting there, doing nothing. I de-cided I would not do anything to make the situation less awkward; I didn't want to make it easy for him to get away with doing nothing. So I sat, absolutely motionless and rigid.

That didn't seem to work. So then I sighed impatiently, sort of a huff.

"Are you okay?" he asked.

"Yes," I answered meekly.

If he didn't find this awkward, why should I?

After about fifteen minutes, he turned to me and said, "It was nice, wasn't it?"

"What was?"

"Walking into the woods and sitting here."

"Yes."

We got up and walked back to the house; I was dazed. I looked at my watch. It was 11:00 P.M. He had an hour left to make his move, and if he didn't do it by twelve, then I would have to, in time to catch the last train, depending on the outcome. My stomach flipped with unease as I realized that it would be like "Cinderella," in reverse. By midnight, instead of escaping, I would be pouncing.

Chapter Six

Oh, I forgot to show you the pool," he said, as we walked back. "And I should take you on a tour of the house."

The swimming pool was in the basement. It was very standard-looking, in a very standard-looking room, except that there were numerous rubber ducks, of various shapes, sizes, and colors, lined up against one wall. I suddenly wondered if he had children or was somehow involved with children. I asked him.

"No," he answered simply.

He took a yellow duck and carried it to the pool, squeezing it once along the way, which caused it to make the classic rubber duck squeak. He squatted, placed the duck on the water, and gave it a gentle shove. It sank. He looked at me, as if to observe my reaction. I wasn't sure what reaction he expected me to have. But he kept staring at me expectantly, perhaps waiting for me to seem astonished. Well, I was sorry if I wasn't astonished, but I wasn't. Even though rubber ducks usually floated, so what if one sank? So what if there was something wrong with it? Damon took another rubber duck and handed it to me, motioning that I should place it on the water. I did, and the duck sank. Damon was staring at me with so much expectancy that I was suddenly struck by the absurdity of it and burst out laughing.

"Okay," I said, "I give up. Why are the ducks sinking?"

He seemed relieved by my question. His intense expression disappeared, and to my surprise I saw that it wasn't just relief, it was sudden mild disinterest.

He waved his hand dismissively and said, "Oh, I'll tell you another time."

I decided I would not satisfy him by begging him to tell me. So I ignored my twinge of exasperation and said nothing.

We went back upstairs and sat side by side on the blue vinyl couch. Conveniently, the glass clock was straight in front of us. It was now 11:32 P.M.

Once again, Damon asked me about my dreams and desires, which naturally led us to the topic of acting, among others. But of all my desires, I didn't mention the one that was the most recent and, right now, the strongest: him.

"I wish this moment didn't have to end," he said, to my delight, at five of midnight.

"It doesn't have to," I replied, hoping this wasn't too forward.

"Yes, it does," he said sadly, and added, "I want to remember the way you're looking at me now. I wish I could take a picture of it, and I would, if I didn't loathe photographs."

"I can look at you this way again."

"I hope, for your sake, that you will be able to, but even if you are, your look will be a shell—perhaps a very beautiful shell—but a shell, empty of your heart, empty of sincerity."

"I don't know what you're talking about."

"I know. I wish it could stay that way."

"You're being enigmatic."

"Yes. Grant me that, just a little longer."

He stared at me sadly.

"What are you thinking about?" I asked.

"The alternative," he answered slowly. "The exquisiteness of it."

"What alternative? To what? You're being so mysterious."

"I asked you to . . . grant me that," he almost whispered.

"I should warn you that you are now officially entering the realm of melodrama," I could not resist teasing. But I immediately felt guilty, for I hadn't noticed the tears in his eyes.

Choosing to ignore my warning of impending corn, he said, "This moment will never exist again; the innocence of it, the selfishness of it. The simplicity and purity of it. The sweetness. And the open doors, the potential, the blank future. Every path is still possible, but soon will no longer be. Is there anything significant you would like to say to me?"

"Perhaps, but it might be a little premature."

"And later it will be too late. But that's the way it is; part of the way things are, part of the sadness. But necessary. And good." He paused. "There are so many things

I would like to say to you now, so many assurances and
reassurances, and truths. It would make things easier for
me. But I mustn't. It would be counterproductive. However, having said even this much has made me feel slightly
better."

"Well, not me."

He laughed. I laughed too, despite my annoyance at his
mysteriousness.

He gazed at me. "You are already slipping away, I see."

I could only attribute this statement to his having sensed
my irritation.

"But no," he continued, "I'm fooling myself. This is but
a pale shadow of what will be." He sighed, and his tone
lost its bitterness. "We've talked about your dreams at
length. Now I'll tell you one of mine: it is the hope that
whatever dreams of yours come true, I will have played
even just a small part in their actualization."

I was touched. Now was the perfect time for me to kiss
him. But that was the problem. It was too perfect; so perfect that it would have been silly.

Dong went the clock, slowly. It was the first stroke of
midnight, making the moment even more perfectly silly
for kissing. Therefore, to create a little diversion, I asked,
"At what time is the last train?"

Dong; the second slow stroke.

"You're not thinking of leaving, are you? I was hoping
you could stay."

Dong.

"I don't know," I muttered, trying to appear thoughtful.
I then looked at him, pretended to be overcome by the
intimacy of the moment (*dong*), and leaned forward to
kiss him.

He moved away, to avoid my kiss.

I smiled faintly, with embarrassment (*dong*), and got up from the couch.

"Well, I should be (*dong*) going," I said, with feigned casualness. The strikes of the clock were tragically making the situation even more awkward and confusing, if such a thing were possible. Not to mention the fact that they were loud, obliging me to raise my voice, making it harder for me to sound casual. "I think the last train is at twelve-thirty," I lied, to make sure I wouldn't miss the last train at 12:40. "Would you mind dri(*dong*)ving me to the station, or should I call a cab?"

I walked to the door, and just as I was about to pick up my overnight bag, he took my (*dong*) hand. I faced him and waited for him to do whatever he intended to do. *Dong.* But he did nothing. *Dong.* We just stared at each other. And then it became awkward. I looked at him sadly, disappointed. *Dong.* I almost felt sorry for him. He seemed pathetic to me at that moment. I turned away again, to pick up my bag, and did.

"No, Anna (*dong*), don't," he said softly.

I gave him another chance. I waited a few moments to see what he would do, but he did nothing, so I finally gently said, "This is getting silly, don't you think? I really should be going."

He took my bag from me, placed it back on the floor, and pulled me toward the staircase.

"What are you doing?" I asked hesitantly, not wanting to ruin the romance, if that's what it was. But then I decided that if that was what it was, it was so little, so late, that there was not much I could do to ruin it, and things could only go uphill from here.

"Making you happy," he answered, leading me up the steps.

"I'm not sure you can."

"I'll give it my best shot."

"And make yourself very unhappy in the process, is that it?"

"It's the least I can do."

"Please, I don't want you to *force* yourself," I said. Sarcastically, of course.

He didn't answer, but just kept pulling me up. He held my hand rather tightly, and I started getting the uneasy sensation that I might not be able to free it if I wanted to.

"Perhaps I should let you know that force is not the greatest turn-on for me," I said.

He did not soften his grip. I had not imagined our trip to the bedroom would unfold in this manner.

"This is very unromantic," I snapped.

All he answered was, "Come."

"I'm not interested anymore. Please let go of me. What you're doing is repellent. Do you care?"

Secretly, I thought: who knows, the approach is not my favorite, but it might turn out to be worth it, or at least interesting.

We arrived at a door at the end of a hallway. When he opened it, I was faced with an unfamiliar sight. Halfway into the room were iron bars extending from the floor to the ceiling, making the back part of the room into a sort of cage.

I immediately turned away and tried to run out, but Damon was apparently prepared for this reaction. His grip was painful, and he dragged me toward the bars. I screamed at him to stop, to let me go. I kicked him, and punched him, and dug my nails into him, everywhere I could. I tore his flimsy outfit. His shirt popped open, a few buttons flew off. But it was all in vain. He flung me inside the cell, and slid its door shut between us.

I tried to slide it open, but it was, predictably, locked.

"I apologize for what just happened," said Damon, panting. "I feel very bad about it."

"Let me out of here!" I shouted. "Why do you have me in here?"

"I'm a little shaken up, and so are you, so maybe it's better if I come back later, when we've calmed down."

"No, don't leave me in here! Why are you doing this? Tell me!"

He paused by the door and seemed to hesitate. He said, "I can't right now. I'm not up to it."

Speechless, I watched him walk out. He left the door to the room, but not to my cell, open. He moved down the hallway and disappeared through a doorway on the left.

I turned and pressed my back against the bars, holding two of them tightly in my hands. For a while I couldn't let go, afraid the cell would suck me in, absorb me, become my master, my container. Then I realized it already was.

Against the left wall were television monitors eye-level on a shelf. Five of them, side by side.

In the far left corner was a regular-looking television set. Straight ahead were two windows, facing the garden. Then the back of the cell branched out to the right, but from where I was standing, I couldn't see to where. I stepped forward, hoping that by some miracle the branch led to a way out.

A bowling ball and a hammer were lying in the middle

of the cell. I was perplexed, but more interested in the branch, which, to my distress, I now saw was just an extension of the prison; a more private area, with a bed, and a night table topped by a lamp and an alarm clock. These homey furnishings chilled my blood; a bare prison cell was scary enough, but one with plush beige carpeting and a comfortable-looking bed was truly terrifying. I tried to block out what it meant.

There was a door on the right, behind which I was further horrified to discover a pleasant bathroom.

I went back to the TV monitors. Each screen showed a different room of the house. I recognized the living room, and although the other rooms were unfamiliar to me (Damon hadn't given me the tour after all), I felt it was reasonable to assume they were rooms of this house, for they all had clouds in them.

On one screen I noticed movement. It was him, walking around in a bedroom. I watched him until he plopped down on the bed and lay back.

I wondered why he had these monitors in here with me, and whether I was being filmed as well. I could see no cameras around the ceiling.

I turned to the windows. They were locked, but not barred. I glanced around the room for a heavy object to break them. The one-story jump couldn't be fatal. But the stay could.

There was the lamp on the night table. And the alarm clock. But then my eyes landed on the bowling ball and hammer, either one of which would do much better. I picked up the hammer, and saw a handwritten note taped to its handle. It read:

Dear Anna,

Here are a hammer and a bowling ball for your convenience, so that you won't try to use the lamp or the alarm clock to break the windows. I should warn you, however, that the windows are made of soundproof, bulletproof glass, and that trying to break them will only bruise them, limiting your enjoyment of the view from then on, in case you care about such things.

It was signed Damon. Unlike in the instructionless entrance hall, now I felt more like an informed Alice in Wonderland.

Using all my strength, I banged the hammer against the window. Then against the other window. Again, and again.

Then the bowling ball, throwing it at the windows.

But all of this made only bruises on the glass. And tremendous noise. The furniture and walls rattled.

I went back to using the hammer, panicked by the words: "from then on." Those words implied more than a few hours. Even more than a day, probably. Actually, what was the maximum amount of time those words could imply?

Hammer in midair, I paused and stared into space, thinking about that question.

The hammer came hurling down against the windowpane: "from then on" did not exclude forever.

After a long time, I stopped hammering and throwing the ball. It was obvious I wouldn't break the glass. I dropped the hammer and went to the TV monitors. Damon was still lying on his bed, apparently undisturbed by the racket. He must have expected it.

So. Damon turned out to be a psycho. I still had a faint hope that this was a game, but it seemed unlikely. And even if it was, Damon was still a psycho.

And the worst part was that it was not so surprising. Looking back, I could not comfortably say, "I would never have expected such a thing from such a person." He made clouds, after all. But in a way, it was those very clouds that kept me off guard, that occupied my imagination too much to let it do its normal job: creating healthy paranoias of things like . . . oh, I don't know, I'll just say what comes to mind—imprisonments, why not.

I rushed around the cell in circles, inspecting every corner. I should never have saved him that night in the subway, arrogant fool that I was. The businessmen had been right: Who the hell did I think I was, Super Cinderella or something?

I searched the room thoroughly, but found no secret door, no way of escape. There was a closet, near the bed, with only a vacuum cleaner in it.

All I could do now was try to find a way to escape psychologically. Maybe there was something I could say, some way I could act, that might persuade Damon to let me go.

Before settling down to think, I took the hammer and stuffed it under my sweater. The metal was cold against my stomach. I hadn't worn a T-shirt underneath, to be sexier. The memory brought tears to my eyes. I sat on the floor, near the bars, against the right wall of the cell, so that I'd be able to watch the TV monitors if I felt like it.

I had to figure out why Damon was doing this, what

his motives were. Then I would know how to approach him. I replayed in my mind the last half hour before he imprisoned me. I mulled over his cryptic comments. He said he wanted to make me happy. Maybe he was now planning to give me jewels and treat me like a princess, having me live in extraordinary luxury, but somehow I doubted this: although my cell was nice, it didn't have that kind of opulence; it wasn't stuffed with satins and precious stones and rose petals and trays of fancy foods and closets full of gowns. But maybe that was because Damon wasn't yet sure what my tastes were, and he didn't want to impose satins on me if I preferred some other cloth.

Or maybe he wanted to use me in some pleasant scientific experiments involving his clouds.

Or maybe he knew I had a crush on him, and he wanted to offer himself to me; exactly the way I imagined he would when he was dragging me up the stairs.

But then I realized that with a psycho like him, even if he did, truly, want to make me happy, that did not exclude death. Maybe he felt I would be happier dead.

But if I came to my senses for a moment and stopped assuming he meant it when he said he wanted to make me happy, the field of possibilities opened up considerably and unattractively, ranging anywhere from torture to torture and death. Not knowing which it was, was itself torture. And would his torture, if that's what it was, be mental or physical? And why the TV monitors?

I frequently got up and changed positions, because I didn't always want to watch Damon sleeping. Sometimes I wanted to and sometimes I didn't, and when I didn't, I didn't want to have to close my eyes not to, so I went and sat against the opposite wall until I wanted to again.

The hammer was by now warm against my stomach. Tense, I pressed it harder into my skin. I hadn't managed to devote even a minute to thinking of a strategy. I was completely unprepared.

Damon came in when I was sitting against the no-looking-at-Damon wall. I was startled.

He was carrying a chair in one hand, and my overnight bag in the other. He took only one step into the room and stopped.

"I'll trade you information for the hammer," he said. "I don't want you hurling it at my head."

I was still sitting on the floor with my legs bent, and there was no way he could have seen I had a hammer under my baggy sweater. I wondered if I had been filmed, after all.

"No, you were not videotaped," he said, as if reading my mind. "I just know that any reasonably intelligent person would try to hurl the hammer at my head. On the other hand, a brilliant or stupid person might not. I'm not implying you're not brilliant. I'm sure there must be some brilliant people who would."

I sat there, considering the offer of trade.

After a while, he said, "You'll still have the bowling ball."

What I was hesitating about now was not whether I would agree to trade the hammer for information—I had decided I would—but whether I would gently hand it back to him or hurl it at his head.

I ended up doing neither, because he gave me instructions: "Toss the hammer at least four feet out of your cell, and out of your kicking range."

I did what he said. He relaxed immediately and bustled

about, placing the chair near the cell, out of my kicking range, and putting my bag against the bars.

He then sat on the chair, and said, "Now I can answer your questions."

"Why am I in here?"

"To receive a present."

"What present?"

"You."

"What do you mean?"

"Just what I said."

"I already have myself."

"You have a certain version of yourself. But I'll give you another version."

"What version?"

"An improved version. If everything goes according to plan, once I'm through with you, the new self I will give back to you will be able to make all your dreams come true."

I was relieved that so far, at least, it seemed he did not intend to kill me. Unless, in his eyes, an improved version of myself would be a dead version.

I said, "I see. So this will be a sort of self-affirmation seminar. Like 'How to Be More Successful' or 'How to Improve Your Self-Esteem'? You'll sit there and tell me I'm great? Or you'll make me listen to subliminal tapes."

"No. But I'm glad you're not too upset to make light of this."

I was furious. "I'm just astonished. And disgusted. I want you to let me out of here right now. I have no interest in your little plan. If you want to make me happy, let me out of here."

"No."

"How long are you intending to keep me in here?"

"I'm not sure exactly. Awhile."

I sighed. "What are you thinking of doing to me?"

"Me? Nothing much. But you'll be doing things to yourself. And you won't do other things. I will alter you. Or rather, I will make you alter yourself. My gift to you will be to take away your freedom of choice for a while. Freedom can be very unhealthy and unproductive. Instead, you'll have freedom from choice."

"Please, just let me go."

"Why?"

I spat out: "Because it's unpleasant to be imprisoned."

"What would you prefer?"

"Freedom."

"What do you want to do?"

"Go home."

"To do what?"

"Oh, please. To live."

"You can live here for a while."

Obviously, I had to think of things I could only do at home. "I want to see my family, my friends, go to my jobs, meet new people, work on my acting—"

"Bingo! We will act. Among other things not worth mentioning right now. But most of all, we'll do some acting."

He got up, and left me gaping.

Chapter Seven

I needed a cigarette. I grabbed my overnight bag, but couldn't squeeze it through the bars, so I looked for my pack of cigarettes with my face pressing between two bars.

Unable to find my pack or my lighter, I got frustrated and poured the entire contents of my bag onto the floor. I still couldn't find them. Why had Damon taken my cigarettes and lighter? Maybe he thought I would set the place on fire. But then why were my Life Savers also missing? Nothing else was gone. I squeezed the empty bag through the bars, and filled it back up slowly.

When I got up and turned around, my eyes landed on what I forgot to ask him about: the TV monitors.

Maybe he liked to be watched. He'd walk around his room naked. That made sense. He already had an exhibitionist streak: walking around in transparent clothes. Why not go the whole way?

I didn't even try to sleep. I screamed a few times during the night, and banged on the walls, and watched the monitors to see if he stirred. I thought about my parents and wondered when they would start getting worried. I cried a bit.

I sat staring out the bulletproof window. My view of the lit woods was blemished by the bruise marks I had caused and was already regretting. How long would it take for the police to start looking for me? Would I be reported missing on the news, eventually?

I got up and turned on the TV, thinking it would comfort me to be in touch with the free world. And maybe I'd come upon reports of missing people, and I'd understand what types of people got to get reported missing. I found a channel that was broadcasting news at this late hour, and to my astonishment I saw *myself* on the news! It was a video of me, taken from the back, running away, with Chriskate Turschicraw chasing me down the street. The anchorwoman was saying, "Ever since two o'clock this afternoon, everybody has been wondering: '*Who* is the pursued woman? Who could this woman be, pursued by the woman who is pursued by the world.' Speculations abound."

Next, a reporter was interviewing random people on the street, asking them who they thought the pursued woman was.

Someone answered, "I don't know who she is, but she must be extraordinary, to be chased by such an extraordinary person."

A man said, "I don't know, but there must be something about her that's different. Otherwise, why would the most beautiful woman in the world wanna catch her?"

Someone else said, "I think she must be a very famous actress or rock star. Or maybe another model."

This time the reporter replied, "But didn't you see the footage of the pursued woman? She doesn't have a model's body."

"No, I didn't see it. I heard the story on the radio. I don't have a TV."

Someone else said, "No, you can tell from her back that she's not someone exceptional. I mean, she's far from perfect, her butt's not like rock. I think she's an ordinary citizen, which is what makes it exciting. It means that any one of us could be chased down the street by someone like the Shell. It's uplifting. You don't have to be someone special, someone famous, to be pursued by people of worth."

I watched, gaping. Maybe this insane broadcast meant that I was only dreaming. Maybe I had fallen asleep on Damon's couch, and everything afterward had not really happened, including my imprisonment. Or better yet, maybe I had fallen asleep at home, after my bath, and had only dreamed that Damon called inviting me to the country.

I opened my eyes as wide as possible to wake myself up, in case this was indeed a dream. I had often used this technique successfully to wake myself up from nightmares. But this time nothing happened; the world didn't change.

The anchorwoman came back on the screen. "The nation asks the pursued woman: please step forward. Let us know who you are. Let us *know* you."

I screamed for Damon. The nation wanted me. I had to step forward. He had to let me step forward. Good excuse to be released. But he didn't budge in his bed.

I stayed awake all night.

*   *   *

At ten of eight, Damon was still sleeping in his bed. At eight o'clock he came in, carrying a bag. He took out a key and entered my cell without hesitating.

I was mildly insulted. After all, I was the caged, angry animal, and what was he doing coming into my cage, risking his life? I felt like an emasculated beast.

"Hi," he said, chewing gum. "You probably didn't get much sleep. We can take it easy today."

He plopped his bag down and was about to sit on the floor against the wall, when I told him about my fame as the pursued woman. I convinced him to watch the news with me until the story came on, which it did, to my relief. When the footage of the chase was shown, I told him that was me, running away from Chriskate Turschicraw. He was surprised, got a kick out of it, but said it changed nothing to his plan: the nation would have to wait to meet me. I told him I wanted the nation to meet me *now,* and that this could be a great opportunity for my acting career.

"Nonsense," he said. "You have to be a good actress. Being pursued by Chriskate Turschicraw might open doors, but it won't win you Oscars. Which leads me to what I want to talk to you about. To prepare myself to become your trainer, I've read many books on acting, which I'm sure you've read as well. I don't think we should follow their theories. We won't follow any theory. We'll just act." He smiled. "I also read some scene books, but I don't think we'll do any scenes from them. I'll write scenes myself that we can memorize and perform."

He took out of his bag a little notepad and flipped it open. "I also took notes of your desires and wishes. I will do everything in my power to make them come true."

"Did you have this whole thing planned from the be-

ginning or did you decide to kidnap me on the spur of the
moment?"

"We were by the river one day when the idea came to
me. I had been trying to figure out a way to repay you for
saving me."

"You realize it's illegal what you're doing?"

"Yes, I know."

"I suggest you try to make me happy in a legal way."

"Don't worry, Anna, the end will justify the means,
you'll see. It's simply a question of delayed gratification."

"What are these TV monitors for?"

"I thought you might feel less lonely if you could see
me doing stuff in the rest of the house. It might reassure
you somehow, destroy an uncomfortable feeling of mystery."

"Yes, it'll make me feel better to see you enjoying your
freedom while I'm in this cage."

With the sudden, un-thought-out urge of a wild animal,
I decided to attack Damon. I threw myself on him and
tried to strangle him. He did not push me away, but instead reached into his bag and pulled out a gun. I immediately stopped my attack and stared at the gun in shock,
not because I hadn't dreamed it possible that he would
have a gun, but because this was a water gun. Damon was
not laughing, or even smiling. The gun was bright orange
transparent plastic.

I rushed to the bathroom and closed the door and
laughed, trying not to let him hear me. I wanted to neither
flatter him nor offend him with my laughter. I buried my
face in the thick bath towel and laughed until my eyes
were wet with tears and I could barely breathe. The
thought of him, in his transparent outfit, shooting his

orange water gun, while his jiggling willy was faintly visible, was overwhelming.

And then I felt like crying, because this giant, insane child was not letting me go. I wanted him to shoot me. I wanted to see the thin stream of water wet my clothing like a wimpy ejaculation.

But I couldn't risk it. Maybe real bullets came out. Maybe the gimmick was that it was a real gun that just looked like a water gun.

"Is that a real gun?" I shouted from the bathroom, knowing he would probably answer yes, just to be strange.

"No."

"Is it a water gun?"

"Yes. But I can hurt you with it."

"How? By throwing it at me?"

I opened the door and looked at him. The gun was no longer in sight. He was sitting on the floor against the wall, flipping through the pages of a book while blowing bubbles with his chewing gum.

From the night table, I quickly grabbed the lamp and alarm clock, which I had unplugged during the night for this purpose, and ran toward him. I threw the lamp at him. He blocked it with his arm and whipped out his water gun and shot me. There was a stabbing pain in my stomach. I screamed and dropped the alarm clock. I looked down at myself and saw a small shard of ice planted in the middle of my abdomen. I pulled it out and lifted my sweater and saw a bleeding half-inch cut near my belly button.

"Ow!" I said. "I'm bleeding!"

From his bag he took out a box of Band-Aids, pulled one out of the box, and threw it at me. It fluttered to the floor. He then took out a bottle of rubbing alcohol and a package of cotton balls and handed them to me.

Blood was running down my stomach, spreading to the top of my pants. I said, "You think I can just put a Band-Aid on this? We have to go to the hospital, to the emergency room. I need stitches."

"No you don't. Disinfect yourself and put on the Band-Aid." His gun was pointed at me.

I started disinfecting my wound. "You said it was a water gun, you liar."

"Ice is water," he said coldly. "I was hoping I wouldn't have to use it, or even take it out at all. That's why I brought it in a bag."

"You deceitful asshole."

He looked hurt. "Come over here." He took me by the arm and positioned me in front of the bed. "Listen," he said. "First off, it can kill. With the ice knife." He shot a large blade of ice into the mattress. "Then there are the shards, which I shot you with. We also have the ice needles, which hurt about as much as getting a shot at the doctor's." He shot one into my pillow. "Then there are the ice threads. Those don't really hurt at all."

"So what are they for?"

"For the hell of it. There's also the boiling water category. The doses come in three sizes: tablespoon, teaspoon, and half-teaspoon. And in two forms: stream or ball of water." He shot all the varieties onto my bed.

"Can't your gun just do a normal, gentle stream of room-temperature water?"

He opened his mouth, aimed the gun inside, and shot a few spurts. He suddenly looked in pain, and I thought perhaps he had used the boiling or ice features by accident. But no. All he said was, "Gross pH."

He then talked about flexibility. He wanted to see how far I could stretch in every direction.

"Show me your bridge," he said.

"My bridge? I don't have a bridge."

"You know, a back bend."

"I know what a bridge is, and I don't have one."

"It doesn't matter how small it is. I want to see it."

"But I don't have one. Not even a small one."

"Sure you do. Do it."

"I can't. I don't even have a speck of a bridge. You could shoot me with the shards or even the dagger and I still wouldn't have a bridge."

He rolled his eyes. "I'll show you your bridge."

"No, you will break my back. It'll be a broken bridge."

"Nonsense." He made me lie down on my back with my legs bent, elbows up and palms flat on the floor on either side of my head, in the proper pre-bridge position. He slid his hands under my waist and tried to force me into a bridge by lifting my middle off the floor. But I wouldn't let him bend me; I kept my back as straight and rigid as a board, too afraid of pain or injury. Damon pulled harder, and finally my entire body (hands and feet included) rose off the floor, my back still perfectly straight. I was balanced on his hands like a seesaw.

He gave up and put me back down, panting from the exertion. "As far as I'm concerned, a person cannot truly be sane if their body is not flexible. I know *I* wouldn't be."

"But you're *not* sane."

"Flexibility is not only important for sanity, it's important for life. You know, deep down people die of stiffness. The root of all death is stiffness. As is proven by rigor mortis."

"That happens after you're dead."

"That's where you're wrong. Rigor mortis creeps up on you imperceptibly before you die, and it's what kills you. You die of subtle stiffness. The intense stiffness you get a short while after death is just the symbolic manifestation, the proof that stiffness is what killed you."

"That's your insane theory."

"Yes, I admit that it's my amusing theory. But it could be true. And to a certain extent we know it is. We all know that being flexible is healthy. It even protects you against accidents. But flexibility is not only important for mental and physical health, it's also important for emotional health. It's an essential ingredient to successful relationships. What is far more fascinating, though, is that it is important in art." He paused and then spoke slowly and intensely, as if imparting me with a very exciting secret: "In my opinion, the most basic, essential quality to genius is flexibility." And he added very quickly: "There were no great artists without it."

He took something red out of his bag and handed it to me. It was a bathing suit.

"Would you mind going in there and changing into this?" he said, waving toward the bathroom.

"Why?"

"Because I'd like to see your body. I need to get a clearer picture of how much work it needs."

"I'm not a piece of meat."

"Hey, you're the one who wants to be the actor. Bodies matter."

He took his plastic gun out of his bag and pointed it at me. "Now go."

I went, sighing.

I took off my clothes, first hoping that the one-piece suit wouldn't be too small, and then hoping it would be, just so he'd have a small failure. But it fit, and it was even somewhat flattering. But not flattering enough to make me feel totally at ease stepping out of the bathroom.

And then I became indignant at myself, and ashamed of feeling uneasy about my body. It was ridiculous; I was a captive. Here was the last place I should let images of tall, thin models that had oppressed women for centuries, or at least decades, add to my oppression.

I tried to comfort myself by remembering the best, and I think only, compliment I ever received about my face: I had been told that I resembled young Elizabeth Taylor, but with slightly lighter hair, and disfigured. "The way Elizabeth Taylor would look if her face had been gently squashed."

I bluntly stepped out of the bathroom.

"Let's see what we have here," said Damon. "We have to work on the legs."

He walked behind me and mumbled, "Forgive me for touching," and squeezed my upper arm, feeling for the firmness or lack of it, I suppose. "We could tone the arms a little more. The stomach is in good shape . . . comparatively speaking. The buttocks need firming, but they will be taken care of along with the legs."

"I'd like a cigarette."

"No, sorry. That's wish number five on the list: to stop smoking."

"I didn't mean it."

"You must have. You uttered it eight and a half times during the few weeks I knew you."

"What are the others?"

"What others?"

"The other wishes on your fucking list."

"*You* know what they are: they're *your* wishes. I don't need to tell them to you."

Still from behind, he placed his hands on my shoulders and pulled them back. "Your posture needs improving. Ah, you see, when you stand straight, your breasts look as young as their age. You're lucky, they are quite large, which means they will still be nicely full after."

I waited for a moment, and said, "After what?"

"After you do things like . . . exercise, and little things like eat . . . healthy, or . . . less." He blew a bubble with his gum, which exploded all over his face. He unstuck part of it and put it back in his mouth, but plenty was left stuck on his cheeks and chin. I didn't point it out to him.

He took some keys out of his pocket and unlocked my cell door. He took my wrist firmly and escorted me through the house.

"Where are we going?" I asked.

"To the most predictable place, considering your outfit."

"Nothing is predictable when it comes to your insanity."

He took me to the pool and said, "Go in."

The gun was casually pointed at me. After trying to object, which did no good, I went down the first rung of the ladder. The water felt weird. It was unusually gentle, light and soft against my legs, as if my skin were numb.

"Continue," said Damon.

I went down another rung. I swung my foot through the water, which offered little resistance. It didn't feel as *solid* as water usually did. It felt the way water might feel in a dream.

It wasn't until I actually lowered myself into the water that I knew, like an animal who knows to stay away from fire, that I should do everything in my power to avoid going in. But before I had a chance to climb back out, Damon yanked my hands off the rail and I fell backward into the water. And I kept on falling. In truth, I sank, but it felt like I was simply falling.

Chapter Eight

It was terrifying. The water was like a form of quicksand, only quicker. I had to kick extremely hard and fast to stay afloat, and do the same with my arms. If I slowed down for an instant, I started sinking again. I tried to swim back toward the ladder, but Damon was there, with his gun, preventing me from grabbing onto the rail.

"Not yet, Anna. You're doing well. Try to get used to it. Just a bit longer. Try to relax."

Relax? The asshole. If I relaxed I would sink. This was not the type of water in which you could pleasantly bob around.

"You're doing great," he said. "It's excellent exercise. Great for your legs. For everything. You just have to get used to it."

"I'm already used to it," I managed to screech, which was a mistake, for I didn't have the energy to spare and I started sinking. My movements were now too weak to get me back to the surface.

A hand violently grabbed my upper arm and yanked me back to the air. As he pulled me out of the pool, his translucent wet trousers clung to his legs like Kleenex.

I coughed as never before in my life. Then I sobbed, sitting with my face in my knees.

I looked up at him and said, "Please let me go. Please." Tears streamed down my cheeks and blurred my vision. I kept repeating "please," almost maniacally, to show him I might be losing my mind.

"Calm down Anna. It's not as bad as it seems. Just remember what we're doing: we're working for your dreams."

"By making me drown? And what the *hell* is wrong with this water, anyway?"

"It's highly diluted."

"*Diluted?* With what?"

"Air."

"What are you talking about? Water can't be diluted," I said, with more authority than I felt. "And certainly not with air."

"Fine, then call it aeration. This water is drenched with air. It doesn't offer much support for swimmers, or rubber ducks."

"So you made me swim in air."

"No, unfortunately. That would have been more fun. You were swimming in airy water, or slightly vaporous water."

"Please, let me go," I said.

"You'll feel better if you just accept the fact that you're here until we reach our goal," he said, settling himself down beside me. "You might as well work as hard as you can."

I was clawing my scalp. "I'm not going to survive. I can't work or function this way. You're a scientist; you know nothing about acting. Even if you did, I wouldn't learn under these conditions. Any talent I might have will be crushed, out of disgust. But if, by some miracle, you did improve my acting and I became successful, that wouldn't make me happy. Success doesn't ensure happiness, especially when attained in this nightmarish way. And isn't my happiness your primary goal?"

"Absolutely. And success in all your dreams may not guarantee that you will be happy, but it'll make it as likely as possible."

"No, there are things that matter to me much more than success, such as having my life unfold in a natural way; having the destiny that is most natural to me. You're not letting that happen."

"What is most natural to human beings is for them to develop their highest potential. The *way* it happens doesn't matter. What matters is that it happens. Now let's get back to work," he said. "We have to find some other form of exercise for you, in addition to swimming in this watair."

"Swimming in this what?"

"Watair. It's my name for it. Can *you* think of a better name?"

"I think so. Watmare. By the way, I plan to devote the rest of my life to making your life hell, if not ending it altogether. Your goal is to make me happy? Well, I will be *un*happy, just to spite you."

"My life is of no importance to me. If it'll please you to make my life hell, then do it. I'll put myself at your disposal. Now, what types of physical exercises do you enjoy doing?"

"Horseback riding."

"I've never heard you mention riding before. But it's not an option, for obvious reasons. What else?"

"Dirt biking."

"Same obvious reasons. And how strange that I've never heard you mention that one either. What else?"

"Fencing. Have you heard me mention that one? Fencing. That's *all* I like doing physically."

"Yes, but you'd have no one to do it with, and if *I* tried, it would be too risky; you'd incapacitate me in a second. I saw how you worked your wand in the subway. You were dangerous."

"Your flattery repels me."

"What other sports do you like?"

"Any sport that consists of swift transportation outdoors."

"I see I'm not going to get much help from you. If you want me to pick your sport for you, that's fine. How about running?"

"Excellent. Especially outdoors and alone."

"Running it is, then."

"Outdoors and alone?" I asked, surprised and hopeful.

"Indoors and supervised."

"I hate running."

"Too late. You tired me and tried my patience. We're going back to your room so you can change into your running outfit."

"Please don't call it that."

"Jogging outfit? Sweat suit?"

"It's not my room. It's a jail. Call it jail."

"Okay, we're going back to jail. But that makes me sound like a sheriff."

We went back, but instead of making me change clothes, he looked at his watch, and said, "Actually, we won't have time to do this right now. You'll have to excuse me for a little while." And he left. It was 1:25 P.M.

Through the monitors I saw Damon go into the living room and disappear behind a door. When he finally came back, half an hour later, his eyes and nose were red: he had obviously been crying.

He handed me sweatpants and a T-shirt, and told me to go change. His voice was stuffed up and nasal from the crying.

"What's wrong?" I asked.

"Nothing."

"Are you upset about something?"

"That's a reasonable assumption."

"What is it?"

"Why do you think there's no camera where I went? Why do you think you couldn't see me on any of the screens? It's because it's not something you need to know, or that I want you to know, or that concerns you. Now please go and change."

"I'm too hungry. I feel faint," I said.

"It'll pass as soon as you start jogging."

"No, *I'll* pass—out."

"We'll see which one of us is right," he said, pointing the gun at me and wiping his nose on his tissue-like sleeve.

I went into the bathroom and changed into the outfit.

When I came out, he said, "Start running."

"In *here?*" I looked around the small cell.

"Yes. Why not."

I didn't deign to answer. I started running from one end to the other, following the L-shape of the cell. After four laps, which took only a few seconds, he said, "You can just run in place if you want."

"Oh goody, that'll be even more fun."

I ran in place, staring at him, hoping to make him uncomfortable.

"I don't like running," I finally said, and dared to stop moving. "It's uncomfortable for me."

He looked concerned. "Is it? Do your knees hurt? Or your back?"

"No."

"Then what?"

"I don't feel comfortable talking about it."

"Ah, you jiggle," he stated, nasally. "Is it your breasts? Do your breasts hurt?"

I so wished I had a heavy object to whack him with. Or better yet, my sword.

"You're blushing," he said.

He got three more imaginary blows. "As a matter of fact," I said, "maybe I don't jiggle. Maybe I just feel as if my feminine organs are being pounded loose and are about to come pouring out of my vagina, if you want to know the truth."

He was speechless for a moment. Then he slowly smiled and said, "No, I think you jiggle."

"Not necessarily. And if I did, it would be called 'bounce.'"

"You're right if we're referring to the breasts. But if we're talking about another part, like the buttocks, it would be called jiggle, I think."

"It's the breasts!" I said indignantly.

"Okay, I'll try to think of something," he said, and left my cell.

He came back, holding an Ace bandage. "This should work."

"What is it for?" I asked, hoping it wasn't for what I thought it was.

It was. "To wrap around your chest," he said. "There's no reason it won't do the trick."

"Yes, there's a very good reason: I'm not getting near that thing."

He sighed. "So what sport would you rather do?" He fell silent, and then said, "Okay. I've got it. I'll just get an exercise machine that you can use in your room."

"My room," I repeated, rolling my eyes.

"I'll get you a Stairmaster or a stationary bicycle. Which one?"

"Oh, don't spend so much money on me."

"Answer."

"Well, if I must, I'll take the bicycle. But a reclining one."

"All right. One recumbent bicycle coming up! Now we're in business," he said, and blew a loud bubble.

"These stock phrases," I muttered, disgusted.

"I'm trying to be cheerful."

"Oh yes, I forgot that stock phrases are renownedly cheery."

He gave me a small sandwich, which I gobbled down. He ate one too.

He then made me do some squatting exercises, while he looked at himself in a hand mirror and tried to unstick the gum from his face. By the time he was done with me, I had cramps and a hard time limping over to my bed.

"Cheer up," he said. "After dinner we'll have the wishing session. It's an important part of the program. It's the more spiritual part, shall we say. You'll get to make some wishes, which I will attempt to fulfill."

Damon left for town, to buy the recumbent bicycle.

I stayed on my bed, staring at the ceiling in a depressed trance. I started crying, and the tears ran into my hairline and itched, and when I tried to raise my arm to wipe them, the pain of a cramp was too great, so I had no choice but to allow the tears to collect in my ears.

It was in this pathetic state that I thought of a plan of escape. It wasn't the type of plan that cool prisoners would have thought of. It wasn't a graceful plan. But maybe it was its very lack of grace that would make it unpredictable and effective. I would try it early in the morning the next day, if I hadn't already escaped by then.

I turned on the TV and found the news. It didn't take long for the story about the mysterious pursued woman to come on again. The nation was obsessed, it seemed. And then, to my surprise, I heard something that made me sit up in bed. Apparently, five women had stepped forward, each claiming to be the real pursued woman. One of them was even interviewed in the newsroom. She seemed vulgar, tacky. How could they think, when they saw me running from the back, that my front would look so tacky? I stayed on my bed, lethargic, until Damon came back.

He entered my cage and paced the floor at the foot of my bed, gesticulating broadly. "I got you an amazing reclining bicycle! The most expensive one. The most electronic one."

"How exciting," I moaned.

"It'll be delivered tomorrow."

"That's too bad: I'll be gone by then."

"Oh? Where will you be?"

"I will have escaped."

"Good for you. Or rather, too bad for you, because you'll be missing out on quite an enviable future, but hey, it's your life."

"That's right, so would you mind giving it back to me? People are stepping forward, assuming my identity. You can't let this happen. You must let me set them straight. Otherwise, by the time you release me, I will no longer exist out there. They will have stolen me away from myself. I will no longer be me. They will be me."

"Really? Women are claiming to be the pursued woman? It doesn't surprise me, come to think of it. But don't worry about it. You should be above all that. Leave them to their petty schemes."

He tossed a videocassette on my bed. "I rented *La Femme Nikita* for us to watch after dinner, after the wishing session. I hope you haven't seen it."

"I don't even get to pick the movie?"

"No, this film might inspire you to view your stay here more positively. It's about a woman who, like you, gets trained and is improved. The similarity ends there, for she gets trained to kill people."

"Why didn't you just rent *My Fair Lady*? That should satisfy your Pygmalion leanings."

"Not a bad idea, but *La Femme Nikita* is more modern, more likely to be an inspiring role model."

"You are like a Nazi. You want to make me into some sort of superhuman. Do you have any German blood?"

"No, I'm out of it at the moment. I usually keep some in my freezer, but I might be getting some more in tomorrow. What did you want it for?"

"That's a really insensitive thing to say to someone who's kidnapped and who might be the one ending up in your freezer, as far as I know. Or in your stomach. Or both. I would then become your excrement."

"Lovely. Okay, I'm sorry, I didn't know you still had any fear that I might kill you. And I don't think I have German blood in my veins."

"Well, then, have you read too much Nietzsche? Doesn't he talk about supermen?"

"I'm not interested in making a superhuman, or superperson. I'm interested in your happiness. If you had told me that your dream was to be a bag lady, I would have given you bags. If you had told me you wanted to find the man of your life and live with him in a house with a white picket fence, I would have searched the earth for him and brought him to you and bought you the house."

"You're insane," I said. "But I'm repeating myself. What if I had told you I wanted you?"

"I would have warned you. But then I would have acquiesced."

"Warned me of what?"

"That having me may not make you happy."

"But then you would have given in?"

"Yes."

"You would have sacrificed yourself to that extent?"

"It would not have been a sacrifice. What I'm doing now is a sacrifice."

"What do you mean it wouldn't have been a sacrifice? Are you saying you're in love with me?"

"Too bad we didn't record it, cause we could play it back and check if I said that. But I don't think I did."

Damon made me stretch again. I got mad: "Did I ever, at any point, say that I wanted to be flexible? *No!* Flexibility is not in the list you so conscientiously made of my desires. So leave me alone!"

But he didn't. He said, "I remember one time when you saw how flexible I was and you said you wished you were as flexible."

"I didn't mean it."

He ignored me. After the stretching, I was allowed to take a bath and relax for the rest of the afternoon, since it was the first day, he said. I took that opportunity to go over my plan of escape.

As for Damon, he worked in his lab. I watched him on the monitor. He typed at his computer for a while, and then, with the big machine in his lab, he made three new clouds, which came out of a sort of horizontal chimney, or exhaust pipe, like a slow, aerial defecation, or birth. He then placed each cloud under a glass cover and left them there.

We had dinner in my cell, at a folding table that he brought in. The food was good considering how healthy it was: dark, whole grain pasta with steamed vegetables, cut up in small pieces. We ate with plastic spoons, for safety reasons. When we finished the food that was on the table, I felt some panic and my scalp was sweating, because nothing was happening: no dessert was coming.

"What's for dessert?" I asked.

"Oh, are you still hungry?"

"What does that have to do with anything?" I answered.

"If you're still hungry, you should eat more. Have more pasta."

"I'm not still hungry. I want dessert. The dessert to this meal."

"There *is* no dessert."

I felt my throat clenching. "Oh, so you *do* want to kill me after all."

He looked confused and pushed the bowl of pasta toward me, saying meekly, "Have more pasta."

I restrained myself from knocking the bowl across the room. "I need sugar."

"Oh. Okay, if you want I can give you a piece of fruit or a yogurt."

"No." I was on the verge of tears. "I want real dessert. Real sugar."

"I'm sorry but I don't think I can give you that. What type of dessert did you have in mind?"

"Anything with chocolate is fine. Some desserts without chocolate will do too as long as they're good, and contain sucrose, not fructose."

"I know it's hard at first, but in a few days your body will adjust to not having sugar or chocolate."

"No it won't; it never does, and even if it did, *I* wouldn't adjust. Believe me, your dealings with me will go better on every level if you give me dessert. So please call up that restaurant now and order some."

"No. But let's try to get your mind off this, and you'll forget about it in five minutes."

"*Demon,* listen to me. If you don't give me dessert, you will regret it. I'm warning you. This is the worst possible thing you could do to me, next to kidnapping me. It's worse than making me swim in the watair. It's worse than not letting me smoke."

"To categorize no dessert as the worst thing is a little premature, wouldn't you say? You've only been here one day."

He didn't give me dessert. He gave me a banana and yogurt. I didn't accept them, out of pride and lack of hunger. I asked him for a cigarette. He refused, saying, "No smokey dokey."

After dinner, he made me sit in a chair against the wall, and sat in front of me with a pad of paper and a pen. He offered me a piece of grape Bubblicious, which I reluctantly accepted. He had one too.

"Okay, you can start now," he said. "Make your wishes."

I stared at him blankly, chewing, and then, in a tone dripping with sarcasm, said, "Hmm, this is tough, every wish of mine is fulfilled. I'm so happy in every way. I couldn't ask for anything more." I paused. "Oh, but wait a minute, I just thought of a wish: that you let me out of this god-awful fucking cage."

"No, real wishes about your life, your future."

"That you give me dessert."

He gave me a reproachful look.

"That I won't be obsessed with killing you when I'm free."

"I told you I want some real wishes. Apart from wanting to be an actress, what else have you always wanted?"

"Why in the world would you think I would *ever* again tell you *any* wish of mine? You must be insane." I paused. "But of course, you are that. You must also be dumb."

"I think you'll tell me because otherwise I'll shoot. Now wish!"

"I wish that you have a life of endless misery."

"Already done," he said, and shot me. I screamed. He was now standing over me, his gun pointed. "Stop annoying me and wish. Otherwise . . . "

"No, don't," I said, holding out my hands as a shield. "Wait. I don't know. I need time to think."

"No, you can't have time. That's the whole point of this wishing session: that you don't have time."

The barrel of the gun was an inch from my forehead, and I found it very upsetting that he next intended to shoot me there.

I tried to come up with a safe wish that would not offer him any opportunity to torture me.

"Okay. I wish that I had a better sense of style."

He seemed stunned for a moment, and then screamed, "No! That's a trick wish. You're just avoiding your real wishes."

He shot me in the collarbone, and I howled and plucked out the shard, yelling, "Do you *have* to use the shards? You could at least use the bullets of hot water."

"*Boiling* water. They don't hurt less," he warned.

"But you already know all my real wishes. I told them all to you when we were friends."

"I want to hear about your other wishes, the things you may not know you want. Getting what we want is not enough to ensure our happiness. Getting what we don't know we want ensures it more. But for that to happen, we have to realize what it is that we don't know we want. Then we can get it. So search deep within yourself."

"I do have some wishes, but I don't want to say what they are."

"Why?"

"Because I'm afraid of your gun. You might not think they're good."

"Okay, I won't shoot. Tell me what they are."

"That you kill yourself."

"Okay, you got that one out of your system. What are the others?"

"Oh my God, I just realized that if you die, then *I'll* die!"

"I'm touched."

"No, I mean literally I'll die. Of starvation."

"Don't worry about it. Give me lots of wishes now. Quick, lots." He snapped his fingers rapidly.

"I would like never to die, nor my family . . . Not to think too much. To be free of any obsessions. Always to see things in perspective. To live a full life and die a painless death (but only if my wish of never dying isn't possible). To go to the moon—"

"Why?" he asked.

"So that I could be in a rocket."

"Why?"

"To experience weightlessness."

He smiled sadly, dreamily. "Don't you think that's a little far-fetched?"

"You didn't say it couldn't be far-fetched."

"What else?"

"To be able to forget what I want, and that you, too, are able to forget what I want and forget about making me want things and forget about making me think of what I don't know I want."

He rolled his eyes and sighed and blew a bubble. "Your wishes are getting monotonous. Give me different ones."

"To jump on a real trampoline. I've only jumped on the tiny ones in sporting goods stores."

He looked at me, and I was afraid I had again gone too far in ridiculing his wishing session. I said, "I'm sorry, you don't like that wish, right? I take it back."

"Are you kidding? On a trampoline you could jog without the jiggle. There might still be some jiggle, but gentler jiggle. And none of the pounding. In addition to the bicycle, I'll get you a trampoline. Now tell me more good wishes like that one."

"I would like you to give me a beautiful antique sword."

"What else?"

"Wait, aren't you going to tell me it's a brilliant idea because it'll make me less homesick and help me concentrate more on your regimen?"

"No. Tell me more wishes."

"I can't think of any more."

"Yes you can. *Think!*"

"That when I'm famous the press won't hound me too much, and will let me have some privacy."

"What else?"

"That's it. I just can't think of any more. I'm not good at this sort of thing."

"This *sort* of thing? What *sort* of thing?"

"You know, things like wishing sessions."

"Okay, we can stop for now, but we'll have another session soon, so you should keep thinking of more wishes, and write them down."

He handed me his pad of paper, on which he had not

written down any of my wishes. He then dismantled his Bic pen, pulling out the flexible inner ink tube by its little writing tip. He handed me the tube with tip.

"Why only this?" I asked, the puny writing tool erect between my fingers like an uncooked spaghetti strand.

"If you can't guess why I'm only giving you the pen's vein, you'll know when we watch the movie. I'm sure you'll manage writing with it."

We stretched out on my bed, his gun pointed in my direction, and started watching *La Femme Nikita*.

"How do you feel?" he asked. "It feels good to exercise, doesn't it?"

I didn't deign to answer.

The scene with the pen came early on. The heroine stabbed it in the hand of a policeman.

"Brava," I muttered.

A few minutes later he said "Huh," as if he had noticed something.

"What?" I said.

"It just occurred to me that if a Bic pen were alive, it would not feel pain. Bic pens are like insects. They're invertebrates. Their skeletons are on the outside and they are soft inside. They would be classified as insects. Or perhaps mollusks. If Bic pens were alive, they, like all invertebrates, would not feel pain."

I stared at him. "What useful knowledge. I'm sure it'll come in handy in my life when I'm around a lot of live Bic pens. I'll rest easier knowing they don't feel pain. Especially considering all the harm I intend to inflict on them."

After the movie, which I could tell I normally would

have liked more than I did in the present circumstances, he took out of his bag some stapled pages, placed them on my bed, and said, "This is a scene I wrote that I want you to memorize tonight. We'll act it out tomorrow."

I didn't answer. He left me for the night. I turned on the TV and waited for the news.

On the monitors, I saw Damon stretch in his bedroom for fifteen minutes. He was incredibly flexible.

The news came on. The story of my chase was not talked about until halfway through the broadcast. They revealed that the count was now up to thirteen: thirteen women had stepped forward claiming they were the pursued woman. In addition, there were reports, from all walks of life, that it was becoming fashionable to insinuate that one was the pursued woman. Even some men were doing it. An expert came on to talk about this phenomenon. His expert insight was that the chase had sparked the public's imagination.

I turned off the TV, bitter.

I read the scene that Damon had left for me, and was appalled. It was about a couple, sitting in a restaurant, who see a movie star walk by, who happens to be me, Anna Graham (although it wasn't my part). The woman in the couple (my part) becomes jealous of her boyfriend's admiration for Anna Graham.

And I had to memorize this absurd, embarrassing scene. For a moment I considered not doing it, but the thought of having to pluck shards out of my body quickly put an end to that fantasy. The dialogue was indescribably ridiculous, memorably ridiculous, which was lucky, for it was easy to memorize, and the scene was not very long. In a

short time, I knew the damn thing by heart and went to
bed. I set the alarm clock for 6:30 A.M. Damon had told
me he'd come in at eight.

I got up in the middle of the night to go to the bathroom,
but my muscles were so sore that I could barely move.
And it wasn't as if I had never worked out before, or never
been in serious pain as a consequence. I had, but not like
this. Nevertheless, I had to go to the bathroom, so made
my way there, bearing the unbearable.

I held on to the counter to lower myself onto the toilet
seat, because my leg muscles were in too much pain to
support my weight.

On my way back to bed, when I glanced around the
corner to see if everything was still the same, I saw a large
vase of colorful roses just inside my cell. I limped over to
them. On the monitor, Damon was sleeping. He must
have quietly brought them in during the night. Near the
vase on the floor was a small white card. With great difficulty and suffering I bent down and picked it up. On it
was handwritten:

Dear Anna Graham,

I hope that these are not too unbearable.
I'm sorry to be giving them to you,
But with them will come more beauty.
Follow your name to understand me.
(5-letter word)

Yours,
Damon

At first I didn't understand. Roses were not "unbearable." At least not to most people.

Then I realized it was a puzzle. As if I didn't have enough stress already.

It was a word game, an anagram, of the word *roses*, which I was supposed to figure out, and which I did. The answer was *sores*. I reread his note and it made a lot more sense now. It felt good to know he felt guilty about my aching body. Maybe tomorrow he would be more gentle with his exercises and with his shards. I went back to bed feeling less vulnerable, thinking my complaining had worked.

I ate the banana and yogurt he had left.

Chapter Nine

Again, I didn't sleep that night. At 6:30 A.M. the alarm rang, and I started my escape plan.

First, I donned armor: I put on my jeans, wrapped a towel around each of my legs, and put on two pairs of sweatpants over them. I wore every top I had: two T-shirts, a turtleneck, and a sweater, after wrapping a hand towel around one arm and the bath mat around the other. I stuffed my pillow under my sweater to protect my torso. Finally, I wrapped a sheet around my head and face, leaving just my eyes uncovered, and a hole to breathe through.

As for a weapon, I took the vacuum cleaner out of the closet and scooped the dust out of its bag. I replaced the vacuum in the closet, and checked Damon on the monitors. He was already in the kitchen making breakfast.

I carefully took the dust in my arms and carried it like a baby into the bathroom. It was actually the size of a baby. I stepped into the bathtub, closed the shower curtain, and waited.

It didn't take long for Damon to arrive. He knocked on the bathroom door for a while before opening it. He drew back the shower curtain. I shoved the dust in his face, leaped out of the tub, and tried to grab his gun on my way out, but failed. I rushed to the cell door. He hadn't locked it. I had noticed the day before that sometimes he didn't bother locking the cage after entering it; he didn't need to, since he had his water gun to control me. But no longer, now that I had my padding. I ran out of the room and down the hallway. Rather, I wobbled (my cushiony armor made me into a very fat person). My aching muscles didn't help things. The bath mat was sliding out of my sleeve. I hopped down the stairs, and by the time I had reached the bottom step, Damon had reached me. He dragged me back upstairs, flung me in the cage with him, locked it, sat me down at the breakfast table, and screamed, "Eat!"

The breakfast consisted of unappetizing whole grain sugarless cereal with skim milk, toast without butter or jam or honey. And orange juice.

I wanted to tell him that I was dying without sugar, that I couldn't act if I didn't eat sugar, that if I ate sugar, I was alive. But it didn't feel like the right time.

I ate through the breathing hole in the sheet.

After we had finished, he looked at his watch and made me sit on a pillow on the floor, with my back against the bars of my cell and my hands behind my back. He handcuffed my wrists to the bars and tied my legs together. He took out of his bag two pieces of cloth that looked like scarves, made of the same thin and transparent material as his clothes, and tossed them next to me. They fluttered lightly to the floor. He could strangle me with them. Or hang me.

"What are you going to do?" I asked.

He left the room. From where I was sitting, I could only make out some indistinct movement on the monitors, which occasionally traveled from one screen to the next. I waited. Damon hadn't made me take off my armor yet. The pillow under my sweater protruded in front of me like a huge beer belly. I was hot.

An hour and a half went by, and then the doorbell rang, which first stunned me, and then threw me into a state of intense turmoil. Damon rushed into my cell and roughly pulled the sheet off my head. He picked up one of the silk scarves and shoved it in my mouth, and wrapped the other one over my mouth, tying it tightly behind my head. I gagged. My nose started running from my choking.

Someone was coming in the house, and if only I managed to make enough noise, I might get their attention. As soon as Damon left the room, I tried screaming, but the only thing that came out was a hum. I tried different pitches of humming, hoping one would be louder than the others, but they all came out at about the same volume. I tried banging my feet against the floor. I tried getting up, but a horizontal bar was preventing the handcuffs from sliding up. I tried banging my head back against the bars, but did not do it more than once—the sound was small and the pain big. I went back to humming frantically. My throat started hurting, and I choked at intervals, and my nose ran more, but I never actually threw up inside my mouth, which pleasantly surprised me. And then I heard voices of men. I stopped humming for a moment, but couldn't make out anything they were saying. I banged my head against the bars once more. The voices faded. I cried. I forced myself to stop that, however, because my nose was getting clogged and I couldn't breathe.

Five minutes later Damon opened the door and ungagged me. This was too bad because it meant the man, or men, was gone. But I screamed anyway, just in case. Damon did not seem to care, which confirmed my fear that they were gone, but I continued, in case he was bluffing, which I knew was illogical, but I wanted to be thorough.

"It's okay," he finally said, "you don't have to keep screaming. They're gone."

"Who were they?"

"The deliverymen."

I was still handcuffed on the floor, but by twisting my head I glimpsed a big machine in the doorway. Perhaps a torture device.

I was not entirely wrong. It was the bicycle, the recumbent bicycle.

"This is so exciting," said Damon, pushing the massive, electronic device into my cell. He positioned it facing the TV monitors and plugged it in the wall.

Sitting on it, he said, "The pedaling is so smooth." He pressed various buttons, lighting up the screen.

Removing my handcuffs, he told me to go change into more comfortable—and fewer—clothes. I felt sad and defeated in the bathroom, as I took off my armor amid the dust.

Damon then made me pedal on the bike and told me to keep pedaling until the screen had indicated that I had burned eight hundred calories.

"Eight hundred calories! But that's two or three hours of bicycling!" I said, horrified. I knew this because I occasionally went to a friend's gym and used the bikes there.

"It's two hours, at the level I'm setting it to. When I come back in an hour, you better've burned four hundred calories. If you haven't, I'll be very mad and you will deeply regret it. Now I'm going to do some work in my lab. Pedal well."

I pedaled, watching the calories add up on the screen and wishing I had a cigarette. Or chocolate, to give me energy. I watched him on a TV monitor, futzing in his lab. I became absorbed by what he was doing.

He took the glass covers off the clouds he had made yesterday and experimented on them. I assume they were experiments, unless he was just trying to kill time.

After an hour, he came in to check on me and saw that I was right on schedule, calorie-wise.

As he was about to return to his lab, I asked him, "Why were you hitting your clouds with raquets?"

He seemed taken off-guard. "I was testing the density of my clouds by checking the speed at which they go through the grooves of the racquet. I was comparing the speeds, or resistance, of the different clouds."

"And why were you sucking them up with eye-droppers and turkey basters?" I asked, panting from the exertion of bicycling while talking.

"I was again testing their density."

"And why were you stomping on them, sitting on them, and trying to slice them with a knife?"

"I was mad because my clouds were not as dense as I had hoped."

"Why were you sitting on the floor with fans blowing around you?"

"I was trying to think of the solution."

"To what?"

He looked at me with a puzzled air. "To increasing their density."

"How do you expect to do that?"

"By changing the way the water is whipped. I told you my bonsai clouds are created by mixing the water in a particular way, with my whipping machine. It's a sort of blender. I can make the blending prongs blend in different positions, create different patterns and combinations of whipping, and vary the speed of whipping." He paused, then told me more: "Whipping is like knitting. It stitches the cloud together, but with floating stitches. I want to figure out how to make the stitches stronger, while retaining their lightness. I spent the last three years of my life trying different speeds and whipping patterns, in the hope of making the cloud's fabric more tightly knit."

"How dense do you want to make your clouds?"

"I want to make them solid."

"Why?"

"It would be nice."

"Do you, by any chance, want them to carry things?"

He shrugged. "Maybe."

"You want them to carry *you*, don't you! You've been too influenced by children's books, where people float on clouds. You're crazy. How could you think it's possible? Clouds are less dense than water."

"Why do you have to be negative? *I'm* not negative about *your* dream of becoming an actress. Why would you be negative about my chances of finding the right way to whip water?"

"Have you tried anything other than changing the way the water is whipped?"

"Of course. I've tried everything I could possibly think of. I've tried mixing the clouds with various chemicals. I even tried mixing them with things like blood, spit, pus, sweat, tears . . . hair. I've spent entire days just thinking, trying to figure out what I must do to the clouds to make them solid. I went to a health food specialist and asked him what vitamins I should take and what foods I should eat to make myself more scientifically imaginative and intelligent. I think I must have a nutritional deficiency of some sort, or be lacking in a vitamin, that is preventing me from coming up with the solution. Or maybe I have a chemical imbalance."

"Because you can't make clouds solid."

"Yes." He sat on the floor, facing me and the bars. "You can stop pedaling, by the way; I see you've just about done the eight hundred calories. I even tried talking to my clouds, to convince them to get more solid, that it's a better life being solid, it's more fun to have substance."

I stared. He looked vulnerable sitting on the floor, his legs spread open into a perfect split. He was stretching.

He went on: "There were times I felt my sanity slipping, like when I tried mixing them with smoke, darkness, and smells." He looked uneasy, and added: "When my sanity slipped even more, I tried mixing clouds with boredom, envy, tendency, and the notion of extremes. But I'm not giving up. I will make it. I must."

"Why must you?"

"Because I want to. No special reason other than great desire."

What followed was an unpleasant stretching session for an hour. He kept repeating, "Flexibility is freedom." He kneaded his chewing gum between his fingers, saying that I should try to be as flexible as the gum. When I didn't stretch far enough, he spurred me on by shooting ice needles at me or sometimes only ice threads that were so thin they felt like what I imagined acupuncture was like. Toward the end of the session he made a little sculpture out of his gum, and presented it to me on the palm of his hand. It was a face, which vaguely resembled mine, but more attractive; a young Elizabeth Taylor without the slight squashing. When we had finished gazing at it, Damon threw the face in his mouth and said, "Flexibility is not only freedom. It is beauty."

He allowed me to rest while he went out and bought a dinky trampoline.

During lunch we had an argument that began when I said, "You are wasting your time and mine by keeping me here. You'll never be able to improve my acting. I'm either meant to succeed or fail as an actress, but you won't make any difference as to the outcome."

"Let me tell you that you sure seemed to be heading for failure when I met you. And you knew it. If I hadn't come along, ten years from now you'd still be struggling."

"First of all, let me remind you that you did not come along: *I* came along. And if *I* hadn't come along, *you* might be *dead!* Which is what I now wish with all my heart had happened."

"Perhaps I would be dead. But what is more important—not just to you but also to me—is that you would be a failure, and unhappy."

I was enraged. And I couldn't think of a good comeback. So finally, I just passionately, childishly, repeated, "Well *you* would be *dead!*"

"Honey, you know who that was that just walked by?"

For a second I thought he was delirious. But then he pointed his gun at me, and it jogged my memory: he was reciting the first line of the scene he had given me to learn the night before.

I snorted at his timing. He was shamelessly taking advantage of the situation, of his position of power, by choosing this moment to do the scene. I told him I thought his scene was stupid, and he said there was no talking about scenes beforehand. He threatened to shoot me if I did.

"Honey," he repeated, "do you know who that was that just walked by?"

"Who?" I recited.

"Anna Graham."

"The actress? Are you sure?"

"Yes. She looked straight at me."

"Was she pretty?"

"Yes."

"More than me?" I asked, feeling like a moron.

"I really couldn't say. Why would you ask such a thing?"

"Answer me."

"Maybe slightly. But it's not her looks that make her so appealing as an actress. She has an amazing personality."

"Better than mine?"

"Better than ninety-nine percent of the population's."

"Does that mean it's better than mine or not?"

"Well, it's better than almost anyone's."

"But better than mine or not?"

"If your personality is better than ninety-nine percent of the population's, then no, hers is not better than yours."

"Is my personality better than ninety-nine percent of the population's?"

"Who can say."

"You can. You just said hers was, so you can tell me if mine is."

"Listen. She's an actress, a frequent indicator of charm and charisma; you run a copy shop, a frequent indicator of . . . probably many qualities, but not specifically charm and charisma. Draw your own conclusion."

"Would you sleep with her if you could?"

"Probably not."

"What do you mean *probably* not? That means maybe?"

"I don't know. It would depend on how you felt about it."

"That means if I said okay, you would do it? You would want to? You would *want* to sleep with someone else?"

"She's not just someone else. She's a great movie actress. That makes it more okay, more excusable, if not acceptable, don't you think? I mean, you could then feel proud to have a boyfriend who had slept with Anna Graham. You'd think to yourself: he was good enough for *her,* so he must be pretty damn good; you know, a pretty good catch. Don't you think?"

"No, I don't think. And I don't think things are working
out between us."

He clapped. "I'd say that was a good beginning. And
you learned your lines perfectly. I'm very pleased. We
should celebrate."

"That was the most stupid scene I've ever heard. Even
pornographic movies don't have lines as bad as yours. But
then again, you are the weatherman passing off as someone who knows anything about acting, so why am I surprised?"

"Your passion and earnestness are funny. I could listen
to them all day, but we should move on to other things."

"That's it? Aren't you going to teach me now, and critique my performance? Isn't that what this is supposed to
be about?"

He shrugged. "I thought you were fine."

"You're keeping me prisoner for *this?* Boy, that's really
useful for me to know, that I was fine. I can feel the Oscar
getting closer, you pathetic fraud."

"I like your mood right now. It's an extraordinarily ripe
mood. Ripe for a contrast. I can feel the creation of the
new mood simmering within me. It's almost ready. I've
got it! Your new mood is happiness. Pure and basic. I
want you to do happiness. Now . . . do it . . ." He said this
like a fashion designer who visualized red as being the
color for the next season.

"What are you blabbering about, you idiot?" I snapped.

He laughed. I didn't.

"In other words," he said, "I want you to act happy.
I've given a lot of thought to what kinds of acting exercises you should do. I came up with this one, which will
consist of me ordering you, unexpectedly and with no

warning, to act out a certain mood, or a state of being, or to adopt a personality trait. Now is the time for happiness."

"Forget it."

"Oh, come now, do we have to go through the whole gun and threat process? Can't we skip it and take it for granted?"

I didn't answer.

"Okay, good, I think you agree. Now please do happiness."

It was pointless to resist. "I'm happy," I said, stiff-lipped.

He laughed. "You'll have to do a lot better than that."

"I'm so happy," I said dully.

He aimed his gun at me. "Well I'm not. You're going to have to make it at least ten times better."

"I'm ecstatic?"

He shot me in the thigh. I screamed with pain and indignation. I was shocked, *shocked,* that he would shoot me over that. I plucked out the shard and threw it in his face.

He performed the now classic throwing-of-the-Band-Aid-at-me. After I put it on my wound, he said, "Do happiness."

"And how would you like it prepared: with jumps in the air and screams of joy?"

"You could."

"For how long?"

"Until I say stop."

"In a minute or so?"

"No. Anywhere from a *few* minutes to a few hours."

"But that would be aerobics."

He sighed. "Do happiness. Just do it. And well."

I clapped my hands once and kicked my foot and said, "Life is great!" but it came out sarcastic, like the cereal tiger, and I got shot again.

I took a deep breath and focused my thoughts and drained every drop of sarcasm from my being, and did happiness: "I'm so happy to be here," I said. "It's like being at a spa. It's great to not have to go to work at the Xerox shop or at the jewelry store. It's like attending an acting school for free, plus a gym for free, and getting delicious meals free, and cage and board free."

I hoped he wouldn't shoot me for the offensive but irresistible last four words. He did frown, but I quickly rambled on to distract him: "And the *anagram!* What a charming way to give a present-slash-message. And the activities! I'm always in suspense as to what new and challenging method of improvement you will have concocted for me." It may be hard to believe, but my tone didn't contain a hint of mockery.

"I'm sorry I don't have anything new planned for today," he said.

"Well that's okay too. This way I'll get to enjoy the old stuff, which is still very new to me anyway."

"Does it bother you to do this mood?" he asked, obviously intending me to demonstrate my mood further.

"Like yeah, it really bothers me to be staying in this gorgeous house with this gorgeous guy giving me all these acting exercises for free. Yeah, I'd much rather be wasting my life at the Xerox shop."

He was smiling with appreciation at my tour de force: being able to say what I really felt while still fitting into his exercise.

He looked at his watch and said, "Hold that thought, I'll be back in a while." It was 1:25 P.M.

I watched the monitors and saw him go through the same doorway as yesterday, at the same time—the doorway that led to the mysterious unfilmed place.

He came back half an hour later, having, like yesterday, obviously cried.

He informed me that I was not yet relieved of my obligation to "do happiness." He brought me down to the pool and made me swim again.

"Don't just stay afloat; advance!"

"I can't," I said. "It's not possible."

"Of course it's possible."

"No."

"Just watch," he said, placing his gun on the shelf with the rubber ducks. He dove into the pool, and flew through the water (since moving through this airy water was more an act of flying than swimming). A moment later he was back at my side.

He heaved himself out of the water. "The secret is to kick your feet as if you were doing the crawl, but with your arms you should do the breast stroke. Just as you would if you were flying."

Speak for yourself, I thought. That's not what I would do if I were flying, and I've never seen anyone fly that way. Except maybe in a dream.

"Advance," he ordered, standing at the edge of the pool. His dripping clothes stuck to his skin. His naked body was quite visible underneath.

"Move it," he repeated, and shot an ice needle in my neck, which hurt less than a shard.

I tried advancing, but he had still not allowed me to

stop "doing happiness," and it was a challenge to keep a smile on my face while I was so frightened of drowning. At one point he said, "You don't look very happy," and he gripped his gun and I forced a bigger smile on my face, and he said, "Yes you do, I was wrong."

He finally allowed me to come out. I climbed up the ladder, the smile hanging off my lips precariously.

He said, "Was it fun?"

"Yes."

"Tell me more."

"It was exciting, so challenging and exhilarating," I said, mustering every last drop of emotional energy I had. "No health club on earth can offer such a workout."

"Okay, you can stop acting happy now."

I hissed, "What's in your head, you twerp? You can't treat a human being this way. I'm a human being! Don't you have any concept of what that means?" I was trembling from the cold and from rage. "Do you think you're God? I never thought it would be possible to feel such hatred for anyone. I'm actually disturbed by the strength of my hatred. If I had a gun I would kill you without a moment's hesitation. I would even kill myself, just to deprive you of me: your plaything."

My lips were starting to curl away from my teeth without my control: I was baring my fangs. "If I get any chance, I *will* kill you. Escaping is no longer enough for me."

I crumpled to the floor and burst into tears, in distress.

He gently placed his hand on my shoulder.

"Don't touch me!" I screamed. "Your attempts to make me feel better will only make it worse."

"I wasn't going to try to make you feel better," he said

softly. "I was just going to say that now I want you to do hip."

"What?"

"Now act hip. Do hipness."

I tried to hurl myself into the pool, willing to put an end to the whole thing through drowning, but he caught me by the waist and said, "I don't feel like rescuing you again today. Please don't make me jump in after you. Be good." He watched me carefully, and added, "Now, have some courage, Anna. Do hip."

"Can you give me a few minutes before you make me do this?"

"That would defeat the purpose. You must do it now."

"Oh God how I hate you," I said, panting. I felt like the little girl in *The Exorcist,* possessed by the devil. I screamed, "Die!"

"Do hip!" he answered.

Fury, and a sort of fever, were destroying my sanity. I was actually snarling. Like a dog. It was the first time I had ever snarled, and I didn't know humans ever did, or could, when pushed to the limit. I crawled away from Damon, over to the wall, on my hands and feet.

He approached me cautiously, like a tamer. He was still dripping. "Anna, be reasonable. Stop making that noise, and come to your senses. Do hip. From the moment the word leaves my lips, it is yours; you have to act it. Now or I'm going to shoot."

He shook the gun at me, which shook me out of my beastly state, or partly. I stared at the ceiling, desperately trying to capture an idea of what acting hip looked like. I had a firmer grasp of "cool" and hoped the two were interchangeable. I took a deep breath and plunged into what I thought might be hip behavior: I began by combing my fingers through my hair, which I did not manage very well, for my hair was wet and tangled, and my fingers got stuck.

Damon took off his wet shirt and dropped it on the floor. It was the first time I saw him genuinely topless. He was predictably well built.

I kept acting hip as he escorted me back to my cell.

We changed into dry clothes, and he made me continue to act hip during stretching, jumping on the trampoline, and dinner. Then we laid down on my bed and watched *Now Voyager,* starring Bette Davis, and I thought I was acting hip, but he said, "You're not sitting in a hip position. It's a nerdy position. Sit in a hip position."

I shifted my legs on the bed. I bent one, and crossed my fingers on my stomach. He seemed soothed. I so wished I had a cigarette or chocolate so I could be soothed too.

Halfway through the movie he said, "Now I want you to do slim-hipped and statuesque."

He was not sane, it was as simple as that. I didn't move.

After a minute, he said, "Aren't you going to change your position? You can't stay in the same position. That's the hip position. You can't stay in the hip position if you're going to do slim-hipped and statuesque."

"Well maybe I'm a slim-hipped, hip, and statuesque person."

"I still think you should change your position."

I sat up a little straighter in bed and pressed my hands against my hips, as if squeezing them closer together.

"What are you doing with your hands?" he asked.

"Making my hips slimmer."

"You call that good acting? I'm not asking you to *be*

slim-hipped, at least not right now; I'm asking you to *act* slim-hipped. And statuesque."

I thought about very skinny people, and remembered noticing the way they often sat: they sat not merely crossed-legged (with one leg simply hanging over the other), but with their leg wrapped around the other, many times, like a sort of vine.

So I tried to do that, and it was not very comfortable, but it earned me some silence, which I assumed meant it was acceptable.

After the movie, he left me for the night, depositing on my bed a new scene I had to learn by morning.

I read it and was appalled and learned it.

I chose not to turn on the TV today. I wasn't in the mood to see what I was missing out on; the attention I was not getting; the opportunities I was not there to grab.

I went to bed. I was absolutely exhausted, having barely slept for two days. I was intending to have a good night's sleep to be in good shape to escape if I had an opportunity.

I did fall into a deep sleep, but woke up in the middle of the night feeling extremely confused and disoriented, because I was all wet and getting wetter by the second. I was being rained on by a large cloud that had drifted into my cage.

My blanket, my pillow, the mattress, and the carpet were wet. I was cold. I shouted for Damon, and sloshed over to the bars of my cell to scream some more, but I was distracted by the sight of five sparkling, dark red stones scattered at my feet. Having worked in a jewelry store, I knew before picking them up that they were garnets. Next to them was a small white card.

Slowly and with agony, I lowered myself and picked up the stones and the card, which said:

> Dear Anna Graham,
> Don't think I'm not aware that this is what you think of me.
> And don't think I'm not aware that you think it's putting it mildly.
> Follow your name to understand me.
> (7-letter word)
>
>   Yours,
>   Damon

The cloud growled at me like a dog. As if responding to his growl, the other clouds in the house started thundering, or rumbling too.

I shook my towel at it, to create a breeze, to make it leave, but it was big and would require a stronger breeze to budge it.

Or the opposite, I thought, suddenly struck with an idea. All monsters had their weakness, their particular requirement for being killed: vampires needed a stake through the heart or exposure to the sun; the living dead had to be burned, I think, or decapitated; and clouds needed to be dealt with, with . . . a particular household appliance I happened to have in my cell.

I took the vacuum cleaner out of the closet, plugged it in, turned it on, and lifted it in the air, aiming its mouth at the cloud.

The vacuum let me down once again. Its suction power was no more effective than its dust in fighting my enemies.

The cloud was not being sucked in, and kept raining on my bed. I threw the vacuum aside.

I needed my escape rest. I looked for a dry patch of carpet on which to sleep, and found one under the monitors. I got some towels to use as blankets. I also took my poor nude pen and a pad, to try to solve the anagram Damon had left me, in case it came in handy to know what he thought I thought of him.

It took me fifteen minutes to figure out that the anagram for *garnets* was *strange*. I would have been better off getting my sleep.

Which is what I then tried to do, but failed. I was not used to sleeping on the floor, pillowless. I needed my bed, and since the cloud seemed to have finished relieving itself on it, I took down the plastic shower curtain, spread it over my wet mattress, and laid on it. Eventually, I wrapped myself completely in the shower curtain when the cloud started drizzling on me again.

Listening to the sound of the raindrops on the plastic, and hoping I wouldn't die of suffocation breathing that hot, humid, scarcely oxygenated air, I finally managed to fall asleep inside the shower curtain.

Chapter Ten

When I told him I had been rained on during the night, Damon was horrified and apologized profusely, saying he should have checked the weather forecast in the living room before going to bed. Despite his remorse, he forced me to keep doing "slim-hipped and statuesque" all through breakfast and through the ensuing bicycling session. Then he told me to switch to nerdy without even giving me a short break during which I could insult him. I had to do nerdy through swimming, jumping on the trampoline, calisthenics, and half of lunch, when he said I could stop, and I was able to insult him to my heart's content while, using spoons, we ate small portions of delicious healthy pasta cut in short strands. And then he interrupted me in the middle of a new insult, and said gently, "You look a little gloomy."

I was stunned by this absurd understatement. I opened my mouth to utter some stinging retort, but noticed the orange plastic barrel of his gun pointed at me, and I replied instead, "Yes, I'm depressed about our daughter, Anna. It upsets me that she's such a failure."

"I know, I feel the same way," he said, "but we should try not to think about it."

I recited stoically: "Moderate failure would be one thing. But such monumental failure. It's heart-wrenching. She hasn't managed to get one acting job, not one penny earned from acting, just classes and Xeroxing and piercing. I don't understand what's wrong with her. I dread it when my friends ask me what Anna is up to. I actually feel embarrassed for having nothing of interest to relate. And I hate myself for feeling ashamed. And I hate myself for even admitting this now."

"You're just being honest. I feel the same way. John O'Connor was telling me the other day about the various accomplishments of the sons and daughters of our unit owners, and then he asked what our children were up to. I told him about our son's graduation and his great job, and I hoped he would leave it at that, not ask about Anna, but he did. In fact, he said, 'And that daughter of yours? That promising one? That ambitious one?' It was really uncomfortable. I felt like a fool."

"It's unfair," I said, "that a decent man like you should have to endure that kind of interaction. We don't deserve this. I often resent Anna for her failure. Her failure is our failure, and how can it not make us feel like bad parents? John O'Connor is right: Anna had so much promise. It's ironic that our son is the one who made something of himself. At first it looked so different."

"Yes, but it does no good to dwell on it. We should think of pleasant things," concluded Damon as my father. Then, Damon as Damon didn't wait a moment to say,

"Wood! You were wood! Wooden, wooden, wooden. You are wood when you're supposed to be water. You were not as good as yesterday. We'll have to do it again later. You obviously didn't like the scene and didn't make much effort to hide the fact. You must be more convincing, more fluid, more liquidy."

I had a floating sensation. My body felt as if it had lost its physicality and turned into an emotion: hate. I couldn't speak, and I had no need to speak. I gazed at him, and I was hate.

We sat staring at each other, me with my hatred, and he closely observing it, as if measuring it, even appreciating it.

Finally, he slowly and deliberately broke the silence: "Now I want you to act telepathic."

I acted telepathic. He watched me doing it for five minutes, and then looked at his watch. I looked at mine. It was 1:23 P.M. He stared at me, as if waiting for me to say something. I just stared back at him.

"You see," he said, "this would have been a good moment for you, since you're doing telepathic, to say, 'You are now thinking of leaving for a little while.' Too bad, you missed a good opportunity."

He got up and started walking out, and I said, "You're intending to come back in half an hour, and you will have cried like a baby—a baby automaton who cries every day at the same time when plugged in."

"Better late than never," he said, and left.

I took up my position in front of the monitors, and sure enough he went into the same unfilmed space, and came back half an hour later having cried.

As for the blasted scene in which I expressed my disappointment with my daughter Anna, he made me do it again during an unexpected session of swimming in the watair. I almost drowned.

While I relaxed in my cell for a short while in the afternoon, I saw an astonishing program on TV. *Geraldo* was doing a "special" about the Pursued Woman. The count had risen to fifty-three since I had last watched the news two days before. Fifty-three women pretending to be me. And Geraldo had invited the thirty most plausible candidates, offering them an opportunity to prove their authenticity on his show. The audience was to decide which one was the real pursued woman. It made me sick and gave me all kinds of unpleasant symptoms.

The women were required to do two things: (1) Be filmed from the back while they ran from the front to the back of the stage. (2) Explain why they had been pursued by Chriskate Turschicraw.

I turned off the TV to soothe my symptoms. Thirty seconds later I turned it back on and watched what could have been my life. Not that it was that glamorous to have the jiggle of one's running butt analyzed, evaluated, and compared to the jiggle of the butt on the original footage. But still, it could open doors.

After the butt evaluation, they voted. And then came the explanation category, where the women told their stories, most of which were banal. Some were far-fetched, without, however, significantly sacrificing their banality. What would the audience have thought of *my* story: Chriskate, in love with a man in love with me. She wants to study me, to be like me. It was the best story. It was unguessable.

Then the final vote took place. The woman who won was called Armory Jude. She didn't look like me at all.

That evening, during dessert (fruit salad), Damon made me do "jumping to conclusions," which immediately gave him the idea to make me do it while jumping on the trampoline. I actually rather enjoyed doing "jumping to conclusions," because it was not so far removed from my natural inclination in my current situation. Unfortunately, Damon realized this right away and made me instead act "tanned." Having never noticed that tanned people had a particular way of acting, all I could think of doing was rolling up my sleeves and my sweatpants, to show off my "tan." I also caressed and gazed at my bare arms and legs to show I was enjoying my "tan." And I spoke in a slightly languorous way, assuming for some reason that tanned people were more languorous, having laid out in the sun all day.

He then left me to relax for an hour, saying we would watch a movie when he returned.

Of course, I knew he would expect me to still be tanned when he came back. I hated doing tanned. I thought about how much nicer "jumping to conclusions" had been, and I decided I would do it again in the future whenever I felt like it.

Suddenly, I was appalled at myself for thinking this way. There *was* no future for me in this house. I could not *let* there be a future.

It frightened me that I did not feel more horror, more panic, more agony; I had accepted my predicament. It was this realization that finally awoke the full extent of my horror.

I rolled down my sleeves and my pants. I would not be tanned when he came back. I would let him shoot me. I would endure the shards as long as I could, or the ice blades, or boiling bullets, or whatever, even if they brought me near death. But I would not do tanned again. Nor any other state of being.

I waited, feeling nervous, but also brave and invigorated, like Joan of Arc or Antigone.

When he came back, he chatted about this and that and did not even notice I had stopped acting tanned, which just showed how absurd the whole thing was. Without telling me that I could stop acting tanned, he told me to do "realist."

I stared back at him and firmly said, "No."

He sighed and rolled his eyes. "I don't have much patience anymore for the whole threats process. From now on I'm skipping the threats and going straight to the shooting. Now do realist."

"No. You can shoot me all you want, until I look like a porcupine and die. I will never do realist or ever again obey any of your orders."

"You shouldn't talk like that. It'll hurt your pride when you cave in and do realist after a couple of shards. Spare your pride. Do realist."

"No. I've never cared much about my pride."

"I'm not kidding. Do realist."

"No."

He shot me in the arm. I barely flinched.

"Do realist," he said.

"No."

He shot me again, in the breast. This one hurt a lot and I did murmur "Ow."

"Do disobedient," he said.

Ah, a trick. If I said "no," I would be obeying him. How to dodge it? No way to. It didn't matter, I wouldn't play his game.

"No," I said.

"Good. Now do stoic."

"No."

"Excellent. Now do realist."

"No."

He was starting to look pained. I could see him trying to decide on a body part to shoot, away from the other wounds. He shot me in the shoulder. That one hurt a lot too and I said "Ow" again.

"Do realist."

"No."

He shot me a tablespoon of boiling water in the stomach.

"Ow."

"Do realist."

"No."

He raised his gun to shoot, but then lowered it. He slowly turned away and walked out of the cage with his head hanging, not forgetting of course to lock the cell behind him. I had won.

I sat against the wall in blissful meditation, pressing on my breast and shoulder wounds.

I had won. Now. Anagram of won: now. Now, I had won. I had discovered his weak spot (or strong spot depending on how you looked at it): he would not harm me seriously.

A few minutes later I heard thunder approaching through the hallway. I saw a big dark cloud flying quickly toward me and clapping loudly. It lit up like a lightbulb for a second. And then again. On and off, it blinked irregularly. And then I saw a lightning bolt spear to the floor.

Behind the cloud was Damon, advancing with long, confident strides, and carrying a large electric fan, which explained the cloud's rapid progression.

He blew the cloud into my cage and came in himself. He grabbed me and shoved me in the bathroom and blew the cloud in with me. I tried to open the door, but Damon was holding it shut.

I immediately got struck by lightning. The pain was revolting; worse than normal straightforward pain. You couldn't tense yourself against it. It was a tricky, very powerful pain that possessed you, and then left you.

I was struck again. I screamed, and tried to open the door, but Damon wouldn't let me out. I climbed into the bathtub to get away from the cloud. Just inches from my waist, a bolt of lightning hit the soap, which leaped a foot in the air, accompanied by its plastic dish. For many long minutes I stayed in the bathtub, which in no way prevented me from getting struck by lightning repeatedly, to the point of almost losing consciousness. I would not do realist. I would rather die. Eventually, of course, I changed my mind and pounded on the door and told him I would do realist. Just as the door started to open, I got struck again and collapsed on Damon. He had to drag me to my bed.

He laid down next to me and was quiet. I wondered if he was expecting me to actively be doing realist right now, but I didn't have the strength to worry about it. I closed my eyes.

After a few minutes I mumbled, "I thought highly of you, earlier, when you stopped shooting me and left. I thought you wouldn't hurt me seriously. That you didn't have the heart to. I was wrong."

"No, not entirely," he said. "I would hurt you but I wouldn't harm you. There's a difference."

I didn't answer and kept my eyes closed.

He went on: "The bolts you were struck with were bonsai bolts, coming from bonsai clouds." He hesitated. "I had to make a decision. There was, to be honest, a small risk that you could have been harmed by the clouds—"

I raised my hand to shut him up, and said, weakly, almost inaudibly, but with extreme indignation: "I *was* harmed."

"You were hurt, not harmed, as you'll see in a week when these disappear," he said, taking my arm and pointing to some marks in the shape of bull's-eyes.

I stared at the marks. I hadn't noticed them.

"You'll find similar ones on your feet and calves, where the lightning exited your body," he said. "Anyway, as I was saying, there was a small risk, quite small. But I felt it was important that I take it. Your future suddenly looked grim to me. I put your life at risk to save your dreams."

I was feeling nauseated from the lightning. I didn't need his words to sicken me more.

He said: "I wouldn't have made you take a risk that I hadn't taken myself. Through my work, I've been struck by lightning more times than I can remember. It's a loathsome experience, disgusting, and every time it happens to me I swear I'll get out of the business. But look at me, I'm still here, all my limbs function, I'm still smart, I'm still normal."

"Normal?"

"Time for the movie."

He put on *Terminator 2* (so that I could "get motivated by Linda Hamilton's muscle tone and general fitness"). It was hard to concentrate on her muscles, however, because soon after the movie started, he said, "Now do clownish."

I stared at him. I was awed by his talent for coming up with the mood that was the most distasteful to me at any given moment.

"I thought you wanted me to do realist," I said.

"That was good for then. This is good for now."

I did my best to do clownish, which was not an easy task after having been struck by lightning.

Before going to sleep, he placed on my bed a scene I had to learn for the next day. I did.

That night, after I went to the bathroom, I checked around the corner to see if by some miracle my cage was wide open. It wasn't, but resting on the carpet just inside the bars was a ruby. The card next to it read:

Dear Anna Graham,
This is what we must do to your old self.
(4-letter word)

                                        Yours,
                                        Damon

I was so exasperated with everything that I didn't want to guess, but it was too easy, and the inauspicious answer rudely barged into my mind, completely uninvited.

The anagram for *ruby* was *bury*.

Chapter Eleven

The days passed. Damon came up with words, key words, and phrases, that he decided to utter when he wanted me to begin a scene. "Act" was one. "Do what you love," was another. There was never any warning, never any time for preparation. His philosophy seemed to be that there was no point in doing a scene if it was not at an awkward time. That's how one learned to act well: through spontaneous slips into character. Sometimes he began arguments between us so that he would then have the pleasure of choosing the ripest moment to utter the word, "Act." Swallowing one's pride was part of becoming a good actor, he said.

And the scenes continued. They often involved ourselves, our lives, our future. In one scene he played my secretary once I became famous. In another he played my acting teacher, Aaron Smith, telling one of his protégés, played by me, that his former student, the now famous Anna Graham, had not allowed him to give her name to another girl. He said he couldn't understand how she became such a good actress, because she was always herself too much, and she was now committing that dreadful sin more than ever. "I'm baffled," he would add. "Maybe I should retire."

And I, the protégé, would say, "Maybe you should. To be frank, you're not a very good teacher."

In one annoying scene, I had to play myself calling Damon a few days after saving him in the subway, and he asked if he really had to see me again just because I had saved him, and was his life going to be plagued by me from now on.

An even more putrid scene was the one where I was reminiscing about my kidnapping to a friend of mine (played by Damon), telling him it hadn't been so bad, that sometimes yes, Damon did indeed shoot me with ice shards, but it was always for a good reason, never gratuitous.

Sometimes he gave me a scene that was the exact duplicate of our normal way of living, our normal routine. Once, he reversed our roles, and he played the captive (without, however, giving me a loaded water gun). Another time we were both captives.

Things stayed the same during the following weeks, except that the trampoline broke. Damon insinuated that it was my weight that broke it. This caused tension on my part.

Another thing that caused tension was that Armory Jude, the woman who had been voted most likely to be me, the pursued woman, got a movie offer. I tried not to think about it too much, but it was hard.

Nothing else in our lives changed. Damon continued

going to the unfilmed room every day at 1:30 P.M., and coming back out half an hour later having cried. Every day except weekends. I didn't find out what it was about.

The anagrams continued. One night there were five rubies on the carpet, next to a note that said:

Dear Anna Graham,
    In case you are concerned, the pain that your beautiful gift brings me lessens when I think that it makes you happy.
    (6-letter word)

It took me a while to figure out that the anagram for *rubies* was *bruise*. He was alluding to one I had given him that morning.

Another night I was astonished to see a moonstone on my carpet; astonished because *moonstone* was so long a word. The note read:

Dear Anna Graham,
    Their beauty depends on their time and place. Their otherworldly air is, strangely enough, more appropriate for life than for acting. Please take them out of your acting.
    (9-letter word)

How could I take them out of my acting if they had too many letters for me to figure out what they were? I tried for a while, but gave up.

I didn't want Damon to think I was interested in his anagrams, so I tried not to ask him for the answer the next day, but I caved in. The answer was *monotones*.

The following night there was a very pretty pink flower on my carpet. I had never seen that kind of flower before. Its leaves smelled sweet. The note read:

Dear Anna Graham,
    Perhaps you are not aware that this is what you are, sometimes.
    (9-letter word)

First thing in the morning, I said, "There's no point in giving me flowers. I know nothing about them. I know stones, from my job, not flowers."

"It was an eglantine," he said.

"And its anagram?"

"Don't you want to guess?"

"It's nine letters long."

"Still, it's a shame not to try. I'll tell you tonight."

I couldn't guess, barely tried, and that night he told me: *inelegant.* This was obviously a reference to the fact that the night before I had thrown some of my meal in his face after he informed me I could stop acting complex.

He kept on writing scripts for me to learn. I discovered that the easiest way to get through the scenes was to plunge into them and do them as well as possible, automatically, detachedly, absentmindedly, on remote control.

Eventually, I learned to slip into character without thinking. Damon said he was becoming awed, not by my acting, but by my efficiency and power to spontaneously don traits.

He made me do a scene in which I was strangling my future son, so I had to pretend to be strangling Damon, who'd be lying on my bed.

He would order me to act sad while we were watching a funny movie, and vice versa.

He would make me pretend I was a teacup or a flower for a whole day, or just a word, like "Otherwise." He didn't expect me to literally act like a teacup, but rather to have its essence.

And what I hated even more than the scenes were the moods. That week he made me do "alert," "impractical," and "spreading rumors." Later he made me do "leech," "nonsmoker," and "fishing for compliments."

Sometimes he made me do a person: "lighthouse keeper," "pool cleaner," or "X-ray technician."

Sometimes the people he made me do were less tangible than that: "former teammate" or "divorced twice."

And sometimes he made me do things that could not be done, like making me act "intramural" or "summarized."

Months started passing. I was not rescued by anyone. I often thought of my parents and what they must be going through.

The clothes I had worn on my arrival were now baggy. And I could tell my body was hard; I no longer felt much jiggle when I moved.

Life always becomes routine, no matter how strange it is. Sometimes, for brief moments, I almost forgot I was a captive, and I was able to laugh with Damon. He remarked on this one day, and I became serious and said, "Just because I hate you doesn't mean I'm not able to enjoy your company, sometimes. Just because I sometimes enjoy your company doesn't mean I'm not unhappy."

And the scenes continued. The one I hated the most was where he made me play my mother thanking Damon for everything he had done for Anna: improving her, making her a good actor, etc. Afterward I told Damon I found his scene preposterous and repulsive, and that I would disown my mother if she ever did such a thing, which she would never do.

He made me do an Oscar speech in which I had to thank him and act moved, with tears in my eyes. He would be sitting in the imaginary audience, and I had to ask him to get up, and I would clap.

After that scene, Damon asked me if acting out these scenes of success would make them less special or exciting for me, in the future, when they did happen. He didn't want to rob me of any upcoming happiness; that would defeat the whole point of what we were doing.

I stared at him and said, "What makes you think there will be any success?"

"I think we're making a lot of progress. I may not be the most expert judge of acting, but I'm noticing changes, which, in my opinion, are improvements."

A theme began recurring in the scenes he made me do. It involved selflessness and having ruined someone's life.

A man who apologizes to his wife for having had an affair. A father who apologizes to his daughter for having molested her. A son who apologizes to his mother for having stolen from her. It was all about remorse and guilt.

And he always played the character at fault.

I accused him of having personal issues, of being unable to judge the scenes objectively. "You need me to satisfy some sick need in you, some weird obsession," I said.

The anagrams never stopped coming. One night there was a piece of satin with a stain on it. The anagram for both *satin* and *stain* was *saint,* which is what he was telling me I sometimes was, probably referring to my rescue of him.

Another night I got a truffle. It was sitting in the middle of a small saucer, on my carpet. The note read, "You should be less this." I ate the truffle with relish. I would ask him for more truffles tomorrow.

At dinner the following evening, he said, "I assume you didn't guess the anagram for *truffle.* Do you want to know what it is?"

"No, but I'd like to have more truffles."

"I'll tell you anyway. It's *fretful.*"

"Have I been fretful?"

"Yes, you have been a bit fretful."

"Oh," I said softly, and slung a pea at him with my plastic spoon.

My favorite anagram was the three different desserts he once left for me, *real* desserts (no bananas or yogurts or anything like that). In fact, they were: a chocolate mousse, a piece of chocolate cake, and a creme brulée. I tried to find the anagram for *fat,* but then saw from the card that the word was supposed to have eight letters. So it was probably *desserts.* I wrote it down and instantly found its anagram by reading it backward: *stressed.* The message on the card was that he wanted me to stop being this. The desserts would certainly help in that enterprise. They were good.

And then the anagrams became weird, comparatively speaking. They became sick. He left me a little dish with fuzz in it. I couldn't figure out what it was. It just looked like dust. And that's exactly what it was, because he wanted to tell me that I would always have a *stud* at my side. Then I again got a dish, but this time with a little *thing* in it, a little hardish reddish thing, which looked like a scab, and it was. This was to let me know I'd be taking a lot of *cabs* once I made it.

One day, I gave *him* an anagram. I asked him to cup his hand for me, and I poured into it my cut nails from my hands and feet, and I said, "This is what you will be when I'm through with you. And I don't mean the animal. Five-letter word."

He left the room carrying my nails and came back later, having guessed the two answers: the one that applied, *slain*, and the one that did not, *snail*. He said it was a good one.

Most of the scenes he made me do were either embarrassing, stupid, infuriating, or humiliating, but rarely frightening. One, however, was. He played someone who knew Damon intimately, and who was giving me some advice. I had very few lines.

"You have to be careful," he began. "There is one thing more important to Damon than your happiness."

"What's that?"

"His unhappiness. If he ever has to choose between the two, he will probably choose the latter. His need for his own unhappiness makes him dangerous. He will do anything to preserve it. You should always be careful, always protect yourself, never let your guard down completely. I'm afraid for your safety in the future. If you ever feel unsafe, don't hesitate to kill him. If you don't, he may end up destroying you. If I knew how to help him, I would, but I fear it's impossible. His pain is intense. His intention to make you happy is the only slight relief he's had from it in years."

"But what is his pain?" I asked. (This wasn't in the script.)

He shot me. "You made me forget my lines." He paused and continued: "Please remember my words: I don't think Damon can ever be normal, ever be sane. The important word here is *ever*. Always remember that. You may not want to, always, but do."

"Will he let me go?" (This *was* in the script.)

"I think so, but there's no way to know for sure."

"Can you try to persuade him?"

"That wouldn't do any good, because I am him."

"Is there anything I can do to persuade him to let me go?"

"Nothing I can think of. But I think you are safe here, because you're here against your will, and as long as that's the case you're safe from him."

"Should I try to escape?"

"You haven't had any opportunities. If you ever have one, by all means you should grab it."

After eight months of captivity I decided to make him believe I had fallen in love with him. It would be hard, but if I succeeded, it could help me escape. So I began.

I stopped complaining, I laughed at all his jokes, I listened with interest to his speeches, I looked at him with admiration whenever it seemed appropriate, and I initiated physical contact by occasionally offering to unstick some of the forgotten gum from his face. He noticed these changes in an amused way.

One day, during a wishing session, I made a wish that he would teach me how to move like him, and how to dance like him. He said it was a very good wish, that it could be useful to me as an actor to move well. The lessons began. We were obliged to engage in more physical contact than ever before. We danced in front of each other, and he wanted me to follow his movements; to flow with him. We were supposed to be waves. But sometimes I wasn't flowing well enough, so he had to help me feel his flow. He would put his hands on my waist and request that I put mine on his shoulders. Then I understood the essence of his movements. And something else happened. Despite my hatred of him, which hadn't subsided one bit, I felt, for the first time since my abduction, a strange sort of physical attraction to him. I knew this was sick, and I think it was simply because he was big and close.

I continued pretending I was enamored of him, but without ever saying it right out. During a wishing session, however, I did tell him I wished he were in love with me.

Out of the blue, one day, Damon said that if my love for him were an act, I was doing a really good job, that he couldn't tell if it were real or fake. He added that if he knew for sure it were an act he would let me go right on the spot because he'd know I was now an excellent actor.

This was a dilemma for me. If he was lying, then telling him the truth would ruin my plan of escape. On the other hand, if he was telling the truth, I could be released immediately by being honest.

I decided to play it safe for a while and assume he was lying. I continued my love pretense.

Just a day or two after this interaction, five of the six monitors in my cell were turned off. When I asked him about it, he said there was a malfunction. The only one still working was the one showing his bedroom.

The same day that the monitors went blank, Damon
spent less time with me than usual: he left me alone in my
cell for many hours during the afternoon. The same thing
happened the next day. I didn't know what it all meant,
but it made me jittery, which was partly why I finally
decided to reveal to him that my love for him was an act.

Finding no good time to do it that day, I planned to tell
him the next day. That night I got one of the sickest anagrams he had ever given me.

It was a little cup, and in it was a drop of half-dried,
yellowish, sticky slime. I didn't know what it was. The
note read:

Dear Anna Graham,
   We will do this earlier than usual tomorrow
night.
   (3-letter word)

I had the feeling the stuff in the cup was body fluid, but
I didn't think it was pee. I thought it might be pus, and it
did fit, because the answer would then be *sup*. I verified
this the next day with Damon and I was correct.

After our early dinner, just as I was asking myself when
would be the best moment to tell him about the fakeness
of my love, he said, "I must confess to you that I know
you're not in love with me. I know it's an act."

I drooped.

He added quickly, "It's not because your acting is bad
that I know this. It's because it would be impossible for
someone in your position to be in love with someone in
my position. But your acting was great."

"So you'll let me go?"

"No."

"Why not? You said that if my love for you was an act, you would let me go because it meant I was a great actor. Were you bluffing?"

"Kind of."

"My acting is still not good enough, is that it?"

"No. Your acting is great."

I huffed. "But still not good enough for me to be released, right?"

"Yes, it is good enough for you to be released."

My heart raced, and I suddenly imagined the dinner I would have tonight with my parents.

"But I will not release you," he added.

"You want me to get better?"

"I don't think you could. At least not significantly. I think you're as good as it's possible for anyone to become."

"So what's the problem?"

"There is no problem."

"Then when will you let me go?"

"I will not let you go, ever."

"Ever!" I yelled. "Why?"

"Because this way we can keep acting out scenes. If I let you go, the outcome is so predictable: you'll be in movies, become a star, win Oscars, blah, blah, blah. Banal. But if you stay, it's less banal. It hasn't been done before. At least not as often."

"What about my happiness? Do you think I can be as happy here?"

"No."

"Then why are you doing this?"

"Because I don't care anymore."

"About my happiness? But it was the goal of your life! You claimed that I would be so happy if I became a great actor, after you shaped me up and let me go."

"Yes, you would be very happy. It's important that you be completely aware of that," he said, facing me squarely. "We have achieved our goal. I have succeeded in creating in you a rich potential for happiness. If I released you now, you would become extremely successful very quickly. And you would be very, very happy. It's more interesting to keep you here. It's a new challenge that will distract me from what I should be distracted from. This way I can see if I can make you happy here. It's harder."

"Damon, I'll kill myself if you don't let me go," I said, looking into his eyes.

"Nonsense. You haven't killed yourself yet. I doubt you'll do it now."

"That's because I had *hope*. And now you've told me there's no hope."

"Well, you can always pretend there's hope. Just enough not to kill yourself, please. Here's your scene for tomorrow. Learn it well."

"No. It's over. I will never do a scene with you again."

"Yes you will. Otherwise . . ." he showed the gun.

"I welcome otherwise. Please give me otherwise, but the big otherwise, the last otherwise. Give me otherwise, *fatally*."

"Read the new scene, learn it, and let's get on with our days."

"I will never read it."

But I did read it. And then I read it again, and again. There was no way I couldn't escape if things unfolded the way they were written in the script. No matter how many times I reread it, I could not find a catch. And it couldn't be stupidity on his part. It was intentional.

I didn't sleep at all, and there was no anagram that night.

I nervously waited for Damon's arrival the next day, but he did not come to my cell until five o'clock in the afternoon, which explained why he had left two sandwiches for me the day before.

He came carrying the dinner tray and two antique swords. I was ecstatic. He closed the cell door, but did not lock it.

We ate our meal politely. More politely than I could ever remember. I tried to be patient. I didn't understand why he had apparently decided to release me in this roundabout way, but it didn't matter as long as it happened.

As we dug into our fake desserts of yogurt and fruit, Damon said, "Act."

"You brought swords," I recited.

"Yes, to cheer you up. You must be pretty upset about the news that you won't be released. If we engage in a little game of fencing after dinner it might help you feel less homesick. Wouldn't that cheer you up a bit?"

"Yes."

"Good. I've never fenced with anyone who actually knew how to fence. I've never fenced with anyone, in fact. It'll be exciting. And then you can give me some pointers; a mini fencing lesson. This way, we're creating a nice dynamic: I gave you dancing lessons and you'll give me fencing lessons."

He ate a piece of fruit and resumed his monologue with his mouth full: "And if we do enjoy ourselves tonight, there's no reason we can't fence *every single night!* This is my first big step in making you happy here. Notice I'm determined to succeed and will stop at nothing."

I had trouble swallowing my banana. Finally, Damon looked at me and said, "Shall we?"

We got up. He walked over to the swords resting against the wall and picked them up. He readied himself with one of them, holding it firmly by the handle, and he handed me the other. He looked nervous, and I was too, until I had the sword in my hand.

We fenced. That's where the scene he wrote ended. What happened after that was not acting.

I soon disarmed him.

"That was great!" he said. "Now you must teach me how you did that." He gingerly went to pick up his sword, but I kicked it away from him.

"Oooh. You must teach me that too."

I picked up his sword and threw it out of the cell.

"What are you doing?"

"I'm leaving."

He rolled his eyes. "No you're not." And he pounced on me, not seeming to care that I was holding a long cutting object that I handled well.

"What are *you* doing?" I said, and slashed his arm. He screamed and looked furious. Things were not unfolding the way I had expected. Blood spread through his white clothing, but the cut didn't look deep, not that I knew much about cuts or had engaged in much cutting of people.

"Hand me the key," I said.

"Why?"

"So I can lock you up, so you won't run after me, and so that the police will find you."

"Oh, well that's useless."

"Hand it to me."

"Forget it. I was nice enough to fence with you, to make you less homesick, and this is how you re—"

I did something I had often fantasized of doing: I smacked the side of my sword against the side of his head. He fell against the bars and looked slightly knocked out.

"Now give me the key!"

He pounced on me again and I gave him a few new cuts. He fell back against the bars.

"Will you give me the key now?"

"No, it's useless," he said, lurching toward me once more, and I again slammed the side of my sword against the side of his head.

He now looked mostly knocked out. I carefully slid my fingers into his pocket and took out the key. To my surprise he started laughing and said, "It's useless. Don't bother."

As I was about to leave the cage, he tried to grab me yet again, but he was weak, and I shoved him back violently. He grabbed a bar and tried to get up, still laughing. I stared at his index finger curled around the bar. I was filled with disgust and resentment for everything he had done. I raised my sword and swung it down on his finger, slicing it off in the middle. It landed a short distance away. Damon screamed. I exited the cell, locking it behind me. Damon looked enraged, screaming and crying. His transparent white clothes were now covered in blood.

I rushed out of the room, unaccompanied, for the first

time in nine months. I flew down the stairs, clutching my sword, frightened because he had said "It's useless." I was tempted to use the kitchen phone to call the police, but had an irrational fear that Damon would find a way to come after me. So I unlocked the front door and ran down the driveway and then along the road. My beige sweatpants and yellow T-shirt were covered in blood. His blood. I was crying, but smiling at the same time. A few cars passed. I tried to hail them by waving my arms and my bloody sword. They didn't stop. I kept running. I passed some houses and considered stopping at one, but was gripped with paranoia that his neighbors were in on the whole thing.

I finally arrived at a restaurant. It looked safe enough, with all those people inside. I entered and walked by tables, looking for someone who worked there. As I passed the people dining, they stopped talking and stared at me. I was a spectacle.

Suddenly, I was gripped with horror and stopped in my tracks: I knew the smells in this restaurant. I looked at people's plates, and in each one was food I knew, food I had eaten for the past nine months. This terrified me. A waiter walked toward me holding a dish that had been one of my favorites.

He said, "What are you doing?"

"You are the restaurant that gave Damon food."

"Excuse me?"

"There is a man who orders food from you every day . . . I need a phone, to call the police. It's an emergency."

I called the police. "Please come and get me," I told them. "Come and get me."

They came five minutes later and drove me to their station. I told them everything. Police cars were dispatched to Damon's house.

I called my parents. My mother answered. Her hello had changed. It was more quiet than it used to be. When she heard my voice, she sobbed. I told her I was at a police station.

"I was kidnapped," I said.

"You were kidnapped? For nine months?"

"Yes, I was held captive. In a cage."

"Oh my God! Are you okay? Did they hurt you?"

"Sometimes. But I'm okay."

"Did they feed you?"

"Not much."

"Oh, Anna." She cried again. "Can you . . . walk?"

"Yes. I can run too. I ran here."

"Did the police catch them?"

"Him. Just one man. I don't know yet, but I think they will, cause I locked him in the cage."

"We were never asked for a ransom."

"I know. It's not that kind of kidnapping."

"What kind is it?"

"The sick kind. I was altered. Against my will."

"What do you mean!" she asked, hysterically.

"Oh no, it's nothing big like plastic surgery. I'm okay. I'm still the same. I just was taught some skills, and stuff like that."

"You were taught to kill?"

"What? No! I said I was taught some skills."

"Oh. Not skills to kill?"

"No! Are you *disappointed?*"

"Of course not, I just thought you said *kill*. I saw a movie, Nikita something, that stuck on my mind."

"*La Femme Nikita*. I wasn't taught killing skills. I was taught acting skills. But I'll tell you later."

"Your father is somewhere in the building fixing air conditioners. He'll be so happy . . ." She choked with emotion.

She then said she would drive up with my father right away and take me home.

The police took me to the hospital to be examined. I then waited for my parents to arrive, while the police continued asking me questions in the hospital waiting room, which I preferred to the police station.

Finally my parents, and my brother, arrived. They rushed through the corridor. As they got closer to me, their faces changed. It was subtle, but I noticed.

And then they all, more or less, gasped.

"You look great," said my mother.

My father gave her an annoyed look and hugged me. "No she doesn't. She just went through nine months of hell. How could she look great?"

"I don't know," said my mother.

The police asked us if we wouldn't mind spending the night in town so that I could be further questioned in the morning. I told them I would rather be questioned all night rather than have to try to sleep in this part of the world again.

Then report came in that Damon had not been found, nor any machines that produced fog, nor any fog (I had told them the house was filled with fog instead of clouds, not wanting them to think I was crazy). They said the cage had been found empty, with its door open. There was only blood, and half a finger.

I was very upset.

The police sent out reports to hospitals to be on the lookout for a man with an amputated finger.

Finally, at 3:30 in the morning, we drove back to the city. My mother cried in the car. And to my astonishment, my brother cried. My father seemed lost in thought. A couple of times he said, "How could anyone do that?"

I slept at my parents' apartment that night. When I woke up in late morning, my mother had a troubled, careful expression on her face, which piqued my curiosity.

"The police called," she said.

"Yes?"

"They know how Damon escaped."

"How?"

"Apparently . . . there were fifteen keys hidden in the cell."

I stared at her, stunned, and said, "No."

She frowned and shook her head. "I told them I found that hard to believe, that I was sure you would have found them. At least one."

I was silent for a while, thinking, and said, "I didn't even look, really. What reason would I have to think he had hidden keys in my cell? What reason could he have?"

"He did it in case he died. So that then *you* wouldn't die. Of starvation."

"Are you guessing, or do you know this?"

"At nine o'clock this morning, while the police were still inspecting Damon's house, a video was broadcast on one of the monitors in your cell. It was a written message on the screen, saying that in case Damon died unexpectedly, or disappeared, or was, for any other reason, unable to tend to you, there were fifteen keys hidden in the cell. Then he describes in detail the fifteen hiding places. Evi dently this video was programmed to go on every day at 9:00 A.M. unless he turned if off each day."

"So where were the keys?"

"I only remember a few of the places, but the police can tell you the others if you want. I know one key was in the rod of the shower curtain. Another was taped behind the toilet. There was one in the leg of your bed. One was inside one of the monitors. Another was hidden in the vacuum cleaner. One was stapled under the carpet. And I forget where the others were."

Chapter Twelve

The days passed, but I had trouble adjusting to the real world. It weighed on me. I was not used to facing life without Damon's interruptions, without having to change into character many times a day. I felt caged within myself. When I fought with people now, it bothered me that I was not ordered, suddenly, to "act singular" or "bald" and was instead actually expected to continue the argument until its bitter end. It was suffocating.

I had the urge to ask my family and friends to make me act in any way they wanted, at any time. But I never dared ask, afraid they would either take advantage or think I was insane. Instead, I settled for ordering myself, out of the blue and at awkward times, to do "angry" or "suspicious" or whatever. And I would do it, subtly, I thought, but probably not subtly enough, judging from people's gazes.

I had other problems as well, other confusions.

One of them was my escape, or that strange thing I had participated in. What had it been? An escape, or a release?

Also, I felt disturbed about having cut off Damon's finger. Especially after hearing about the keys.

And that was another problem. The keys. Fifteen, no less. They touched me. They moved and affected me. I didn't need these new emotions in my emotion salad, a huge salad composed of already too many miscombined, hard-to-digest states: slices of sadness, slivers of stress, crushed exhaustion, ripe indignation, bits of bitterness, anger rind, grated outrage, hard-boiled horror, soft-boiled perspective, steamed embarrassment, a teaspoon of denial, cubes of contempt, superiority peel, canned tolerance, crunchy curiosity, dried humor, leaves of relief, a pinch of guilt, melted melancholy, and a dab of fresh fear.

And now I was adding chunks of being "moved" and "affected"? Movement and affection were not good ingredients to add to my salad. My brain would throw up, or my heart, or my soul; wherever emotional fruits get digested. A brain throwing up; how does that manifest itself? Is it insanity? Yes, it must be; insanity is the vomit of the brain.

But since one has little control over one's emotional salad, the fifteen keys did, in fact, move me, and there wasn't much I could do about it. In addition, I was furious at myself for not having searched the cell more thoroughly. What kind of a kidnapee was I?

But the biggest problem I had after my return to the real world was that I no longer knew what I wanted to do with my life. I was tempted to abandon acting, just to spite Damon.

After thinking about it, I decided that the great victory, of course, would be to not let Damon make any difference to how I ran my life.

Nevertheless, something was frequently on my mind: the pursued woman. Armory Jude, the female impostor who had pretended she was the legitimate pursued woman, had, during my kidnapping, starred in three low-budget movies, due to all the attention she got. She was considered a mediocre actress with no future, but still, it was better than nothing. Nothing—that was what I had. It made me jealous; it disturbed me. It made me wonder whether I might not like to be in her shoes. I was nagged by temptations to reveal to the media that I was the real pursued woman. I fantasized about it. I tried not to, but couldn't help myself. I decided to go and ask my mother for advice.

I agreed to bout with her, as this was the best way for us to have a serious conversation.

The clink of our foils echoed in the entrance hall of the building to which my father was the super. We bouted in silence for a few minutes, absorbed, ignoring the doorman or the residents who went in and out.

Finally, as we continued, I broached the topic: "Have you heard of the pursued woman?"

"Yes, of course."

"Well, I am the real pursued woman. The other one's a fake."

"You feel pursued? *Are* you pursued?"

I sighed. My mother's mind was best described by saying that it was beside the point. She thought beside the point, and she talked beside the point, as I was sure was often the case with geniuses. It was actually an asset for fencing. To win at fencing you had to move and attack and even think in a way that was beside the point.

"Not now," I answered. "I'm not being pursued now, but I was then. Don't you follow the news? The pursued woman isn't being pursued now, she was pursued then, just one afternoon. And I *am* the pursued woman! It's me!"

"How do you know?"

"What do you mean how do I know? I was there, being pursued by Chriskate Turschicraw, the Shell. And we were being filmed by the paparazzi. I was wearing that sweater you gave me for Christmas. Remember, the yellow one? Don't you recognize it from the video?"

"Okay, and?"

"She's getting some pretty interesting movie roles. It just seems unfair, since I'm the real one."

"But is it a worthwhile achievement to be chased down the street by someone famous? Couldn't you just ask Chriskate Turschicraw, since you seem to know her, to hook you up with some connections?"

"That would be asking for a favor, whereas the chase is something that just happened. I wasn't trying to get anything. On the contrary."

"Still, I don't think it would be very dignified to go in that direction. It would be degrading, don't you see that?"

"What would be degrading?" asked my father, marching toward us from the elevator. His foil was at his waist, as always, and he joined in on our bouting. My mother briefly described my dilemma.

"Degrading indeed!" he said, stabbing me. "Don't you have any sense of pride?"

"Not really," I replied. "But you both know that."

*   *   *

Despite my lack of pride, my parents' advice had appeased my tormenting temptation to reveal my true identity to the media. I felt more at peace and was only left with occasional fantasies of confronting the fake pursued woman and saying to her, "I am the real you."

I resumed my job at the Xerox shop and my job piercing ears at my uncle's jewelry shop. I made every effort to live my life as before. Which also meant: I started going to auditions again. Everything was now just like before, but not for long, because something extraordinary happened at the auditions: I got the parts. Although it may be hard to believe, I had not predicted it. Not that I expected *not* to get parts, or that I thought my acting hadn't improved; I simply hadn't allowed myself to think about it, afraid I would get wrapped up in the dynamics of caring, consequently getting stressed and anxious.

I wasn't comfortable, or even pleased, with this turn of events. It complicated my plans about my life staying the same. In addition, and on a separate level, it was offensive. Those auditioners may as well have been saying: "Yes, it was worth it. We would not be hiring you if you had not gone through such pain. Damon was absolutely right all along, down to the last shard. He did a good job. And now you will be rewarded."

At first my only consolation was that I was unhappy, which meant Damon had lost, which made me happy. But then I lost even my unhappiness. It was hard to be unhappy with so much respect and admiration coming my way. I tried to maintain at least my original bitterness, but it wore off too and became harder and harder to recapture. Since I couldn't feel bitter, I settled for acting bitter.

And of course I did it wonderfully. But acting it did not make me feel it. So I was unhappy again, which made me happy. I wished I could send Damon a postcard saying, "Witness my splendid unhappiness, you bastard."

Now that I was getting parts, I had to either give up acting or go with the flow. There was, actually, a third option, but it was too absurd to consider: I could systematically refuse the parts I was offered and keep going to auditions. My life could then be just like before, except the part about getting the parts.

I decided instead to go with the flow. I didn't like it, but what choice did I have? Giving up acting meant Damon had ruined my life, and refusing parts meant I was nuts.

But I would not just go with the flow, or be dragged by it, or controlled by it: I would *lead* the flow.

I turned down the four parts I was offered, because that would have been "being dragged by the flow" (for they were student movies). I got a new head-shot of myself, which I sent to three agents. All three called, I met them, was interviewed by them, and got accepted by them. The one I chose seemed intelligent and down to earth, yet nurturing.

I auditioned for a low-budget science-fiction movie. I got it. I also auditioned for a low-budget, imitation Jane Austen movie. I got it. I was able to accept both offers because one started filming after the other ended.

This advancement in my career didn't make me happy the way it should have, nor unhappy the way it might have. I felt vaguely bewildered and blank. Although my decision to lead the flow was yielding results, it didn't take away the unpleasant sensation that Damon was still controlling my life. I didn't feel free.

This changed as soon as the filming of the science-fiction movie began. I played a good scientist who fought the bad scientists, and the whole movie alternated between me being tough while destroying the bad scientists, and me screaming my head off while being tortured or on the verge of being destroyed. I felt exhilarated and happy. Everything else in my life, like who was controlling whom, or petty issues of freedom, seemed trivial. I was absorbed in the moment.

I then immediately went off and did the imitation Jane Austen movie. Since all the Jane Austen novels had been made into films, the screenwriters came up with a plot that was vaguely similar to one without being one. It was also vaguely similar to my life, although they didn't know it. The story contained a theme of transformation that had a whiff of familiarity and that occasionally brought me bad memories. The story was about a plain and homely girl, played by me, who is suddenly possessed by ambition and decides to transform herself into a more desirable person. But not wanting people to consciously notice the change, she decides to do it very gradually. There were also the essential Jane Austen ingredients, such as me and the other female characters whispering, giggling, gossiping, being obsessed with men. And some romantic intrigue. On the whole, this movie as well was a lot of fun to work on.

Nevertheless, I often thought about Damon. Sometimes, I thought I missed him. I wondered if this might be an emotional hallucination. In any case, I did wonder what happened to him and his amputated finger.

I started seeing the cellist/stripper/etiquette-expert/ Weight Watchers counselor, Nathaniel, again. He had gotten back in touch with me after my return from my kidnapping. At first he was struck by my physical transformation, and then he wanted to know every detail of what had happened to me, and once he knew, he became concerned, and then obsessed, every time he saw me, with whether I had seen Damon again; whether Damon had attempted any form of contact.

"No, why would he?" I asked.

"I'm sure he will. It's inevitable."

I interpreted this statement as sick jealousy.

I asked him how Chriskate was doing.

"She has a boyfriend," he said. "You really helped her get over me. I thank you. Chriskate has become much more sane, easier to deal with. She and I even have lunch occasionally, as friends."

"I'm glad she's happy. But I'm surprised. I didn't think she'd ever get over you. I didn't get the impression I was being of the slightest help to her."

"Maybe she just needed time to digest your wise words, whatever they were."

Nathaniel and I, by the way, became lovers. It happened after the filming of the imitation Jane Austen movie, and it was his doing. Under normal circumstances, I would resist the sexual overtures of a man in whom I had no strong romantic interest. But I didn't care anymore. It all seemed of little importance. So I allowed Nathaniel to play with me. And he made good and constant use of me. The more he noticed my indifference, the more his usage became urgent. When I say I was indifferent, I don't mean unaroused. I was indifferent to the fact that I was aroused. And I was indifferent on a more general level as well. He claimed he loved me. He said this made him happy because he never thought he'd be capable of loving someone like me.

"Like me? What do you mean like me?"

He didn't want to say. I pressured him to no end. I withheld sex. He finally insinuated that what he meant by "like me" was someone whose degree of beauty was not significantly above average. I laughed. Insults to my degree of beauty had never bothered me much, but even if they had, I could not have been offended in this case: he hadn't been able to love Chriskate, the most beautiful woman in the world.

During the usage, I was passive. He used me like an object, and he used me with fascination. Sometimes he had sex with me as if wishing it to be an insult to me. I didn't know why, and I didn't care, and maybe I was wrong anyway. It was never anything specific he said, or anything violent he did. The attempted insult was all in his thrusting. That's where I got the vibe of it.

And then, he turned out to be right: I saw Damon again. It was on a crowded subway platform. I saw him far away, tall, looking at me above people's heads. He moved toward the exit. I was rooted to my spot, and then made a dash to intercept him.

He was gone. I called the police who had worked on my case, and told them about it. They said I should be careful; that I should not go alone to deserted places. I repeated that this had been a crowded subway platform.

They said they knew, but that regardless, I should not go alone to deserted places. I said okay, but what should I do to catch him. They said I should keep doing what I was doing.

"Which is?" I asked.

"Ask the help of a nearby police officer, if there happens to be one."

I reminded them that that wasn't what I had done: I had tried to catch Damon myself. They said they knew, but that they were sure that if there had been a police officer nearby, I would have asked for his or her help.

I was relieved when the absurd conversation ended.

I wanted Damon to be caught. He had altered my life against my will, and *so what* if it turned out well? That was beside the point. It was the principle of it that mattered.

If he were to be caught, it would make an interesting trial.

When I told Nathaniel I had seen Damon, he became agitated, said he wasn't surprised, asked what my plan was for next time. I told him I had no plan. He said that was okay, that I shouldn't scare Damon off or he would be harder to catch.

A few days later, I was walking down the street and saw Damon driving by me slowly in a car. He was looking at me with a very focused expression. He seemed to be scrutinizing my face. I stood still on the sidewalk and watched him drive away. At the last moment, I looked at his license plate, but its number was covered with masking tape.

*   *   *

A couple of days later, I went off to star in a medieval movie, thinking it would be fun to fight with swords while acting. I was offered the part before they even knew I fenced, and they were very pleased when I gave them a demonstration. I had finished the Jane Austen movie a month before and had been able to rest, but my encounter in the street with Damon caused me to be plagued by thoughts of him during the filming, which spoiled my enjoyment of the experience and of my fighting with the swords. I did my job anyway, and well, but I was in a constant state of anxiety. That's when, and why, I first came up with the germ of the idea for my plan.

Two months later, the medieval movie was done. And a few weeks after that, my first two movies came out in theaters simultaneously, due to the fact that one had been delayed and the other had been completed unusually quickly. It was the most exciting moment of my life, and I wanted to savor the experience to the fullest. I bought myself a pair of Rollerblades, donned a black coat, a hat, and a beard and mustache that Chriskate had left behind at Nathaniel's apartment and which he lent me for my purpose. With my beard flowing in the breeze of my skating, I spent my days zooming from one theater to the next, watching my movies, watching people's faces watching my movies, devouring their facial expressions, and listening to their comments. I always brought a notebook with me to write down what I heard, what I saw, and my impressions of both. I also brought a small tape recorder to capture the sounds of the audience in relation to the sounds of the film. Nathaniel came with me sometimes, when his multiple jobs schedule allowed it. We would sit at opposite ends of the audience, and he would report back to me his findings, so that I'd have a double dose of information.

Then we'd go back to his place and have sex, often, because the beard turned him on when he was in a good mood. When he was feeling low he'd ask me to take it off.

After spending about a week watching my movies every day, all day, I was still at it. And one day, as my beard fluttered in the wind and my black coat flapped behind me like a cape while I was skating down a one-way street to get to a distant theater, a car slowed down next to me. It was Damon.

Through his open window, he said, "Are you happy?"

I saw his amputated finger resting on the steering wheel. "Did I escape?" I asked.

"Are you happy?" he repeated sincerely. He wasn't referring to the job I had done on his finger, as I thought for a second, but to the job he had done on my life.

We both slowed our rolling and came to a standstill.

I glanced around to see if there was a policeman nearby. There wasn't. But there were some male pedestrians. I didn't know what to do.

I turned to two of the men, pointed at Damon, and said, "Help! Stop this man! He stole my wallet!" This, I thought, sounded better than saying, "Stop this man! He kidnapped me!"

The two male pedestrians only stopped their walking; not the man. They remained standing there, staring at the woman in the beard on skates who had forgotten to adopt a man's voice when calling for their help. And Damon drove away.

I reproached myself later for my lack of resourcefulness. Yet I still had no idea what I could have done.

Nathaniel reproached me too. He said I was stupid, that I had scared Damon off.

"So?" I said.

"You'll have a harder time catching him now. He'll be more careful."

"How am I supposed to catch him? I can't have an undercover cop following me every day."

Something good started happening at around that time, but, still unnerved over my encounter with Damon, I wasn't able to appreciate it fully. This good thing was that my two movies, both of them, became sleepers. First I noticed it myself: each day the theaters got a little more crowded. And the things I heard people say when I followed them afterward were good. From my past experience going to movies and overhearing people's comments, I couldn't remember if this was usual. So, to check, I went to a few other movies and compared. I got the distinct impression that people said more good things about my movies.

Another indication I got about my movies being sleepers was a call from the director of the science-fiction movie, telling me so. Then it was a call from my agent, telling me so. Then I heard it on TV. And the TV said it was because of me; because I was in both. I thought it very nice of it to say that, but I wasn't sure it was true. Then the critics said it too. And the TV wanted me to go on it

and talk. Many times. I did. One time I went on Joe Let-
terman. I had trouble being completely present for the experience, because thoughts of Damon still harassed me; I
was a little more subdued and tired than I normally would
have been. And magazines interviewed me. I had to pose
for their photo shoots. Out of all my experiences involving
acting in movies and then promoting them, posing for
shoots is what made me by far the most uncomfortable. I
had never been photogenic. Nothing required my personality as little as being photographed, and I was not good
at things that didn't require my personality. The result is
that I looked either utterly expressionless or overly ex-
pressionful. I could never find a middle ground and just
look natural. The frustrated magazine photographers always had to resort to catching me by surprise, which
wasn't very convenient for them, since it drastically fouled
up the carefully planned poses and backgrounds they had
dreamed up for me. They'd grab shots of me while I was
getting my makeup touched up, for example, or they'd
discreetly instruct the lighting person or the stylist to distract me for a moment. *Click*.

And then I got an offer to star in a medium-budget
romantic comedy. I turned it down for two reasons: I
wanted to finish relishing in peace the release of my first
movies, but mostly, I was having nightmares about
Damon and I wanted to take it easy for a while. I needed
to recuperate from my last encounter with him.

The seeds of the idea for my plan wafted through my
mind, but I still didn't pay much attention to them.

Until it happened again. A week or two had passed, and
I was just starting to recuperate, to feel stronger, when the

car slowed down next to me and he asked me once more if I was happy. But then another car honked behind him, and another, and he drove away without getting an answer. There still was masking tape over his license plate. I had a relapse. I could feel it right then and there, before his car had even disappeared from view. It was dark and heavy and sickening, this relapse, and I turned around and walked home staring at the pavement, my eyes unfocused, and my beard still in my bag, not to be used that day to watch my imitation Jane Austen movie for the fifteenth time.

When I got home I had an excited message on my machine from my agent, informing me of an offer from a major director, to star in a huge-budget movie and get paid a huge amount of money that no actor with as little experience as I had ever been paid. As I sat on my bathroom floor listening to the message again, all things came together at once in my mind; all things that mattered— and two things did—became clear: I would accept the offer, and I would go ahead with my plan. The latter had developed in my brain on my way home, so I already knew more or less what had to be done.

I hired workmen to make some changes in my apartment.
I began taking many leisurely walks in the streets.

Finally, it happened again. The car came, slowed next to me.

"Are you happy?" said Damon.

I didn't look for a policeman. And I didn't answer. I just looked sad. Fortunately, I was not wearing my beard, or it might have gotten in the way of looking sad. And then, with the skills Damon had taught me, I made my eyes moist.

"Are you happy?" he asked again, with more concern.

I continued looking at him sadly and started walking away.

"Wait!" he said.

I stopped.

"Please come back."

Trying to look reluctant, I slowly went back to him.

"What's wrong?" he asked.

I shrugged, shook my head, looked choked, and softly said, "Nothing."

"Tell me. Is it that you want me to be arrested?"

I looked at him and didn't answer.

"If that's what's making you unhappy, I'll turn myself in to that traffic cop right there, right now."

I couldn't suppress a small smile. His offer was tempting. But my plan was better.

I sighed and closed my eyes and gave him a long, devastated look before walking away.

"Anna! Wait!" he said, and partially came out of his car. "Come back Anna!"

But I didn't go back. I walked away, my head hanging.

I left my window open at night. And I lingered on the balcony before going to bed. My apartment was on the second floor, and there was a fire escape.

It didn't take long.

The following night he came.

I was lying in bed as he entered through the window. I

was still afraid of him. It may sound silly, but what I was afraid of, was of being kidnapped again.

As he wiped off his translucent white pants, which had gotten dirty from the windowsill, he said, "I know that this is probably a trap and that you'll either kill me or have me arrested." He struck me as funny just then, and I had trouble not laughing. He added, "But I want to know why you seemed so unhappy."

"I don't really want to talk about it," I said, leaning on one elbow in bed. "It's no use."

"You must tell me. Please."

I acted hesitant, and then put on my bathrobe. "Okay, we can talk." I shuffled into the next room, motioning for him to follow. He did. I turned on a small light.

He did not pay particular attention to the eight- by eight-foot, cloth-covered cube in the middle of the room.

"Sit down if you want," I said, pointing to a couch against the wall. "I'll get something to drink."

But before I left the room, he said, "So this is the moment when you signal the police that I'm here?"

"Hardly," I said, but I said it with a smile because I was an inch from the doorway, which I went through the next instant and slammed the door, which locked automatically, and that was that.

That was that. But that was not all.

I opened a fake closet in the wall that divided our two rooms, propped myself up on my captain's stool, and looked at him through the one-way mirror.

He was at the door, trying to open it. Then he went to the window, which faced the building across the street and which was soundproof, bulletproof, one-way, and locked. He tried to open it.

The whole room he was in was soundproof. Therefore, on my navigation board, or my panel of commands, I switched on the two-way microphone and spoke into it: "Take the cover off that big square thing there."

He pulled off the cover, looking a lot like those men in commercials who pull sheets off new cars.

Underneath the cloth was a brand new cage with all the necessary accommodations: bed, bath, and toilet.

It took a bit of work to convince him to go into the cage, requiring me to say things like: "You are in a cage already. The room you're in is a cage. I just want you to go into a smaller cage. No big deal. And life is a cage anyway. Right? So what's the difference."

That didn't do it. So I added, "I won't release you until you go in the cage. And we can't have our little conversation until you go in the cage. Due to our past, I can't feel safe while talking to you unless you're contained."

It was the threat of no conversation that did it.

"But it's just for the length of this conversation?" he stupidly asked, as he stepped in.

"Yes," I answered, and slammed the door behind him with a simple press of a button on the control panel.

I hadn't lied. A conversation can last a lifetime.

I switched off the two-way microphone and laughed like a villain, a wicked witch, a mad scientist, frightening myself a little in the process.

I was so happy it was indescribable.

I unlocked the door and went back in the room within which Damon was caged. I sat on a lounge chair, facing him.

Damon said, "Can you tell me, now, why you're not happy?"

What an admirably focused, one-track mind he had. Like me.

"Did I escape?" I asked.

"I don't understand that question. And before you explain it to me, tell me everything I want to know. Why aren't you happy?"

He was right, I would let him ask the questions, for now. I didn't want to clutter this beautiful, precious, sacred moment with my own needs. Let the experience be stark and bare, composed mostly of his reactions and yearnings. I would sit back, observe, and relish.

"Oh, I'm *very* happy," I answered.

"I don't mean right now. I mean in general."

"I'm actually very happy in general. The only slight blemish on my happiness was the knowledge of your existence."

"That means I succeeded. It worked."

"If I could go back in time," I said, "I would not choose to go through what I went through with you."

"Even if the result is success in your career and great happiness?"

"That's right."

"Well, it doesn't matter. All that matters is that you're happy now."

"*Idiot!* You could have made me happy without *kidnapping* me. You could have helped me, encouraged me, offered to make me do all your acting exercises. I would have gone along with it."

"It wouldn't have worked," he said, turning the bathtub faucet on and then off, to check if it worked, I supposed. "I'm surprised you can't see that. I was able to push you way beyond the levels you would have attained if we were friends." He flushed the toilet, which worked too. "It worked because it was against your will."

"It doesn't matter. You had no right."

As I got up to leave the room, he asked to be let out.

"No," I said, "we haven't finished conversing. We'll continue tomorrow."

I left, and my irritation was gone soon after. I tried to sleep, but couldn't, because I was so happy. A few times I got up and looked at him through the one-way mirror. He was taking a bath. I was pleased in the same sort of way a cat owner whose cat is using the new scratching post the first day it was bought is pleased.

Early in the morning, I opened the door quietly. Damon was sleeping. In a soft singsongy voice I said, "Hello Damon."

He rose, and stared at me through the bars of his cell. His hair was sticking up.

I sat on the lounge chair and beamed.

"You do look happy," he said.

"Yes, I'm so happy. You have succeeded, like you said."

We chatted. He asked about my life since my return to it. I told him everything; about the parts I got, the people I worked with, how easy it had been to find an agent, how shocked I was when I was offered practically every role I auditioned for. We laughed over this, and he looked moved, with tears in his eyes.

"I'm so happy Anna. I'm happy that it's worked out so well. And thank you for being so generous in sharing it with me."

"I hope you'll be as generous in answering my own questions."

"Absolutely. Shoot."

"No. I'm still digesting the present. I'll save them up for later."

At about noon, he started getting antsy, I could tell. I assumed he was anxious to get out. But it was something else.

At 12:30 P.M. he said, "I need a TV."

I found this interesting. "Is that so?" I said.

"Yes."

"Why?"

"I can't say why."

"But you *must* say why. Or no TV."

"It's very important. I need a TV," he said, clutching onto two bars.

"So that you can build an escape device out of it?"

"No. There is something on TV that I must watch. It's extremely important."

"What is it?"

"It doesn't matter what it is."

"Yes it does. Some programs are not suitable for criminals."

He looked at me earnestly.

"At what time is your program?" I asked.

"One-thirty."

The words rang a bell. One-thirty was the time when he used to disappear every day for half an hour and come back having cried. Could TV-watching be what had been going on in the unfilmed room?

I fetched the *TV Guide* from my night table and came back flipping through its pages. Among all the shows playing at 1:30, I was stumped as to which one Damon could be interested in. Laughing, I read the selections out loud to him, glancing up at him reproachfully after each title: "*Harry and the Hendersons, Stories of the Highway Patrol, Papa Beaver Stories, The Bold and the Beautiful, Gourmet Cooking, Charlie Brown and Snoopy, The Look,* etc."

Perhaps it was one of the children's shows, which, come to think of it, would fit well with the eccentric, childlike side of his personality.

"Which one is it?" I asked.

"Will you get me a TV?"

"We can't let you miss one of these shows."

"Will you get me one," he whispered sadly, which piqued my curiosity even more.

"Why not." I went into the other room and unplugged my TV. I carried it into his room and placed it on a little table, facing his cage.

"Could I have some privacy now?" he said.

"I want to watch TV too. It's my only TV."

"Please, could I have some privacy?"

"Did you give me sugar when I wanted it?"

He didn't answer.

"Therefore," I said, "I think I'll be watching TV at one-thirty."

At 1:25 P.M. I told him, "Okay, it's almost one-thirty. What channel do you want?"

After a long sullen pause, he murmured, "Two."

I switched on channel two and looked in the *TV Guide.* I screeched. "*The Bold and the Beautiful?*"

He sat, stone-faced, staring at the set.

We watched the soap opera, and he cried. I could tell he was trying to restrain himself, but tears rolled down his cheeks anyway. I handed him a box of tissues, which he did not touch.

Why he was crying was beyond me. The show was not sad. Even though I hadn't seen previous episodes, I was pretty sure I wasn't missing some deep level of sadness. The actors were appropriately beautiful (their boldness was less apparent), and they had names like Ridge, Brooke, Thorn, Sally Spectra. There was also a beautiful legless character in a wheelchair, called Stem.

"Why did you cry?" I asked afterward.

He didn't answer.

"*I* didn't cry," I said. "And I'm sure I'm not less sensitive than you."

He was silent.

"If I wanted to treat you the way you treated me, I would now torture you until you told me why you cried. But dammit, I don't have an ice gun. I guess I could get ice cubes out of the freezer and throw them at you until you cave in."

He still didn't tell me why he cried.

I went for a walk that afternoon. I was eager to experience the sensation of being out walking, while having someone locked in a cage in my apartment.

And I wasn't disappointed. It was a great, rewarding feeling.

I stopped by a gourmet store and bought caviar and smoked salmon and unpasteurized Camembert and two baguettes. Then I bought champagne and went home.

I looked at Damon through the one-way mirror. He was sitting in bed with his chin in his palm. I felt bad. I went in there cheerfully and said, "I bought a good dinner to celebrate."

"Celebrate what?"

"Your captivity."

While we were eating, he said, "I hope you don't eat things like this all the time, or it won't be long before . . ." and he raised his eyebrows meaningfully, not bothering to finish his sentence.

"Why did you leave your finger behind, after I chopped it off? Why didn't you take it with you and try to get it sewn back on?"

"Oh, there are lots of reasons for that," he said, eating caviar, and sucking on some of his remaining fingers. "First, I wanted to accept the punishment you had given me. I deserved it." He picked up his glass of champagne and said, "Shall we drink to that?"

We clinked glasses through the bars of the cage, and drank.

He continued: "Second, I thought it would be a nice souvenir of you and from you, this absence of finger. An irreversible souvenir."

We clinked our glasses to that one too.

"And third, and most importantly, it would remind me of the sacrifice I had made for you, the thought of which would cheer me up in moments of melancholy, making me feel better about myself."

He extended his glass to get it clinked again. Instead, I threw my champagne in his face and stared at him impassively.

He blinked from the sting in his eyes. He clinked his glass against one of the bars of the cage, drank, and resignedly said, "Everyone is entitled to their own reasons for leaving a finger behind."

"Did I escape?" I asked.

"No, of course not; you were released," he answered, wiping his champagne eyes with his napkin. "I gave you a sword."

"Why did you fight me, then, and resist my departure, and push me to the point cutting off your finger?"

"To give you the illusion of escape. I was afraid that if I released you in a straightforward manner and told you the truth, which was that we had achieved our goal and that you were now ready to conquer the acting world—I was afraid you would be more resistant to this destiny that I had so painstakingly planned for you and prepared you for. Whereas," he stressed the word by holding up his plastic knife, "if you thought you had escaped, or even if you weren't sure, you would then have a sense of control over your life and over your future, you would feel powerful, self-reliant, and self-satisfied at having gotten yourself 'out of this jam.'" He made the quote marks in the air with his remaining fingers.

Chapter Thirteen

The days passed. Damon kept asking why I wasn't releasing him, and I said it was because our little conversation wasn't over yet. He got into the habit of frequently throwing things at me: his toothbrush, toothpaste, soap, the roll of toilet paper, the stopper from the bath, his shoes, his watch, his plastic cup to brush his teeth. I wanted to believe he was not really trying to hurt me, but I couldn't, particularly when the heavy metal stopper hit me in the cheekbone, cutting me slightly. I then would shout at him some French words that a French friend of mine said to her cat when it was being bad: *Méchant!* (bad); *Arrêtes!* (stop); *Fais gaffe!* (watch out).

During many hours a day I would sit on my reclining chair outside his cage and watch him and talk to him, and, on the whole, get what I began to call "my Damon tan." I enjoyed these sessions; they charged me up, like a battery. I kept a bucket of ice cubes by my chair, from which I practiced my aim when he annoyed me. My spirits were very high in those days. Damon was my human pet, my hobby, my adviser, my therapist. I asked his advice about all sorts of things. We'd have deep, serious conversations about issues, such as: me. Mostly me. For example, he'd tell me how I should deal with such and such a person. And then he would throw his razor at me with great force. When I asked him why he did that, he said it was because it was normal.

Every weekday we watched *The Bold and the Beautiful,* and Damon cried. I never understood why. The plot of the show concerned itself with the romantic problems of a family of successful fashion designers, and how one character, the long-lost legless brother, Stem, was making everyone's life better.

"Why is that so sad?" I would ask impatiently. "Why are you crying? I think it's kind of nice that Stem told Brooke that Ridge really loves her. It means they'll get back together. So why are you crying, god dammit! Tell me!"

"Please be quiet," he'd say, putting his hands over his ears.

As an experiment, I made him watch *The Young and the Restless* one day, which ran an hour before the other soap. And he didn't cry. It was therefore something about *The Bold and the Beautiful* that devastated him. I scrutinized his face, while he watched, and tried to detect a pattern to his crying, but found none.

Occasionally, I would be interviewed at night on live TV, about the movie I was doing, and then go home. After throwing things at me when I entered, Damon would tell me he had seen my interview and found it great.

When the interview wasn't live, we would watch it together, our feet propped up on things, just like friends, the
only difference being the few bars between us. We would
drink mint, peach, raspberry, and cocoa liqueurs, and eat
unpasteurized cheeses, and chocolate truffles, and Damon
would laugh at my jokes to the interviewer or scowl at a
stupid question of theirs.

As the evening would wear on, Damon would try to
control me from the cage, saying, "Okay, you've had
enough truffles now. If you don't moderate yourself, I'll
have to confiscate the box."

I would then stare at him and stuff three truffles in my
mouth and chew them noisily, making sure he saw lots of
glistening brown paste rolling around my tongue and over
my teeth.

"Oh, Anna," he'd say, covering his eyes. "What are you
doing to yourself?"

I responded once by throwing a truffle at him, which
left a circle of cocoa powder on his cheek before it
dropped to the floor. Damon carefully picked up the truffle and placed it on the edge of his bathtub. "I am confis-
cating this truffle until you control yourself."

I had twenty more in the box, and I threw another one
at him, and he repeated the procedure until he had six or
seven truffles lined up on the edge of his bathtub. Then I
got bored, and low on truffles, and stopped.

Damon wanted to listen to music. So I got him a tape
deck, which I placed outside his cage, out of his reach,
so that he couldn't fabricate an escape device out of it.
I played him some of my tapes, including the one of

Nathaniel playing the cello, without, however, telling him that Nathaniel was my boyfriend, or that I knew him in any way, or that I even had a boyfriend. Nathaniel's cello compositions made a strong impression on Damon. He seemed mesmerized, and didn't want me to play anything else. My questions to him, of course, yielded no results, and this happened in the following, rather typical, manner:

"You really like this music?" I asked.

"No, the word *like* doesn't apply here," he said, stretched out on his bed. "I feel a communion with it. It reminds me of certain emotions I've felt, and of other emotions that were not mine but were present in the atmosphere around me during a time in my life."

I threw an ice cube at him. "What were these emotions?" I asked, staring at him intently through two bars.

"The same old thing, Anna. The same old thing I can't tell you about."

"That thing that makes you cry during *The Bold and the Beautiful*?"

"Yes. It all goes back to the same old thing."

"Will you ever tell me what that thing is?"

He was thoughtful for a long time, staring at the ceiling, his arms clasped behind his head. "I don't know. I'm not having much success imagining a time when I would feel compelled to tell you."

I threw another ice cube at him, which he then brushed to the floor, so it wouldn't wet his mattress, I suppose. "To tell *me* or to tell anyone?" I asked.

"I don't know. Anyone, perhaps. Perhaps you more than some others," he said, glancing at me.

"If I tortured you, would you tell me?"

He chuckled. "It's hard to know in advance. What kind of torture?"

"Is there any kind that would be more likely to work?" I said, walking circles around his cage.

"I don't know right off. Maybe if I were inclined to think about it, I might come up with one that might strike me as being more likely to work. But I'm not inclined to think about it."

"Is there any other circumstance under which you could foresee telling me about that thing?"

"I'm not inclined to think about that either right now. Could you please put the music back on."

I did, hoping I might find out more from his facial expression than from his words. But I didn't, as it turned out, even though he kept listening to the tape over and over, that day and the next.

Three days later, not having seen Nathaniel since the acquisition of my new man-pet a week before, I agreed to have dinner with him at a restaurant. I informed Damon of this.

"You have a boyfriend?"

"Of course, what did you think?"

"Nothing. It's good. You just never mentioned him."

"That's true. And I also never mentioned that he's the one who composed and played those cello pieces you like so much. I mean: that you feel such *communion* with."

"Really? That's funny," he said, without smiling.

During dinner, Nathaniel said to me, "Something weird is going on that you're not telling me."

"No."

"Yes. Something has happened, hasn't it?"

"Like what?"

"You tell me. Have you met somebody? Are you interested in somebody else? Or is it Damon? Have you seen him again and you're not telling me?"

"Yes. We're cohabiting."

"Just tell me the truth. It's fine if that's what it is. I just want to know. Please."

"That's not what it is. But I think you're taking our relationship a bit too seriously. Maybe we should take it easy for a while."

"No! You mean sexually? Sexually, that's fine, but not as friends, not as people. I don't want us to take it easy as people."

I was touched. "Okay, but then ease off a bit, okay?"

"Sure. Are you living with someone?"

"No. Are you kidding?"

"Just answer me."

"I did."

"Prove it then. I want to see your apartment."

"Why?"

"You haven't let me see it in a while."

"No."

"If you don't, I'll assume you're living with Damon, which is fine, I just want to know the truth."

"First of all, why would you assume such a thing? And second of all, I don't care what you assume."

"You should. If you tell me, or show me, that you're living with Damon, it's fine. I'll be sad and jealous, but I'll accept it. But if you leave me in a state of assumption,

I will react to it; I'll notify your parents and the police. I'll tell them you're living with him."

"Do you think this endears you to me?"

"I don't care!" he shouted, slapping the table with his palm. "I just want to know the truth!" He was on the verge of tears, and added: "If you do show me your apartment, though, you must do it right now, so that you don't have time to hide anything."

I thought about this for a minute, and then said "Okay." I didn't want to risk having Nathaniel talk to my parents or the police, filling their heads with this absurd idea that I was living with Damon. And anyway, I had locked everything sensitive before leaving: Damon's room and the new closet with my control panel.

I took Nathaniel to my apartment, and he noticed the new closet, and the open sofa bed.

"Who's been sleeping here?" he asked.

"Me."

"Why?"

"Because the heater in my bedroom is broken, and I can't have someone come in to fix it because it's too messy in there."

He marched toward my bedroom door and tried to open it. "Why is it locked?"

"Because it's so messy. I don't want anybody to see it. It's embarrassing."

"This is too weird. I want to see your bedroom."

"No."

"What kind of relationship do we have if I can't see your bedroom?"

"A not very important one."

"Why are you being cruel?"

"I'm just being factual. I don't want to lead you on."

"You could be living with someone in your bedroom."

"Yes, I could be. And I lock him in when I leave my apartment."

He laughed. The tension seemed to have eased, but suddenly his body stiffened. "Where's your TV?"

"It's in my messy bedroom."

"Why?"

"Because the person I'm living with, in my bedroom, enjoys watching TV."

We laughed, and I added: "Particularly that soap opera *The Bold and the Beautiful*."

At this remark, his eyes opened unnaturally wide.

As I stared at him staring at me, it occurred to me that I should write a letter to those producers of *The Bold and the Beautiful*, asking them if they had noticed a phenomenon involving men and their show, and if so, could they explain it to me.

Finally, he turned away, mumbling to himself, "This doesn't necessarily mean anything."

"But maybe it does mean something," I said. "And if it does, Nathaniel, what does it mean? What is the meaning of *The Bold and the Beautiful*?"

"None, as far as I know."

"Then why does it disturb certain people, like you?"

"And who?"

The conversation went nowhere. I had sex with him, to put his mind completely at ease. It was an interesting sensation to have sex while someone was in a cage nearby.

Nathaniel wanted to see me again, a couple of days later, as was normal for a lover, but I had very little desire to

see him. I kept making excuses. He got paranoid and suspicious again. So I saw him.

"You look unhappy," said Damon, when I came home
after being with Nathaniel. With the remote control to the
tape deck, he turned off the cello music, which he had
rarely stopped listening to since I had introduced him to
it.

I plopped down in the lounge chair. "I want to break
up with my boyfriend, your precious cellist."

"Why?"

"Because he threatened to tell my parents, and the police, that I'm living with you. Can you imagine?"

"What gall the man has."

"I know."

"So you told him?"

"No. I mean, not seriously. He's paranoid."

I wasn't exactly telling Damon the truth. Nathaniel had
not, this time, threatened to tell my parents anything. I
wanted to break up with him because for some mysterious
reason—a reason I didn't want to delve into too deeply—
the thought of him having sex with me didn't appeal to
me anymore. Not that it ever had. But now, I didn't even
feel neutral or indifferent about it. I was opposed, turned
off; I had an actual aversion to it, and the strange thing
was that it didn't have much to do with Nathaniel.

Damon was wrong. I was not unhappy. I felt cheerful
and liberated at the thought of breaking up with Nathaniel, light and playful. I imagine it was the same sort of
feeling people have after taking a laxative that worked. I
didn't know if I would have the courage to do it, though.
I felt sorry for him. But I soon forgot about it as I spoke
of other topics with my pet.

*   *   *

Two days later, Chriskate Turschicraw called me, saying she had something important to tell me and asking if we could meet somewhere. We met in a coffee shop. She was disguised in a black wig and sunglasses. She informed me that she had not stopped loving Nathaniel, that she had simply put on a show, hoping to perk his interest. She told me frankly that she was distressed that I was going out with him and that she needed to tell me about something that happened in her past with Nathaniel.

"A few years ago," she began, "when I was just starting out as a model, and not very successful, I fell in love with Nathaniel. He told me he found me wonderful, but that there was just one thing preventing him from being outright in love with me. He said there was something about me that turned him off, and that thing was that my nose was slightly too long. One millimeter too long, to be precise. Nobody had ever told me I had a long nose, so I was surprised. I was very sad and asked him if he was sure that meant he couldn't love me. He said yes. I thought that was the end of *that* dream. But then he said there was a possible solution: I could get plastic surgery. I agreed to do it. He gave me the name of a good surgeon, offered to pay half the price of the surgery, and gave me precise written instructions to give to the surgeon as to how my nose should look. I had it done and went back to see Nathaniel once it had healed. I was very nervous because I wasn't sure the result would be exactly what he had wanted. But it was. He said the surgeon had done a very good job and that the length of my nose was exquisite. I assumed this meant he would be able to love me, but I was wrong."

"What happened?" I asked, suddenly realizing I had been gaping for a while now.

"Well, I sensed a certain reticence on his part, so I asked him about it, and he said there was one other thing that he found problematic and was trying to overcome. It was that my eyes were slightly droopy; the skin above my eyes covered my eyelids a tiny bit. He said that plastic surgery could easily take care of that. He once again gave me carefully written instructions to give to the surgeon. He assured me that after that there would be no more obstacles to his love for me. So I had it done."

"And?"

"And he loved the result. He said it was beautiful. I asked him if he thought he could love me now. He seemed uneasy. He said, 'Well, there is one other thing, but I hesitate to ask.'

" 'What is it?' I asked him.

" 'If your top lip could be a tiny bit fuller.' "

Chriskate's story was very distressing to me. I couldn't contain myself any longer: "And didn't you object, at any point, to this charade?"

"I did. Right then I got a bit angry and said, 'Why are you toying with me this way? Is this your last request?'

" 'Yes,' he said.

" 'And you'll love me?'

" 'Yes.'

" 'Okay, I'll do it, if you assure me that it's a token of love, and not a whim.'

" 'It's not a whim,' he said.

"So I had it done, but he still seemed unable to love me."

"And did he again ask you to alter yourself?" I asked.

"No. He was going to give up trying to love me. I'm the one who finally asked him to feel free to tell me if there was any other alteration I could make that might have the slightest chance of arousing his feelings. After begging him to tell me, he did. It was some other triviality involving my nose. I had it done. Needless to say, it happened again and again. Each time he told me there was only one more alteration before he could love me. In short, I ended up going through fifteen operations that altered my face ever so slightly, but crucially. The alterations were mind-boggling in their subtlety. And each one made me more successful as a model. Please don't tell anybody about this. It's not something I'm proud of. It was great for my career, but it never did win me Nathaniel's love."

I promised her I wouldn't tell anyone.

"After I became the most highly paid model in the world, I started suspecting that my appearance had nothing to do with whether Nathaniel could love me. I knew there had to be something else, which apparently you have. That's what I so desperately wanted to find out when I met you."

I could not imagine what that thing might be.

Needless to say, Chriskate's story made it extremely easy for me to break up with Nathaniel, which I did that same afternoon, by phone, after expressing my horror to him over what he had done. He tried in vain to apologize and explain his vile act.

"I was unable to love anybody," he said. "I desperately wanted to love someone, and I was convinced it had to do with their appearance, but now I know I was wrong. I know I was sick to think that way. And anyway, it wasn't *so* horrible what I did to her, was it? She got to become very successful and she can now get any man she wants."

"Except you."

"That's true. But please forgive me, I'm not like that anymore. I realize it was terrible to prolong her agony. I'm sorry, but I was in agony too. I had never been in love. That was agony. I thought I was incapable of being in love with anyone. I thought there was something wrong with me."

"There is."

"Please don't break up with me over this. I'm a totally different person now. If you break up with me over this, I don't know what I'll do to myself."

"Don't worry, I was going to break up with you anyway, but I was holding off out of guilt. I don't have the guilt now. That's the only difference."

"I still want us to be friends, at least."

"I don't see how it's possible now that I know what you did to her."

"Please."

"If you need anything from me, any favors, please ask. After all, I perhaps owe you my life."

"I ask for your friendship."

"Well, that's asking a lot."

"Well, I gave you a lot."

"That's true. Okay, I can try to be friends with you sometimes. But you must know I'll feel differently about you from now on."

"Okay, I'll accept that for now. But I hope you'll change your mind. I hope you'll see I'm a different person. I'm who you thought I was before she told you all that."

*   *   *

The filming of my big-budget movie began. Luckily, most
of it was to be filmed in New York.

When I came home each day, I'd tell Damon all about
the filming, and he seemed to relish every detail. He
couldn't get enough of them, down to the hair color, shoe
color, and smallest gestures of anyone on the set, be it the
director or the gofer. He also wanted to know my feelings:
every nuance of my happiness, all my surges of excitement, little racings of my heart, swellings of pride, or
blushings, or whatever. We would talk about these things
for hours, until either he or I would bring up the importance of being rested for the next day of filming, and then
I would go to bed.

The day came when I had to leave my pet alone for two
weeks, to go on location for a small section of the movie.
I bought a small fridge, which I placed right outside Damon's cage, within his reach. I bought him lots of cans of
tuna, of spaghetti, of fruits, of vegetables, mini cartons of
long-lasting milk, cereal, crackers, olive oil. Unlike him, I
didn't have the heartlessness to leave my victim without
chocolate, so I left him nine bars of dark Lindt chocolate,
and boxes of cookies, and hard candies.

I wanted to buy him a few clothes, since he only had
what he was wearing, but I had no success in finding
men's clothes made of translucent white silk. So instead,
I bought him a roll of silk fabric with which he could sew
himself some clothes if he needed them. I left him a sewing
kit that didn't have more than one needle, and whose pair
of scissors was tiny, very blunt, and round-tipped, to prevent any possibility of escape.

"I don't know how to make clothes," he said.

"Neither do I, but it can't be that complicated. I'm sure you can figure it out if you feel like it."

Before I left, I set up a video camera hidden from Damon's sight by the one-way mirror. I programmed the camera to start filming him every day at 1:30, while he watched his soap. By placing another mirror at the other end of the room, I was able to get a shot of both his face and the TV screen at the same time.

The last thing I did before leaving was give Damon a custom-made telephone that had no keypad, no numbers that could be pressed. I, and only I, could call him, because I, and only I, had his phone number. There was, of course, the risk that a stranger might dial his number by accident. Damon could then ask for help and be rescued, and I might get arrested. But he had kidnapped me first, so how much trouble would I really be in?

The risk had to be taken anyway. I left Damon in the cage, with his phone, and I went on my trip.

I called him every day. It was fun, having a pet to call. One time he didn't answer, which worried me, but I tried to convince myself he was doing it for just that reason. A day later he did answer. The cello music was playing in the background, as almost always.

"Why didn't you answer the phone yesterday?" I asked.

"Oh, did you call? I was out shopping."

For a second I was alarmed, but then said, "For what?"

"More silk. I've made myself three costumes already, and I was getting bored again."

"I'm glad you're keeping yourself busy and you haven't

lost your sense of humor. How are the bold and the beautiful ones doing?"

"Fine," he said, at once sullen.

At some point I would have to figure out what it was all about. I called him once at 1:45 P.M., in the middle of his soapie, to see what he would do. He picked up and immediately hung up, without saying hello.

Another time I called him at 2:00 P.M., right after his soapie.

"Hello?" he said, sounding all stuffed up and nasal.

"What's wrong? Are you okay?" I asked, feigning surprise and innocence.

He sighed. "What is it?"

"Are you crying? Why are you crying?"

"I just watched *The Bold and the Beautiful*."

"Yeah, and?"

"And nothing."

"Why do you find it sad?" I asked, hoping this was a turn of phrase I hadn't used before and that he might respond to it. I couldn't help but feel that all I needed was to discover the magic words, the magic phrasing of the sentence, and I'd get an answer.

But this phrasing was not the right one, for he just sighed and was silent until I changed the subject.

We chatted about my work. He was supportive, saying he was sure I was doing a great job, the best they had ever seen.

And my work *was* going well. No matter how good an actor I had become, I think I was even better knowing I had Damon locked up in my apartment. It endowed me with an air of power and calm that I might not have had otherwise.

*   *   *

Finally, the trip came to an end, and I returned to my apartment. Before going into Damon's room, I looked at him through the one-way mirror. He was lying on the floor of his cage, on his side, wearing a long white gown, and watching TV. As he watched, he was raising and lowering his top leg like a ballet dancer, causing his gown to bunch up around his thighs. After a few reps of this, he lowered his leg and rested it on the nearby toilet seat.

I entered the room only after having donned my fencing armor in case he threw things at me. He had so much to throw, and he did throw, immediately: cans, the sewing scissors, more cans. I took everything away. I counted the cans; the empty ones and their lids, as well as the full ones, to make sure he was rid of all of them—lids could be used for cutting me.

"So, you made yourself a dress," I said, as I took off my fencing gear.

"Yes," he said, raising his arms and modeling it for me. "It's A-shaped. It flares out at the bottom to provide me with freedom of movement. Do you like it?"

I shrugged and made a neutral sound. It was indeed A-shaped and flared out at the bottom. It was also coarsely cut and sewn. It was sleeveless, horrid, and looked like a costume from an abusive insane asylum. I'm proud to say it was better than anything I could have made.

When I handed him dinner, he stabbed my hand with the sewing needle I had forgotten to take away. This brought back memories of the ice shards he used to shoot at me. He now held the needle between his thumb and forefinger, ready to stab me with it again.

"Give it back," I said, and he threw his dinner at me.

"Why are you doing this?" I asked.

"I'm in the cage. And I've been in here for two weeks, alone. It is appropriate for me to do this."

I sat on the easy chair and ate my dinner on a tray. We talked about how my filming had gone. Two hours later, when he was getting hungry, I gave him a sandwich in exchange for the needle.

I didn't leave the apartment for three solid days, to compensate for having been away so long. At night, I carried my TV back into my living room, to secretly watch the tapes of Damon watching *The Bold and the Beautiful* during my absence. I got the results I had hoped for. Not knowing he was being filmed, he was less inhibited than he had been in my presence, and I was finally able to detect a pattern to his crying.

It had to do with the legless character, Stem. When Stem would come on the scene, Damon would cry a little more. This also happened when Stem left the scene. I had a feeling Damon's grief over *The Bold and the Beautiful* had to do with his past, with that terrible thing he sometimes alluded to having done.

To catch him off-guard and witness a genuine reaction, I confronted him with an extravagant guess, out of the blue: "You cut off Stem's legs, didn't you?"

He stiffened. He wouldn't speak to me for the rest of the day.

So I did some research. I called an acquaintance of mine, Jeremy Acidophilus, who did menial labor at *Screen,* a magazine on movies and celebrities. He had just gotten his job back after having lost if for a few months when he had asked for a raise.

He was able to find out for me the name of the agency that represented Stem, or Philip Jessen, as was his real name.

I called it and left a message saying I needed to speak to Philip Jessen urgently about someone he knew, whose name may or may not be Damon Wetly.

I kept the phone at my side at all times that day and evening. The next day, while I was chatting with Damon, I got the call from Philip Jessen. Without asking me any questions about my reason for calling, he asked if I could visit him in person. I said I would fly there on the next plane out.

When I told Damon I was leaving again, he got mad and asked for how long. I said it wouldn't be long.

I arrived in L.A. that evening and went straight to Philip's house in Beverly Hills. A housekeeper opened the door and led me to a den where Philip was waiting in his wheelchair. I sat down, was served tea, and got straight to the point.

"Who is Damon?"

"My brother."

I let this sink in, and asked, "Why does he cry when he watches you on TV?"

"Does he?"

"Yes. He does."

"It's a long story. Who are you?" he asked, and then quickly added, "I mean, I know who you are, from your films, but you only recently came on the scene. Who are you in relation to my brother? How do you know him?"

"Damon kidnapped me."

"Why?"

"To thank me for having saved his life in the subway."
I explained that Damon had decided to make me happy
by making my dream of becoming an actor come true.
Then I abruptly asked, "Did he cut off your legs?"

"No, why?"

"He often referred to something terrible he did in his
past. And I thought it might have to do with you."

"No, he didn't cut off my legs, although he probably
feels he did."

I begged him to tell me what happened. I claimed it
would help me cope better with my kidnapping. After
looking thoughtful for a while, he agreed. But first, he
asked:

"Do you know where he is now?"

"I think in New York."

"Are you in touch with him?"

"Sort of."

"How? Letters, phone, meetings?"

"Meetings, I guess. He drives up to me in the street and
asks me if I'm happy."

"Oh, how unpleasant. I had no idea he was so imbal-
anced. Next time he does that, you can tell him his brother
wants to resume contact. That might help him regain some
of his sanity. Did you try to have him arrested?"

"Yes. But they didn't find him."

Philip then told me the story of his past with Damon,
which turned out to be stranger than the most melodra-
matic plot lines of any soap opera, including *The Bold
and the Beautiful*.

Philip said that before he was an actor, and before he
became legless, he was a plastic surgeon. His story re-
volved around a third man, a former friend of his, who

was also a plastic surgeon, named Ben. Ben was apparently extremely talented and ambitious, as well as extremely unethical and unhinged. One day he performed plastic surgery on a young girl without the authorization of her parents. Later, he actually kidnapped two children and worked on them as well, without the authorization of their parents, nor their own. The police searched for the criminal. Philip found out by chance that it was Ben. Ben begged Philip not to report him, and Philip agreed, but Philip's brother, Damon, who hated Ben, sent an anonymous letter to the authorities revealing the culprit, and Ben was arrested and released on bail while awaiting trial.

At that point in the story, Philip paused, and softly said, "And that's when Ben came . . ."

He was then silent for a long time, and I said, "He came where?"

"That's where the story really begins. Or ends. Could you please stop drinking your tea while I tell you this. It's very hard for me."

I put down my cup.

"Ben came to my house one evening while I was having dinner with my daughter and Damon, who happened to have stopped by earlier. Ben had a gun. He handcuffed us, gagged us, and drove us to his house. He took us to the basement, which was divided into two rooms. He left Damon in the first room, tied down, and brought my daughter and me into the second room. Two heavy chairs were bolted to the floor, facing each other, ten feet apart. He sat my daughter and me down, and tied us up. Soldered to the arm of my chair was a gun, aimed at my daughter in the opposite chair. Ben tied my hand around the gun's handle. He ungagged my daughter, but not me. She screamed and cried.

"Ben then talked to me, said absurdities like, 'You had to turn me in, didn't you. Making someone beautiful; there could not be a more atrocious crime. I should have left these girls to their happy lives of ugly ducklings. Your daughter is far from ugly, poor girl. She doesn't know what she's missing, right? Don't worry, I won't give your daughter a life of ugliness, at least not for long. I'm not saying I won't disfigure her. No, I'm not saying that at all. I will, in fact, disfigure your daughter in such a way that even after years of plastic surgery she could never regain her present appearance. But that's irrelevant, because immediately after I disfigure her, I will continue to torture her in extremely painful ways; ways that will also be, after, let's say, about half an hour, fatal. Now, I'll tell you what your choices are. I have generously given you the option of putting an end to the torture *at any time,* by killing your daughter with that gun. Granted, one way or the other, she'll end up dead. But still, I'd say, it's not bad.'"

Philip paused. My breathing seemed loud to me in the silent room. So I stopped breathing.

"And he did what he said," Philip went on, staring at some point behind me, squinting a little as he spoke. "He first disfigured her, cutting off pieces of her face. She was screaming. He burned her in various places, punched her, cut off some of her fingers, and then an ear, and then her tongue, her lips. I didn't shoot her. He continued torturing her, bringing her closer to death, until she had stopped crying, and all you could hear was her pained breathing, her wheezing. And finally the sound of her breathing stopped. Ben felt her pulse and said, 'Okay, that's done. I won't reproach you for not having spared her the slow death. Everyone makes their own choices. Although, I should have known that about you and spared myself the trouble of soldering the gun to the chair.' "

Philip was quiet for a moment, staring at me intently before going on: "Then Ben dragged me into the room where Damon was, and ungagged me. I was in shock and didn't speak. Ben said, 'You may think I'm kidding, but I don't think that what happened in there was quite enough of a punishment. I will also cut off your legs. This may seem a bit anticlimactic, but I don't care; I think it's a good idea, especially in the long run, when the pain of your daughter's death fades a little and you try to start your life over again. The missing legs will be a good, vivid reminder that it's not so easy to turn over a new leaf.' Damon was thrashing, screaming through his gag. He wanted to tell Philip that he was the one who sent the letter, not me. But he never got a chance. And *I* certainly wasn't about to correct the misunderstanding. I didn't need to lose my brother now too. As Damon kept thrashing, Philip looked at him and said, 'You don't need to see this,' and he whacked him in the head with his gun, knocking him out. The blow sent Damon into a coma that he came out of only a month later.

"Ben then put me under anesthesia, and I woke up in my house, sitting in a wheelchair, by the phone, my legs missing. Damon was slumped in an easy chair next to me, unconscious. Tagged to his clothing was a note: 'Don't know why he hasn't come to, yet, the wimp.'

"I sat there, in a trance, remembering what had happened to my daughter and unable to move. Finally I called an ambulance for Damon. We were rushed to the hospital. They informed me that I was fine, that the amputation had been done very well. Damon was kept at the hospital, on life support.

"The police tried to find Ben, but he had disappeared and to this day has never been caught. When Damon came out of his coma a month later, he wanted to find Ben, of course. He said his purpose in life would now be to find Ben and kill him. I told him I didn't want him to. Through much persuasion, I made him promise me to never look for Ben, never go near him. I didn't want to worry about Damon's safety. He then said that he would devote his life to helping me. I refused this offer as well, saying I preferred we didn't see each other, because the sight of him would constantly bring back the tragedy. I told him I would contact him when the memory of what had happened had become less vivid and painful. He left, very upset. It's been eight years. That was the last time we spoke."

"And there was never any trace of Ben?"

"No. I've been afraid, over the years, that Ben would find out that Damon was the one who turned him in, and that he would again seek revenge. The police and hospital personnel, at the time, agreed not to reveal to the press that Damon had written the letter. But three years ago, a journalist wrote a big piece on me for *Soap Opera* magazine. He was fascinated with my story, and delved deeply into the case. He spoke to doctors, nurses, and the police. Somehow, he found out that Damon had written the letter, and he mentioned it in the piece. I was worried that Ben would see it and go after Damon. I actually wrote to

Damon then, telling him to be careful. He sent me back a postcard saying he was fine, and has continued doing so once a month, ever since."

Philip and I finished talking in the early hours of the morning. I was to sleep in the guest room, but ended up unable to sleep much at all and wishing I could take a plane back to New York immediately. I was scheduled to leave later in the morning, right after breakfast.

My departure had to be slightly postponed, however, because while we were having breakfast, Philip said, "There's something I hesitate to bring up."

"Yes?"

"I really hesitate to bring it up, because you'll think it's very strange of me."

"What is it?"

"Well, it's a favor I'm tempted to ask of you, but if I do ask it, you must absolutely refuse if it's at all distasteful to you."

I started feeling tense. "Okay. What is it?"

"I don't know if I should ask it. It's embarrassing."

I wasn't sure he should ask it either, whatever it was. "Does it have anything to do with Damon or anything we talked about?"

"No."

I grew more worried. I picked up my teacup and mumbled into it, "Well, it's up to you if you want to ask it."

"Okay, I will ask it, but only if you promise not to let it destroy your opinion of me."

Beads of sweat formed on my forehead.

"Oh, I'm sorry, you look so uncomfortable," he said. "Forget I said anything. It's not important."

"Oh, okay."

"But just so you don't imagine terribly perverted things, all I was going to ask is if you wouldn't mind throwing me off a diving board. That was all. There are so few women I meet who give me the urge to be thrown by them. But it doesn't matter. Did you inquire about the flights back to New York?"

I felt I had to be polite. Meekly and hesitantly, I said, "I wouldn't mind throwing you off a diving board."

"Really?"

"Yeah. But why? What does it mean?"

"I don't know. And I prefer not to think about it too deeply. It depresses me."

He got on the phone, and I heard him say, "I met a woman I want to be thrown by. She said she'll do it. Do you mind if we come over?"

We took a cab to the house of a friend of his, who had a pool. The friend turned out to be Philip's very good-looking costar, Ron Moss, who played Ridge on *The Bold and the Beautiful.*

It was a strange sensation to lift half a man. Philip was of course lighter than a whole man. I carried him in my arms and climbed onto the diving board. I felt doubly nervous with Ridge looking on.

I asked Philip, "Do you want to be thrown in head first or—" I was going to say "feet first," but stopped myself in time. I couldn't very well say "stump first." Nor could I say, "genitals first," even though that's where he ended. And I couldn't get myself to say "butt first" either. So I left my question unfinished, which turned out to be fine.

He said he wanted me to choose which end of him I would throw in first, that that was part of the pleasure for him.

So I decided to throw him butt first, which I thought would minimize the damage, in case of a bad throw.

As he fell in, he seemed to relish the moment; he opened his arms wide, as if doing an inverted swan dive.

He then swam toward the edge. Ridge pulled him out of the water and placed him back in his wheelchair.

I flew home having made a decision.

Chapter Fourteen

I decided I would set Damon free. Worse than that, I would enter Damon's cage, to prove to myself that I finally understood him and that he wouldn't hurt me, kill me, or lock me in the cage. It was also to show him that I trusted him. I wanted us to be friends if possible. I wanted us to be normal people, standing in front of each other out of our own free will. What an interesting sensation it would be, to have a conversation with Damon without one of us being the other's captive.

When I arrived home, I peeked through the one-way mirror. Damon was jogging in place in his cage. I donned my fencing armor. Before going in, I peeked again through the mirror. Damon was on the floor, doing pushups.

As soon as I entered the room, he got up, panting, and clapped the floor dust from his hands. He glanced around his cage, grabbed some tuna cans and threw them at me. They bounced off my mask. He threw every object he had, including the can opener. Then he plopped down on his bed, tired, and said, "How was your trip?"

"Very enlightening."

"Enlightening?"

"Yes."

"And what aspect of life did it enlighten?" he asked, his hand encountering something hard in his sheets. He uncovered the object: another unopened can of tuna. He threw it at me.

"The aspect I couldn't understand," I said.

"That goes without saying. What aspect was that?"

"I'm not in the mood to talk about it right now."

"Oh? And what mood are you in?"

"I think . . . I'm in an insane mood."

I approached the door of his cage and unlocked it. I stepped inside, holding on to the bars to make sure I wouldn't fall down from fright.

We stared at each other, barely breathing. He looked frozen, and I wondered if he was afraid of me. The possibility made me laugh. Just one laugh: one loud, awkward, nervous, "Ha!" The sound of it was so funny and silly that two more came out of me, equally funny and silly. I held my breath to block the others.

Damon got up and approached me. His hands reached toward my face, and he pulled off my mask.

He gazed into my eyes for a long moment and kissed me.

I didn't care how insane it was; how sick and embarrassing—not to mention banal and unoriginal, not to mention dangerous—to be kissing your assailant. The only two things that made it slightly less objectionable were that he was my *ex*-assailant and that I had been his assailant too, since then.

We kissed passionately, and astonishingly lovingly, for two mutual assailants. I was able to forget, for a few moments at a time, the possibility that he might suddenly turn around and lock me in the cage. I was able to forget, and then I would remember, and then forget again, when his enthusiasm, like a wave, transported me away from thought.

Slowly, gradually, we started making love. But we had barely just begun, when I jumped off the bed, grabbed my clothes, and ran out of the cage. He grabbed his clothes and ran after me at a phenomenal rate. I rushed down the stairs and out of my building. He followed me. When we were in the street, we stopped running, got dressed, and I said, "Why are you running after me?"

"I'm not running after you. I was running out of that cage, that room, and your apartment before you had a chance to lock me in again. Why were you running?"

"For the same reason."

"That doesn't make sense. I couldn't have kept you locked in, while going in and out of your building as I pleased. As soon as people found you missing, the first place they would check is your apartment."

"That's true," I said, and was tempted to suggest that we go back upstairs and continue where we left off. But then I came to my senses. "No, actually, you're wrong. You could find a way to sneak me out of the building and take me back to a cage in some house in the country."

"Huh, I hadn't thought of that."

"Is that supposed to mean you wish you had thought of it because you think it's a good idea?"

"No. I just meant: huh, I hadn't thought of that legitimate reason you could have to be afraid of me in your apartment, the same way I'm afraid of you."

I nodded. We kissed again. Between kisses, I mumbled, "What are we going to do?"

"The options are limited. We could wait till we're no longer afraid."

"No! That would take too long. It could take days, or months, or years, or never happen."

"I know. Even hours would be long," he said.

It was too cold to stay outside, especially for Damon, who could not wear opaque clothing. So we decided to go to a movie theater. We sat in the back row and continued kissing, never looking at the screen. I felt as if I should be wearing a seat belt.

Amid the kisses, we had a brief exchange.

"Why did you walk into my cage?" asked Damon.

"I had an urge."

"What brought it on?"

"I always had it, I think."

"What made you act on it?"

"I'll tell you one day."

He kissed me again and slid his hand under the elastic waistband of my skirt. This was not tolerable. Our pitch of frustration became simply cruel. Halfway through the movie, we went to a nearby diner and locked ourselves in the ladies' room. We did not let ourselves be influenced by movies: we did not make love standing up. We did it on the floor, which was more exciting. The floor of a public bathroom, just large enough to accommodate our horizontal bodies. It was not excessively dirty. It had just the right amount of dirt to add grit to our sex.

We spent a few more hours together that day, during which we mostly rode up and down the city on a bus, because a bus was warm, safely public, economical, and offered varied scenery. On that bus, Damon confessed to having been in love with me from the beginning, but having not wanted to tell me for fear of ruining the effectiveness of his training. I became gloomy at this reminder of my days as a kidnapped person.

He said, "I'm sorry I kidnapped you to make you happy. I know you feel it wasn't worth it."

"Even if it was worth it, you had no right to do it," I said.

We spoke in earnest whispers, so as not to be overheard by the other passengers.

"I know," he said. "But I wanted to make you happy in a completely selfless way. Beginning a romance with you would not have been selfless. It might have made you happy, but it would have made me happy too."

"What about when you were in the cage? How did you feel about me then?"

"I loved you at all times. In the cage, I loved you. When I threw cans at you—" He lowered his voice, because an old woman who was within earshot was staring at us with what appeared to be either shock or disapproval. "I loved you."

"Then why did you throw them at me?" I asked.

"To put on a good show of wanting to be let out. And because part of me *did* want to be let out."

"Then why didn't you just let me know how you felt about me?"

"I didn't want to impose myself on you. I didn't want to offer you anything that you didn't want. On top of it,

it's hard to think of smooth moves to perform from behind bars." He paused. "Remember, my plan had been to
give you what *you* wanted; not my version of what I
thought or hoped you wanted."

When Damon and I parted that first night, he said he
would be sleeping in a hotel, thinking of me, and that he
would call me the next morning. We were still afraid of
each other.

I hadn't told him about my visit to his brother Philip's
or about Philip's desire to see him again. I thought it might
cause turmoil or agitation within him, and I didn't want
that to happen; not before finding out how this strange
new twist in our relationship would evolve.

That night, it felt lonely to no longer have my pet in his
cage. The sight of the empty cage was disturbing, like a
fish tank whose occupant had passed away and been
flushed down the toilet.

I walked into the cage and touched the things he had
touched. I touched the edge of his bathtub. I used his toilet
to see what it had been like for him, for weeks, to use that
toilet. I took a bath in his tub. I turned on the TV and
watched it while sitting on the floor, the way he had. I
turned on his cherished cello music with the remote control, and I listened to my ex's compositions, wondering if
listening to them from behind the bars would help them
move me the way they had moved Damon. Not really, as
it turned out.

I slept in his bed that night.

Damon did call me the next day. We spent it together,
again in the safety of publicness, and in bliss. We had sex
in three different public places: a fitting room in the men's

section of a department store, a church, and, late at night, between two moving subway cars. A hotel room would have been too risky, not public enough: he could knock me unconscious and sneak me out in a big bag or something. And I could do the same to him, of course, from his point of view.

We saw each other again the next day, and for a while almost every day after that. Always in public. We were extremely demonstrative by necessity; the city was our bedroom.

He would watch me while I finished starring in the big-budget movie, whose last few scenes were being shot in town. We gazed at each other between takes, he standing a ways off, out of the way. It was unsettling to see Damon—my trainer—right there, watching what he had taught me, or rather, what he had forced me to teach myself.

After that first day, we never mentioned our imprisonment of each other. We acted as if it never happened. Understandably, it was a touchy subject.

When our lifestyle seemed too impractical, we tried to reason with each other about our mutual distrust. I tried to persuade him that he had nothing to fear from me.

"I'm the one who opened the door of your cage. Why would I now want to harm you or imprison you again?"

"I can say the same to you. I came into your apartment to find out why you were unhappy, yet knowing it was probably a trap. Why would *I* want to harm you or imprison you again?"

"Because it *was* a trap and you might want revenge."

"Then why did I kiss you when you came in the cage? Why didn't I just yank you in and lock the door?"

Sometimes we got to a stage in our convoluted conversations where the whole thing felt silly to both of us and it seemed obvious we could trust each other. We would then gingerly head for my apartment, with the intention of taming privacy, but as we got closer, we became more quiet, more anxious, and our steps slowed.

"It doesn't feel okay," I would finally say.

"I'm relieved you said it first."

"The only way I can imagine myself feeling at ease alone with you in my apartment is if you're in the cage."

"And that is precisely why I don't feel at ease going to your apartment."

Our discussions on the topic went in infinite circles. And yet we kept having them every time it felt uncomfortable, or seemed like a shame, to lock ourselves in a rest room somewhere.

I still hadn't told Damon that I knew about his past and had met his brother. I felt guilty about not having told him, and I often had the urge to tell him, and sometimes I was on the verge of my urge, but then I never did, always coming up with some excuse or other: the present excuse was that I wanted to wait until we'd figured out how to tolerate privacy together. Our relationship would then be more solid and more likely to withstand any damage my confession might cause. So I waited.

Progress on the privacy issue only really got going one day when I caught a cold from lying with Damon in the cool spring grass in Central Park. I decided the time had come for things to change.

While Damon was nursing my cold in a deli, making sure I drank my herb tea and ate my chicken soup, I said, "I wish you could nurse me in my apartment."

"Me too."

"It would be so nice. You could take care of me in my own bed. We could rent movies. You could take advantage of me while I have my fever."

"Maybe we should try it again, try walking to your apartment and see if we can actually make it upstairs this time."

"No, we won't try, because when we *try* we don't succeed. We will actually *do* it this time. But after some preparations. I'll take down the cage; have it removed. I'll take the lock off the door to my bedroom. And then we'll force ourselves to go up, and we'll stay there, no matter how unpleasant or scary it is to be alone with each other. We'll stay there until the discomfort wears off. It'll have to, eventually. Don't you think?"

"It's a great idea. It's the only solution."

A few days later, workmen came and dismantled the cage and took it away. A locksmith came and took off the lock.

Damon and I walked to my apartment in grave silence, our hearts pounding. We arrived at the door to my building, walked in, walked up, did not stop at any point. I unlocked my door. The sight of keys made us both shiver with dread. Damon actually looked away, at the wall, until the door was unlocked and the keys were out of sight.

I gave him a nervous tour of my remodeled apartment. He approved. We sat on my couch and drank tea, making polite conversation. After forty-five minutes of this, I got carried away by excitement, because my plan was working: we were actually existing in the same room together, not separated by bars, not protected from each other by the presence of other people, and not threatening each other in any way. I flung myself around his neck and kissed him and said, "I love you."

He smiled, and laughed, and told me he loved me too, and pushed me back against the sofa and became passionate, like in the rest rooms and the movie theaters, but of course even more unrestrained.

For a week we stayed in my apartment, doing only a small range of activities, but doing them over and over: conducting sensual and erotic experiments, renting movies, eating all sorts of things. The only times we went out were to buy more groceries. I would put on my boots and my winter coat, not bothering to get dressed underneath, and he'd wear his usual transparencies.

The days passed and I still didn't tell him about his brother, because I felt more days had to pass before I could.

So more days passed. We started going outdoors a bit. We had sex between moving subway cars a couple of times, for old times' sake, despite the danger, and dangerous it was: Damon would hold me firmly, and I would jokingly remind him not to let go of me. But once, which understandably turned out to be the last time we did it there, he did. I caught myself in the nick of time, while simultaneously getting a vision of what would have happened to my body if I hadn't. He said he was sorry, that the jerkiness of the ride had made him lose his grip on me. He seemed very upset that I had almost been squashed, and for a while he wouldn't stop hugging me and burying his face in my neck, even as we walked away from the scene of my near death.

*   *   *

I still worked a lot, but also managed to devote much time to Damon. I would leave the sets as soon as the scenes were shot; I didn't linger to socialize with the other actors. I never had dinner with them.

I'd spend time studying my lines while Damon did his research. Sometimes, he would ask me if I needed help, but he was always very careful because he knew it was a touchy topic. He tried to be very delicate, and very respectful of whatever answer I would give him, which was no thanks.

One time, to make our relationship as normal as possible, and so that he wouldn't think I resented him too much, I casually asked him if he could help me with my lines. He tried to respond calmly, and said okay, and sat near me, but it was clear he was a bit nervous. I recited my lines while he looked at the script, and I got them right, so he had nothing to correct. He just smiled normally at me when I was done. I pushed it a step further, because I couldn't resist, and I was curious.

"Do you have any suggestions? Any thoughts on my delivery?" I asked.

He cleared his throat. He must have known I was torturing him on purpose. "I thought it was very well done." His voice was gentle. "Very subtle and interestingly nuanced."

I waited to see if he would say more. He sensed this and added, "I'm only a scientist. You're now at a level of acting that is way beyond the realm where I can offer any useful opinion."

I think he was afraid he had said too much, that he had been presumptuous, for he looked down at the floor humbly, as if wishing he could go under it.

I observed him, amused. However, not wanting to be excessively tormenting, I breezily said, "Well, thank you for your help," and changed the topic.

He seemed relieved.

One day, I started having a new urge, that type of over-powering, irrational urge, like wanting to enter your assailant's cage or be thrown off a diving board: I wanted to introduce Damon to my parents. I had told them I was dating somebody, and they had expressed great interest in meeting the person, asking if he was an actor too. I told them he was a scientist. When they asked what kind of scientist, I changed the subject until I could think of a good answer. I discussed the possibilities with Damon. He didn't hesitate as to which scientific profession he wanted them to think he had.

"Tell them I'm an experimental astrophysicist, that I build experiments that fly in space. Telescopes and spectrometers that are launched on sounding rockets and satellites, that kind of thing. I can tell them all about it if they're interested. Who wouldn't be? I think I know enough jargon to pull it off."

I laughed, amazed. "Why do you want them to think you're an experimental astrophysicist?"

"It sounds good. Nothing sounds better, in fact. Who wouldn't want to be introduced as an experimental astrophysicist?"

On the whole, Damon thought my urge to introduce him to my parents was insane and self-destructive, but he wanted to please me, and therefore acquiesced, despite the great peril he felt he was putting himself in.

And he was not entirely wrong: my parents were still obsessed with capturing my kidnapper. They were constantly calling the police, asking if there was any progress, if anything had turned up. My father, especially, was persistent and indefatigable in his efforts. He wanted the monster behind bars, he said. Considering all these factors, I don't know why I had such a strong desire to make the introductions, but I did. I simply thought Damon was wonderful, and I wanted them to see just how wonderful my new boyfriend was. I loved him so immensely, so intensely, so far.

I tried to reassure Damon and myself: "Why would they start suspecting who you are? I'd have to be insane to get involved with my assailant. They don't think I'm insane."

There was only one thing Damon and I had to work on before the meeting: his clothes. My parents knew that my assailant had worn, at all times, transparent clothing.

I discussed with Damon the possibility of his wearing opaque clothing. He said he wasn't sure it could work for him, because it would be like trying to breathe on very little air. He could only do it if he was extremely calm, but any slight turmoil would make him start suffocating.

He hadn't worn opaque clothing in years, and yet he was willing to try it now, for me. He practiced it before the dinner and did fine; we even had sex while he remained dressed opaquely.

On our way out, however, we argued about up to where his shirt should be buttoned. I said high. He said low—preferably open all the way, as far as he was concerned; it would help him breathe. He had wanted to wear shorts and his usual sandals. I had told him it was out of the question, and that he should look at the bright side: at least he didn't have to wear a tie. He had gone pale at the mere mention of the word.

We had finally settled on a thin, green, short-sleeved shirt; a ripped pair of blue jeans (the holes calmed him slightly); rain boots that were vaguely translucent; and, most important, one leather glove to cover up his missing finger. My parents knew all too well that I had chopped off Damon's finger; they not only knew it, they were delighted by it, and bragged about it often to their friends.

The meeting was to be held at my parents' apartment. We were to have dinner there.

I still had not told Damon I had met his brother. He was about to meet my parents, and he had no idea I had already met a member of his family. I felt bad, but also felt it was important to keep it a secret, for now. I wanted him to be as calm and relaxed as possible for the meeting. Once we had crossed that threshold successfully, I could be open.

Right before ringing my parents' doorbell, Damon and I were still wresting with the buttons on his green shirt. Finally, he got me to let him keep more than the top two buttons open; I got him to keep less than the top four buttons open.

My parents were innocent and pure in their expectations, unsuspicious. They were ready, willing, and hopeful to have nothing but the highest opinion of my boyfriend. And it began well. They seemed pleased immediately. Their smiles, already broad when they opened the door, broadened when they got their first glimpse of Damon.

He made a good impression in opaque clothing, despite

showing a lot of chest; he was attractive. They took his coat, which of course he was not wearing, but carrying. My father extended his hand toward Damon's gloved hand, to remind him to take off the glove. I noticed this just in time.

"Andy has a birth defect," I said. Damon and I had decided that Andy would be his new name for my parents, and we had practiced using it, to prevent blunders. "The skin on his left hand is fragile, and can't be exposed to daylight or hard angles. It has to be constantly protected by that glove, because if it gets injured, which happens very easily, it doesn't heal by itself: it has to be taken care of by a doctor."

I estimated that this was more than enough information to assure that my parents would leave his hand alone. And sure enough, they politely ignored his hand. But not for more than five minutes—at least not my father. He said to Damon, "You know, I'm a hemophiliac."

Damon nodded and uttered a little "Oh."

"Are you one too?"

"Not exactly."

I begged my father to shut up. My mother seconded me. So he did.

We had drinks. My father updated me on the lack of progress the police were making in capturing my kidnapper. He turned to Damon:

"Isn't it terrible what happened to Anna? I don't know if she's told you all the details—I assume she has. For someone to do to another human being what this man, this Damon, did to her, he must be a deranged monster, don't you think, Andy? Don't you think it's the most abominable thing, what he did to her?"

Damon replied, "Anna hasn't told me much about it, but she did tell me it was horrible. Despite the success she's achieved in her career she doesn't think it was worth it."

"Of *course* she doesn't think it was worth it! Do *you* think it was worth it?"

"Only Anna can decide that. And she did decide it wasn't worth it. But I must say I have a vested interest in the issue. If Anna had not been kidnapped, she probably would not then have been at the cast party where I met her. So if you find me hesitant to condemn her kidnapper, it's undoubtedly for that reason."

My mother chuckled, charmed. My father looked uncertain as to how he felt about that.

In a misguided effort to win my father over, Damon said, "The kidnapper made a mistake in kidnapping Anna. It was poor judgment on his part, and he undoubtedly feels bad about it now, especially if he somehow knows that Anna feels it wasn't worth it. Poor man. I pity him." After being silent a moment, Damon added: "I suspect he was in love with Anna and wanted to make her dream come true."

"Yes, exactly. There is no excuse for that," said my father.

During dinner, my mother said, "Andy, what does your work consist of, exactly? I'm fascinated."

"I build telescopes and detectors to see the sky in X ray. These optical systems are then sent out of the atmosphere to gather their information. Now I'm working on a European project called XMM, which stands for X-ray Multi-Mirror. It has three co-aligned telescopes, two of which will be equipped with reflection grating spectrometers. Those spectrometers are what I'm working on. It's really a spectroscopic mission, rather than an imaging one. The imaging missions always bring back nice pictures and are good for P.R., but spectroscopy doesn't excite the public much. Nevertheless, it *is* the spectroscopy that produces the most scientific breakthroughs. Usually black holes could only be identified spectroscopically, for example. Anyway, it's really a big project involving scientists from many countries, and it'll be launched in two years or so. Nothing like the small homemade experiments that I launched on sounding rockets in the past. Those were like bottle rockets by comparison."

Damon seemed to greatly enjoy describing his fictitious job. He even added, "It's a very sexy field."

"It does sound sexy," said my father.

"Sexy like fencing. The same kind of sexy," said Damon.

My father nodded, and my mother dreamily said, "Yeah."

As Damon continued describing his work animatedly, he became less careful with his gloved hand; he moved it naturally, as if it were not gloved, which was a big mistake. In allowing his hand to move so naturally, he was actually allowing it to look very unnatural: he didn't notice that where the glove covered his absent index finger it remained, at all times, stiff and pointing. Damon and I had talked about this phenomenon and that he would have to be careful about it. But he was not being careful enough. To my distress, I noticed my father's gaze rest upon the straight, frozen finger, and then, to my horror, I noticed that his eyes would not leave that finger. As soon as Damon noticed my father's gaze, his other fingers froze

as well. He stopped talking, drank, and desperately resumed his occupational explanations, trying to recapture
my father's interest: "I'm interested in observing the life
cycle of stars and the gases that they're made of. You see,
stars form out of collapsing clouds in the galaxy."

"Clouds of what?" asked my mother.

"Mostly hydrogen," answered Damon, "and small
amounts of other elements, like helium, carbon, oxygen,
and dust. Often the cloud material is in molecular phase.
When the clouds' self-gravity exceeds their sustaining
pressure, they tend to collapse, give off heat, and when
they become dense enough, they begin to burn and turn
into stars. The less dense parts of the clouds might be
blown away by the stars' radiation pressure."

I couldn't believe he was talking so much about clouds,
a topic too close to his real occupation, which I had finally
told my parents about, after my escape. I was sitting too
far from him to kick him under the table, so I shook my
head at him, mouthing the word *cloud*.

He immediately changed the topic: "I used to work at
Oak Ridge National Lab in Tennessee, doing surface
physics with Dr. Dennis Zilkha. There I spent months
measuring surface reactions between oxygen and this
wonder-alloy nickel aluminum. For a while there was a
lot of interest in nickel aluminum. It's light, has high-
tensile strength, and is resistant to heat, so there were
plenty of potential applications for it as a material."

Damon had not succeeded in diverting my father's attention from his finger for even a second, and now Damon
was becoming distressed. How did this distress manifest
itself? He unbuttoned a button on his shirt. My mother,

who still had not noticed his pointing finger, did clearly notice the unbuttoning. My father, vice versa.

Damon shifted in his seat. He was suffocating subtly, and so discreetly. He lowered his ungloved hand under the table and was doing something there with it, and because I knew him, I knew that he was trying to take off his pants. It was tragic. His gloved hand remained in sight; I'm sure he was too afraid to move it, in case it broke the spell of paralysis that seemed to have befallen my father. Damon was still talking about experimental astrophysics, which didn't work on my mother, who looked surprised and uncomfortable, but politely didn't say so; and which was wasted on my father, who wasn't about to notice any undressing, as long as the finger remained rigid. Consequently, Damon was being driven mad. As casually as he could, he pushed his shirt off one shoulder. His ungloved hand was back under the table and he was clearly trying to lower his pants, but he was having a hard time of it without getting up. Out of frustration, he yanked his shirt off his other shoulder, causing the fabric to stretch across his torso, where the next button, looking ready to pop off, was holding the two halves together. Both of his shoulders were now bare.

My father got up from his chair and went to the kitchen, saying, "Does anyone want garlic salt?" He came back carrying the garlic salt and his fencing epée. He sat down, sprinkled some garlic salt on his food, and asked Damon if he wanted some.

Damon said, "No thanks," and went on compulsively: "There are all kinds of cool ways to tell what's happening on surfaces, like Auger electron spectroscopy [AES], X ray

photoelectron spectroscopy [XPS], and low-energy electron diffraction [LEED]. You can measure the chemical
environment of surface atoms using XPS, literally see the
surface order with LEED diffraction patterns, and get
complete surface atomic composition with AES—"

Damon stopped talking when my father took his
sword, slid it between Damon's index and middle fingers, and bent Damon's empty glove finger backward
until it was flat against the top of his hand. Everyone
was silent.

"You're Damon," announced my father, red-faced, full
of outrage and triumph.

Damon jumped up from his chair. He had successfully
lowered his pants. He now finished taking them off, and
then his shirt, and then his underwear. His boots had been
taken off ages ago and were lying under the table. Lastly,
he whipped off his glove, which for an instant revealed
his amputation, and ran out of the apartment (which was
on the ground floor), and through the lobby, stark naked.

The stripping was what saved him: my parents were still
in their chairs, too stunned to move. I grabbed a raincoat
from the hall closet and chased after him. He had run past
the doorman, who was laughing when I passed.

I found Damon huddling in a doorway a few doors
down the street. I wrapped him in the raincoat, which
unfortunately was black and opaque. He pushed it away,
saying, "I can't." He was crying.

I walked with him, trying to hold the raincoat around
him, to cover him up as much as possible.

"Don't touch me with it," he kept repeating and
punching it where it happened to touch his skin.

I was annoyed at myself for not having brought his

transparent clothes as a precautionary measure. Who did I think he was: a normal person?

When Damon calmed down slightly, we stopped at a corner to get a cab. While I tried to hail one, I ordered Damon to hold the raincoat in front of him, shielding the oncoming traffic from his nudity, which of course did no such favor to the pedestrians and shopkeepers behind him, where a small crowd soon gathered.

A cab finally stopped and took us to my apartment building. Before we got out, I luckily noticed, also disembarking, my parents, who had just arrived in another cab. I begged our driver to speed us away. My parents shoved themselves back into their cab and sped after us. It didn't take us long to lose them.

Our next most attractive option was to go to a hotel, but since we estimated that no hotel would welcome a naked man, I decided that we should go to an often deserted little park by the river, supposedly to think of what to do next, but actually I was secretly hoping that Damon would get cold enough to agree to wear the raincoat long enough for us to check into a hotel.

But he didn't. We stayed in the park for a while. Damon was sitting next to me on the bench, naked and shivering, his teeth chattering, and sometimes crying. Finally, even *I* was getting cold, and I couldn't bear to see him frozen, so I thought of another plan.

I decided to take him to Stress Less Step, a massage parlor close by, which I learned, after a quick phone call, stayed open until 10:30 P.M.

The staff at Stress Less Step didn't make a huge deal out of seeing a naked man walk in, perhaps because anyone walking in would end up naked anyway.

While Damon and I warmed ourselves in the sauna before our massages, we lamented the fact that he had not worn a mitten instead of a glove at the dinner; it would have made so much more sense, on every level, even with regards to the birth defect excuse. I then tried to soothe him, stroking his hair and speaking comforting words, in the heat, while my teeth burned.

After our massages, my masseuse came out and told Damon, in front of me, that I had been very tense. Then his masseuse, who overheard her, said "You don't know what tense is unless you've done him. I wasn't able to loosen a single knot."

I was sorry to hear this, because I had hoped that Damon might now be relaxed enough to wear the raincoat to a hotel. I asked him, just in case, and the answer was no. But then he nudged me, looking at the reception desk. He was motioning toward the curtain that hung behind the desk and that covered the window looking out on the street. It was made of white lace. It was ample.

"Lace?" I said. "It's not exactly the same."

"It'll do," he whispered. "It has holes everywhere. It's like being naked."

I went up to the receptionist and asked him if we could buy or rent his curtain; that it was of utmost importance, and that we were willing to pay any price and to return it tomorrow or even later this evening. The man eyed Damon, and then agreed, as if understanding the purpose of my request. He asked for a large deposit, three-fourths of which he would give back to us upon the return of the curtain. The withheld portion would be used to dry clean the curtain, he said.

As he was unhooking it, I asked him where the nearest

hotel was. He told us it was the Regency, around the corner.

Damon wrapped himself in the curtain and we walked down the street in this fashion to the Regency Hotel. We never got to find out if the Regency would allow us to check in, for the doorman wouldn't let us through. So we kept walking, hoping to come upon another hotel. We did: the Pierre. This time we would be sly.

Damon stayed outside, out of sight, while I went inside and checked us in. Then I fetched him, and we were able to get in without anything worse than glares.

It was a relief to finally be alone in a room with his impractical nudity. We sat on the bed and hugged and commiserated. We went to bed early.

The next morning, while Damon waited in our hotel room for what was supposed to be only a short time, I went to my apartment building to fetch his transparent clothes. To my surprise, my parents were there, keeping watch outside my building, with real, lethal antique swords at their waists.

"How long have you been waiting here?" I asked them.

"Since yesterday," said my mother.

"Don't you have anything better to do with your lives?" I walked into the building, and they followed me.

"No," answered my father, climbing the stairs after me. "We have nothing better to do than to save our daughter, who has lost her mind. We want an explanation. Why did you bring your own kidnapper to dinner?"

"I love him."

"You *love* him? But he *kidnapped* you!"

"Well, now I love him."

"Why?" asked my mother.

"Because he's great."

"But he *kidnapped* you!" repeated my father.

"Well, I kidnapped him too," I said, unlocking the door to my apartment. "So now we're even. I kept him in a cage and I fell in love with him. I got to see him living. And I got to find out about his tragic past."

My father forced his way into my apartment, and said, "No past can justify what he did to you. And how remarkable can one's way of living be, in a cage?"

"Not remarkable. He was human and enchanting."

I took Damon's transparent outfits out of the closet: his shirt and pants, and the gown he had made for himself. My mother grabbed them from me, said to my father, "Look, it's his clothes," and held the shirt by its shoulders, letting it hang in front of her. My father took his sword out of its holder and slashed the shirt to shreds, and then held the pants while my mother did the same to them and then to the gown.

This was a problem and a drag. There was only one thing left for me to do. I left my apartment and walked to the nearby fabric shop. It was a bridal fabric shop, which I entered with my parents at my heels, their hands on their swords, like guards.

For a variety of reasons, ranging from the fact that there was a generous selection of lace, that the translucent silk there was not very thin nor very translucent, and that Damon had seemed to enjoy the holes in the curtain tremendously, I decided to buy lace instead of silk. I was attracted to one roll of lace in particular, called "embroidered tulle scallop lace." I read the label: $13.50 per yard, imported, made of polyester and rayon. It was off-white, supple, satiny, and very see-through due to the fact that much of it consisted of tulle and not of embroidery. The little embroidery there was formed a pattern of birds.

I asked the salesperson if there happened to be an employee in the shop who might be interested in immediately sewing a rough, basic outfit for a six-foot-three male. The person I was talking to was willing to do it for a good deal of money and said it could be ready in an hour.

I was relieved that my parents didn't grab the whole roll of lace and slash it to bits. I went to a pay phone outside with the intention of calling Damon and telling him why I was taking so long, but after I dialed the first three digits of the Pierre Hotel, I realized my parents were on either side of me, watching me like hawks, ready to pounce on the opportunity to find out where Damon was. I hung up the receiver, feeling sad that he would be wondering, all naked and fragile, where I was.

I had to take more drastic measures or my parents would follow me to the Pierre. I went back to my apartment, still followed by my parents, and grabbed my pepper spray. I also took my antique sword—the present from Damon—which had allowed me to escape from him and would now allow me to rejoin him safely.

Just as I was about to leave, the phone rang. It was Damon, wondering what was taking me so long. I was ecstatic to hear from him.

"My parents slashed your clothes," I explained. "I had to go and have an outfit made for you, and now they won't leave me alone, so I came back home to get weapons. I won't be much longer."

My parents grabbed the phone from me and insulted Damon and tried to find out where he was. I threatened them with my spray and got the receiver back. I told him I'd see him as soon as I managed to ditch them. When I hung up, my mother tried to trace the call, but without success.

I left my apartment. They followed me.

I had half an hour to kill before Damon's costume would be ready, so I sat in a café. My parents pulled up chairs and sat at my table. I didn't bother using the weapons on them quite yet, since they knew I was headed back to the fabric store anyway.

They tried to make me regain my senses. They threatened to have me kidnapped by a cult-deprogrammer.

Finally, the half hour was killed, and I got the outfit from the tailor in the fabric shop. My parents immediately tried to take it from me. I threatened them with the pepper spray. They drew their swords. I drew mine. I backed out of the shop. The salespeople stared.

It suddenly dawned on me that perhaps I should consider getting a bodyguard. I was, after all, a star. And I could afford one. A bodyguard who would carry a sword around and fight my parents on their own miserable level.

I hailed a cab and shook my weapons at my father, preventing him from getting in with me. "I'm twenty-eight years old!" I shouted. "Leave me alone! I can do what I want!"

He hailed another cab and hopped into it with my mother. They sped after me. This time it took a while to ditch them, their driver being more skilled than mine.

I eventually went back to the Pierre Hotel and gave Damon the precious outfit. He liked it, and it suited him well, although it looked even more strange than his usual costume of translucent white silk.

When I told him all the trouble I had had with my parents, he grew sad and sullen, but didn't want to talk about it.

We returned the curtain to Stress Less Step, and that night I decided to take him to dinner at Auréole, a very good nearby restaurant that I hoped would cheer him up. But it didn't. I asked him again why he seemed so down.

He said, "I think I should leave. I'm causing too many problems in your family."

"What do you mean: leave?"

"Just for a while. To let things settle down, to let your parents calm down."

"I don't think that's necessary. I'll talk to my parents. I'm sure I can improve things."

"I doubt it. And even if you can, it'll take time. On top of it, there's a project I've been wanting to work on. Unbeknownst to me, what I needed was time to do nothing but think, and my stay in the cage gave me that time. I came up with ideas. And then our last few weeks of happiness together inspired me, they opened up my imagination even more. It may sound corny, but they provided me with the poetry I needed to give life and meaning to my ideas. But I'll miss you."

"How long will you be gone?"

"Oh, I don't know. Maybe a month, maybe less, maybe a little more. But we can visit each other, perhaps, after a while, when your parents aren't stalking you as much."

That night, in bed with him in the hotel room, I cried.

I hoped that by the next day he would have changed his mind. But he didn't. When we had lunch, he seemed even more depressed than the night before. He said he was sad to be leaving, especially at a time like this, and that he would miss me. He wasn't even sure he'd be able to concentrate on his work.

"Then don't go. Or let me go too."

"Your parents would suffer. This is really the best thing to do, for now. I'm sure you can see that." He was speaking in a whisper, his head bowed over his plate, and I almost expected to see tears splatter into his soup. In his lace, he was beautiful and foolish-looking at once.

I could take it no longer. I said, "Damon, I saw your brother."

He slowly lifted his face and gazed at me stunned, so I went on: "I met him, I spoke to him, and I know all about your past."

"Are you serious?"

"Yes."

"When was this?" he asked, his tone growing urgent.

"That time I went to L.A. Before I freed you."

"How is he?"

"He's fine."

"What did he say about me? Does he still hate me?"

"No. Never has."

"But he hasn't wanted to see me in years."

"I know."

"Why the hell didn't you tell me you saw him?"

I was hurt by his tone, but understood it. "I didn't want it to affect what was happening between us. I'm sorry. I meant to tell you, so many times, but I didn't want it to change things. We were so happy."

"You were selfish."

"Yes, for both of us."

"No, not for me. I would have appreciated knowing."

After a long silence, he added, "And that's why you came into my cage."

"Yes."

"You felt sorry for me."

"No. I mean, of course I felt sorry for you, but that's not why I came in. It's because your past gave me an excuse to forgive you. And I *did* want an excuse. I had been wanting one for a long time."

"I can't blame you for being selfish and keeping this from me. At first you were more selfless with me than I deserved."

"I hope you'll still feel that way after I tell you that your brother wants to resume contact with you. I'm sure it's something you would have wanted to know sooner. I'm sorry I didn't tell you right away."

I never saw Damon so surprised and excited. "Are you sure? Did he actually say it or are you assuming?"

"He said it. His words were, 'Tell Damon I want to resume contact. Maybe it'll help him regain some of his sanity.' The reason he added that last part was because I told him you had kidnapped me and all that."

Damon insisted that we pay for the bill right then, before we had finished our lunch, so he could go back to our hotel room and call his brother.

I offered to wait in the lobby to give him privacy while he talked on the phone, but he said he no longer wanted to hide any part of his life from me.

He was able to reach Philip at home, and they talked for about half an hour, catching up on the last eight years of their lives. He told Philip he'd been watching him on *The Bold and the Beautiful* every day, and then added,

"Oh, she told you already." He also told him about his invention of small clouds, and that he was trying to make them solid. "You'll have to see them," he said. Finally, he told Philip that we were in love, and then he laughingly informed him that I had kept him in a cage until just a few weeks ago. At that point Damon handed me the receiver; Philip wanted to speak to me.

"So," said Philip, "you didn't tell me you had my brother locked up while you came to visit me."

I chuckled.

He quickly added, "I'm very happy for the both of you, and I hope you'll come and visit me again. And don't tell him you threw me off the diving board or he might get jealous."

I laughed.

Damon discussed with Philip his plan to fly out to L.A. that evening to visit him.

As soon as he hung up, Damon made love to me, adoringly and cheerfully.

Then he wanted to go to Bloomingdale's.

"Why?" I asked.

"I can't keep wearing this outfit; it's too embarrassing, this lace."

"But I don't think they have transparent clothes for men there."

"I'm sure I'll manage to find something better than this."

"I doubt it," I said.

At Bloomingdale's, he headed for the men's department, on the main floor, where there was not the slightest piece of transparent clothing in sight. I knew; I had searched before.

But Damon didn't look around. He went straight to the turtleneck department and grabbed a *very* opaque, dark blue one. I looked at that piece of opaque clothing as if he had lost his mind and was handling a very dangerous material that he was highly allergic to and that could have disastrous consequences when handled improperly, like how a nut is, for people allergic to nuts. He took off his lace shirt with almost as much eagerness as he had taken off his clothes for my parents two days ago. He donned the hazardous turtleneck.

He then grabbed a pair of pants from a rack, took off the turtleneck and handed both items to the salesman in order to pay for them. The salesman eyed his bare chest, and mumbled some kind of disapproving comment like, "The store doesn't approve of improper attire."

"I understand," said Damon. "Forgive me." And Damon put the shirt back on as soon as he had bought it.

He then took off his lace pants, and for a few seconds was completely naked from the waist down, which caused the salesman to loudly say, "Excuse me sir, this is absolutely unacceptable in this store. If you don't put your clothes back on this instant, I will call security, and action will be taken against you, which I can assure you will not be pleasant. You will be punished according to the policy of our store, which consists in being deprived of your privilege to return your purchases for a full refund."

By the time the man had finished talking, Damon had finished putting on his new opaque pants. I took his lace clothes out of the wastebasket where he had deposited them. I thought this was wise, in case of clothing intolerance or a delayed allergic reaction.

But I wasn't around him long enough to find out. We embraced each other—he passionately, me tearfully—and he was off to L.A.

Chapter Fifteen

Damon's visit with his brother had lasted a few days and had gone well. It had left him feeling relieved that they had resumed contact, but pained at the sight of his mangled body. What was most upsetting, he said, was the extent to which the child's death had scarred his brother's expressions.

After visiting his brother and before returning to me, Damon worked on an invention that had nothing to do with trying to make clouds solid. Even though we spoke on the phone every day, he wouldn't tell me more about it.

During Damon's absence, I tried to persuade my parents to accept my relationship with him. I begged them; I even fenced with them willingly. They threatened to cut me off. I threatened to cut them off.

"He's dangerous. You can't be safe with him," said my father.

"Yes, I can be, and I have been, and I will be."

"Don't you care what this does to us? You are ruining our health. Not one moment passes these days when we are not stressed."

"He's not dangerous anymore," I said. "What made him dangerous has been resolved. He can even wear opaque clothing now."

"Oh boy, the mere thought of that dinner and his strip-tease gives me a headache. It's easy to say he's not dangerous, until we find you lying dead in a ditch somewhere."

"And then won't you wish you had listened to us," interjected my mother.

"He's an extraordinary person," I said meekly.

"Why? Because he can make small clouds?" said my father. "That's the most useless thing anyone could ever do. What good is it to anyone?"

"And he's working on an invention now that sounds very remarkable," I said.

"I'm sure humanity can do without it."

Neither they, nor I, made any progress. Perhaps they softened a little more than I did, but they refused to make any promises to behave in a more civilized manner, to stop chasing me in cabs, to stop stalking my building, etc.

The next person I had to deal with was Nathaniel. I had seen him on rare occasions, and he had been acting so miserable since I broke up with him, despite my willingness to remain friends of sorts, that I asked him about it. He finally said: "You broke up with me. I accepted it. You agreed to remain friends. But you haven't been acting like a friend. You've become secretive and uncommunicative."

"I told you it would be different," I said. Nevertheless,

to make him feel better—or worse, I'm not sure—I told him all about my involvement with Damon.

To my surprise, he was entertained by my story of the cage, and of my meetings with Damon in public places for safety reasons, and of my overall love affair with my own kidnapper.

The only thing he reproached me for was having introduced Damon to my parents.

"What were you thinking?" he said, a bit harshly. "That was an ill-thought-out move on your part; it was bound to fail miserably. Now you may have alienated him."

I was annoyed by his pessimistic attitude, but said nothing. The visit ended well; Nathaniel seemed in good spirits—considerably cheered up, in fact—to my slight confusion. I wondered if I understood anything about people.

While Damon was away, my friend Jeremy asked me to baby-sit his cat, Minou, for a while. I missed Damon and welcomed the company, even though I was busily working on a film almost every day.

Three weeks after Damon left me and the city, he finished his invention. He still wouldn't tell me what it was, but said he'd be back in a week and would show it to me then, after doing some more tests on it. He added that he couldn't wait to see me.

To my surprise, when Damon came back, he was wearing his old transparent clothes. But now he was also wearing huge, clunky metal shoes. I was very happy to see him and hugged him as soon as he walked in the door—or rather, as soon as he wobbled in (due to his weighty shoes). He kissed me and held me tightly. In my arms he felt unsteady, as if tipsy or tired. He sat down in a chair and was smiling expectantly, perhaps waiting for me to say something.

"How've you been?" I asked.

"Very well," he said, nodding and still grinning.

"Have you had trouble wearing opaque clothing?"

"No trouble at all. I'm dressed like this today out of necessity. But don't ask me about it right now."

"Did you bring your invention?" I looked at his big shoes.

"Yes."

He got up and walked to the middle of the room. He unlaced his shoes. So I was right: the invention involved his shoes.

He slipped one of his feet out of one shoe, and then slowly, delicately, slipped the other foot out of the other shoe.

"Do you remember how badly I wanted to make clouds solid?" he asked.

"Yes."

"Well, I failed. So then I thought: if you can't solidify them, join them."

"What do you mean?" I asked.

He gently hopped once. But the word *hop* is not accurate because it implies coming back down right away, which he did not do, at least not very quickly and not before having practically reached the ceiling. I understood then what he meant when he said he had joined them.

I felt weak.

Still, the explanation for what I was seeing had to be less far-fetched than that Damon had become a cloud. "Have you become bionic?" I asked.

"No. Just light."

And he hopped again, and started leaping around the room, like a gazelle, practically hitting the ceiling each time, and doing it in slight slow-motion at that. His white flimsy clothes were fluttering and his blond hair was flowing. He looked like a privileged person.

After a while he stopped and stood in front of me. He took my hand.

"Raise me," he said.

He was indeed very light. He couldn't have weighed more than two or three pounds. I continued raising him until he was above my head. I slowly waved him over me.

Once down, he said he wanted to go to the car to get his accessories. He put his shoes back on and went clunking out. I went with him.

He took some bags out of his car, and we went back upstairs.

He opened his carrying case and out drifted a live rat. It floated in the air around us, trying to run away, but going nowhere, really. Minou, the cat I was baby-sitting, was transfixed. I had never seen a more miserable rat or a more excited cat.

"I had to experiment on rats before experimenting on myself," explained Damon. "I'm sorry about it. I'm not in favor of testing on animals, but I didn't know what else to do in this case."

He then pulled out of his shoulder bag some hypodermic needles and a tourniquet.

"Bring out the scales!" he exclaimed.

"What scales?"

"I know you have scales."

"I just have one."

"No kitchen scale?"

I brought out my human scale and my kitchen scale.

He got undressed and stepped on the human scale. He weighed two pounds. He wrapped the tourniquet around his arm and injected himself with a clear solution. We watched the scale, and within a few seconds he lost one pound.

"I want you to bring me closer," he said, stepping off the scale.

"To what?" I said.

"Zero."

"Why?"

"Cause then I can do even more fun things."

"Like what?"

"Like swim in air or be blown by your breath and stuff like that. The lower the weight, the more fun it gets. But don't let it reach zero or I'll die."

"Do you mean you'll die, as in: you'll be upset, or you'll die literally?"

"I mean the latter, and therefore the former as well. If I become completely weightless, I'll be more cloud than human, and there's no turning back. I won't regain my weight, I'll just eventually rain. Not right away. It takes a few days or weeks. But once you rain, you lose your life. You become a puddle."

He placed one needle and the tourniquet on my kitchen scale, which he then set to zero.

He stepped onto the kitchen scale himself, trying to find his balance.

"Watch the scale and tell me what you see," he said.

"Are you sure you want to do this?" I said.

"Yes."

"What if my scale is inaccurate and you've reached zero and it says you haven't?"

"Don't worry, it'll be fine."

He was about to inject himself, when I shouted, "Wait! Are you sure you got all the air bubbles out?"

"The liquid is weightless. You can't get the air bubbles out."

"But if you inject yourself with air, it can be fatal."

"I *am* air, or rather, cloud. It doesn't matter."

He injected part of the solution into his arm, and waited.

After a few seconds the scale steadied at eight ounces.

He injected himself again, and his weight went down to four ounces. He continued giving himself tiny doses of the solution, bringing himself closer and closer to zero.

"How close do you want to get?" I asked.

"Quarter of an ounce."

"That's crazy. My scale's not that good. You can't trust it at that level."

"I've done it before on my own kitchen scale, which is no better than yours."

"I don't believe you. How could you tell how close you were getting if you had no one to tell you?"

"I used mirrors."

He kept injecting himself with small doses until I lied to him and told him he had reached a quarter of an ounce, when he actually weighed half an ounce.

"Are you sure you're not fibbing?" he said. "I think you're fibbing, but let's try it anyway."

He stepped off the scale. "Oh yes, I feel heavy."

Naked, he jumped in the air, reached the ceiling, and slowly drifted back down like a balloon. Before he landed, he started kicking his legs vigorously and doing the breast stroke with his arms, as if trying to swim in air. And then he landed.

"*An-na.* You *fibbed.* I'm not supposed to land when I do this."

He went back on the scale and said, "I'm sure I weigh at least three-quarters of an ounce, which means I will inject myself with enough serum to eliminate half an ounce."

"If you do that you'll be dead. You weighed half an ounce, okay?"

"Okay. Don't lie to me anymore, or it can be dangerous. Be very truthful, very accurate."

He injected himself and we waited a few seconds. I then told him he had reached his ideal weight.

"Good. Now I'm as heavy as a Bic pen."

He stepped off the scale, jumped toward the ceiling, and did the breast stroke and kicked his legs. He succeeded in not landing. He slowly, very slowly, advanced in air.

After a minute, he stopped and landed. He was panting from the exertion.

"You know, I'll have to get a more sensitive scale so I can get closer to zero, because a quarter ounce still requires too much effort to stay up in the air for long. I bet that if I could get down to one-twentieth of an ounce, I could stay up in the air with as little effort as staying afloat in water."

We then played around. He asked me to blow on him, and I did: I blew him upward, I blew him away. I fanned him away. I opened the window slightly to create a draft. I tapped him like a balloon. He swam after the rat.

We even tried to have sex. When he was on top, he weighed nothing, which was pleasant on the one hand, but impractical on the other. The way we finally managed to do it was with me on top, pinning him down so he wouldn't float away.

Then came the serious question, as we laid side by side, the weight of my arm holding him down.

"Do you want me to try it too?" I asked.

"That's not up to me. It's entirely up to you if you want to try becoming light. I'm not going to pressure you or even encourage you. I'm pretty sure it's safe, health-wise, even in the long run, but I can't be absolutely certain."

For a moment I had a horrible vision of ourselves, a few months down the line, vomiting and shriveling up, due to having been injected with this potion.

"Is it fun? Becoming light?" I asked.

"Yes. It's like being an astronaut. But God forbid, if you reach zero by accident, you'll be like that rat, doomed to rain and die any day. I've already had three rats rain on me. It's something to think about."

"You won't let me reach zero, right?"

"No. I would rather rain a thousand times than let you drizzle once."

"Okay, I'll do it."

Damon made me light. He gave me a tiny dose at first, to see if I tolerated it, and if I wanted to go further. With that first injection, he made me lose ten pounds in about fifteen seconds. I giggled nervously. I felt giddy and, of course, light. It felt good.

As I soon found out, being twenty pounds lighter felt

even better. But no matter how good that felt, it was nothing compared to getting down to a quarter of an ounce. I had to perform the injections on myself, after a certain point, because any touch from Damon would have altered my weight on the scale.

Being light, very light, was not much like anything I had ever experienced. It reminded me vaguely of the liberating feeling one gets when someone offers to carry one's bag.

We bounced in slow motion around the apartment, danced and swam in the air.

Then we walked down the street with our heavy shoes (he gave me a pair of shoes like his) and took Damon's car out to the country, to a deserted road, and while one of us drove, the other was pulled through the air by a thread attached with Scotch tape to the roof of the car. When we had exhausted the fun in that, we left the car and climbed trees using only the tips of our fingers and the lightest pressure. We sat on branches no thicker than chopsticks. We swung off leaves.

When the weight came back, it came back slowly, which meant we started landing just a little quicker than usual when we jumped off the top of trees. We drove back to the city and injected ourselves again and waited till night so we'd be less visible when we drifted outside. We went to deserted streets and made sure no one was around, and then climbed up the walls of buildings. We lowered ourselves down to the East River. We held on to threads that we tied to the railing, so as not to be blown away. It was a very warm night.

The next day Damon bought a scale that allowed us to get down to one-tenth of an ounce: the weight of a jumbo-sized paper clip. And later that day we weighed in at one-twentieth of an ounce. We had so much fun at that weight. We didn't need to be any lighter.

That night the rat rained.

We spent the next two weeks enjoying our weight loss, playing with the freedom it gave us, injecting ourselves frequently and not spending much time at our regular weight. It was wonderful to hang on to birds. Or kites. Or one of those helium-filled party balloons, which would carry us up. When we'd let go of the string, we'd drift around or back down (depending on the breeze), like ordinary balloons. We rode on the backs of dogs and other small animals.

Walking on our hands was no problem anymore. Even walking on our fingers. We could run on the points of our toes, and jump that way, like ballerinas without needing toe shoes, and land that way. We could walk down the street on our bare points for hours if we wanted to and didn't care what people thought.

We could do flips in the air, and if we fell on our faces, it didn't hurt, and if we fell on our heads, we didn't break our necks.

As far as I was concerned, it wasn't possible for anyone to overestimate how much fun this was. If there was a heaven, weightlessness must be what it consisted of.

Due to our tremendously light weight, we were able to walk on water. And sit on it. We sat on rivers and took long walks on lakes and short walks on ponds and puddles.

We liked to sit on electric wires, like birds, and smooch. And then, when we got bored of sitting, we walked on those wires like circus performers, and when we lost our balance, we didn't fall, but drifted to the side.

The one thing we couldn't do was fly in rain. A few dozen raindrops weighed more than we did and made us sink to the ground, unless the breeze was strong enough to compensate.

The only really dangerous thing for us to do was to jump off the edge of a cliff or a roof or a tree while absentmindedly holding something in our hands, like a rock. Then, of course, we plummeted to the ground unless we had the presence of mind to let go of the rock before crashing.

But otherwise, walking off cliffs was fun. We called it "diving." We'd stand on the edge, take off our shoes, and push off for the wind to carry us.

Gliding until our weight returned was exciting, but we invariably regretted it afterward, when we landed far from our shoes. Sometimes we'd land in very undesirable places.

Once, we landed in the middle of a forest. The ground was prickly, which, while we were still relatively light, was fine, but as our weight increased, our bare soles began to sting.

A note about our shoes: I preferred the loafer style, to the style with laces, like Damon's. He liked to hang on to the laces with his toes while he bobbed in the breeze. I liked to be able to slip out of my shoes in a bookstore and float up to a high shelf. There was a big risk of getting caught, of course, which was why I always made sure to pretend I was *climbing* up the shelves, not floating up.

Damon and I also did some weightless socializing. For

fun we went to cast parties, wrap parties, and every other sort of movie party. We wore normal clothes and our heavy shoes. I think people noticed that we moved strangely. We had to be careful not to leave our muscles relaxed, otherwise our arms would be floating at our sides, like in a bath. It required hard work and concentration to look heavy when we were light. Of course, since our hair was weightless too and floating around our heads as if we were under water, we had to do something about it. We wore wigs in the style of our own hair. Sometimes we wore hoods instead. At home, after the parties, I loved to stand in front of the mirror and whip off my wig or hood and see my hair drifting around.

It was so sensual to cavort around weightless that we often became extremely aroused. But it was hard to have sex while being light; a bit like being on Prozac, from what I'd heard. To replace gravity, we had to use sheer muscles—but a whole different set of muscles than those required for traditional, weighty sex. We had trouble making each other stay in place. We were like two big balloons, laughing with exasperation, laughing so hard we'd feel spent, as if we'd succeeded.

Eventually we figured out we had to be intertwined in order to have light sex; I had to wrap my legs around his like vines. And once we got the hang of it, the floor was what became annoying. Our smallest movement would make us bounce up in the air, for many long seconds, and then we'd land. It was distracting to have the floor bump into us repeatedly during sex. We'd land in unexpected ways, like on our sides, but only for a moment, because we'd pop up again at the next movement. Sometimes we would slowly drift back down head first. When this wasn't the case, I'd kick the floor away impatiently with one foot, but when I did that too hard, we'd hit the ceiling, which could also be irritating. And, like a fly buzzing around us, the floor always came back, no matter how many times we'd shoo it away.

This was why we decided to have sex in the wind. We did it in the sky over the ocean at night. We hoped no one would see us. I wondered if we might get arrested for public lewdness. The wafting aspect would surely over-shadow the erotic aspect. Nevertheless, we avoided the full moon, not wanting to be back-lit.

We were carried with an uneven rhythm. The wind twirled us, flipping us over and over in the sky, like a dead leaf.

Our lovemaking tended to be gentle without gravity. And sometimes that was frustrating, when our passion was too strong to tolerate gentleness. We craved weight, the weight of our bodies on top of each other. Weight was sexy, as it turned out.

We'd be drifting and hugging gently, being loving. Like a spider patiently waiting on its web for an insect to land, Damon was waiting for a handle to come along. When that object came, Damon would grab it and slam me against the wall, the railing, the ladder, the seesaw, the root, whatever, anything resembling a handle or narrow enough for him to hold on to behind my back. Then the lovemaking could be stronger, almost as if we had weight. He bore into me with all the strength in his arms, revealing the frustration he felt.

And sometimes it was me. When his back bumped against the trunk of a tree, I latched onto the branches on either side of him, and I pinned him there and savored him, wrapping my legs around him and the trunk. But then, unable to resist sinking my fingers into his hair, I let go of the branches. He pushed us away, and we went off, drifting again.

We were like insects making love anywhere.

After the first two weeks of being light almost all the time, we cut down to twice a week, because of my work. Sometimes we still got light every night. It was very addicting. Not literally, that is. There were no withdrawal symptoms when we did an experiment and stopped for a week.

I thought I had the solution for making my parents come 'round to liking Damon. After having heard them so often say things about Damon like, "He's a loser, he's pathetic, he's mushy, he's pretentious, he's common, he's evil or insane, in any case dangerous, he'll make you unhappy," I could prove to them that he was extraordinary by shooting up for them and showing them I could float.

Understandably, they were horrified at first when they saw me injecting something into my arm. They said Damon was influencing me to take drugs.

Then I started floating.

My father said, "That's what drugs do. They give you the illusion of floating."

"Is this an illusion?" I said.

"Probably."

"Come on! Am I *hallucinating* that I'm floating?" I yelled at them from the ceiling.

"I don't know if you are, but we are. The fact is, someone here is hallucinating; there is a hallucination going on."

*   *   *

For Damon and me, it seemed things could not get better, that nothing could come between us. He continued to help me with my lines occasionally, when I asked him to. We lived in harmony. But then something did come between us.

It started when we sank into a routine. Flying was no longer new, and Damon became gloomy. He mentioned to me that he was having sick thoughts. When I asked him what they were, he just shook his head and said he couldn't tell me. I wondered if they had to do with a desire to be unfaithful. I asked him and he said no. Then I asked if they had to do with a desire to kidnap me again. He said no.

I mentioned to Nathaniel that Damon was having bad thoughts. He wanted to know what they were and urged me to find out.

But I had already tried and failed. And anyway, something else began happening, something that sort of overshadowed the issue. Damon started trying to kill me.

At first I wasn't sure if it was just my imagination.

He backed his car toward me, and if I hadn't jumped out of the way, it would have hit me. Once, when I weighed my full weight, he almost pushed me off my balcony, supposedly by accident, and another time it was supposedly playfully.

He "jokingly" put a pillow on my face for a long time, until I was practically suffocating. I don't know what would have happened if I hadn't fought him off as hard as I did. And when it wasn't a pillow on my face it was his hands around my neck. And he'd press. Nothing came of it, but it wasn't pleasant. And he looked very tempted to press harder and longer, unless that was my imagination too.

And I noticed he felt drawn to my sword. One night I woke up and he was standing over me with the sword raised, as if about to stab me, and I wasn't sure if I had caught him just in time, or if he had been standing that way for a while, not really intending to do anything. I'd see him in the kitchen sometimes, holding the big kitchen knife and staring at me in a dreamy way.

Granted, these attempts seemed ambivalent, but they preoccupied me. I felt depressed. I didn't want to bring up the topic with him, because I didn't want to acknowledge yet that there was a problem in our relationship.

I racked my brains as to what could be his reason for wanting to kill me; what could be his logic. Finally, it dawned on me what his sick thoughts were: he was afraid our relationship might be losing its initial excitement. To rectify this problem and to put spice back into the relationship, he tried to scare me by pushing me toward oncoming subways, for example. I was relieved that that's all it was.

I mentioned to Nathaniel that Damon was trying to kill me.

"What do you mean he's trying to kill you?" he said, very upset. "Doesn't he tell you he loves you?"

"Yes, all the time."

"Well then it's ridiculous what you're telling me. You're paranoid or something."

I told him the many instances of Damon's murder attempts, and then I told him my theory about Damon's need for spice.

"I don't think he's trying to kill you. I think he's just

goofing off, being playful. And I don't think he's doing it in a calculated way to add spice."

A few days after this conversation, Damon said to me, "There is an issue we haven't addressed."

"What is it?"

"The fact that I try to kill you from time to time."

"So you do try to?"

He nodded. "I'm afraid so. I didn't want to admit it to myself, but I can't hide from the truth any longer."

"Well, I'm sad to hear it. I was hoping it was my imagination."

"What do you think we should do about it?"

"Are you asking whether we should break up?"

"I don't think I could live without you."

"You may have to if you kill me."

"I know. That's why I'm tempted. The misery would be so acute."

"Maybe I could try to make you miserable in other ways. I could take on lovers. I could be mean to you. No, I probably couldn't. I love you too much. Can't you just use your willpower to control yourself?"

"I do. I try to resist the temptation to kill you, and I have, till now, succeeded, but it's a war within me. When the pain is so bad my logic is forced to accommodate it, the logic gets twisted into unnatural shapes."

I told him not to worry, that we'd work through his urges to kill me.

Deep down I believed he wouldn't actually go through with it, that he just needed to regularly scare himself about it.

*   *   *

Damon began to get notes on his windshield wiper that said things like, "Prepare yourself," and "Not much longer now." At first he wondered if *I* had put them there. Then we both wondered if my parents had. When I questioned them, they denied it. Soon the notes said "Brace yourself," and "Better late than never."

While I was visiting Nathaniel one day, he asked, while ironing his laundry, how I'd been, if things were still going well with Damon: "He hasn't tried to kill you recently, has he?"

"Sometimes he does, or at least he's tempted to, but as we're both aware of the problem, it's under control. It makes a big difference when you have good communication; you know, when the channels are open."

"Yeah, that's true. You know, there's something I want to tell you," he said, moving the iron carefully over the sleeve of his blue shirt.

"What?"

He sighed and, without looking at me, said, "I care a lot about you."

"I care about you too."

"I want you to know that I care a lot about you, and I love you, and I think you're an extraordinary person. You are so wonderful, and I never want you to think that you did anything wrong or that anything is your fault, but most of all, as I said, I never want you to think that I don't care about you tremendously, no matter what I do, no matter what happens."

At that point Nathaniel started to cry over his blue shirt. He placed the iron aside. I went over to him and put my arm around him and tried to comfort him.

"Please don't," he said. "You're making me feel worse."
I stopped.

"I didn't think this would happen," he said, "that I would cry. I am moved by my own speech. Something, you see, is making me sad."

"What's making you sad? What?" I felt dishonest for asking, because I was sure I knew: he was just heartbroken that I was in love with Damon and not with him. I finally suggested this idea.

"No, it's not that exactly," he said. "I can't tell you quite yet. I want to compose myself."

He tried to stop crying by closing his eyes and repeating to himself, "Think of Santa Claus, think of Santa Claus."

The phone rang.

He picked up the receiver and, still crying, said into it: "Etiquette hot line."

He listened for a moment and said, "No, you can't dunk. Dunking is not good table manners. You're welcome."

He hung up. He breathed deeply and looked more composed.

"Can you tell me now?" I asked, hoping I wasn't being too pushy, especially now that he had recovered and might feel more embarrassed by his display of grief.

But to my surprise he answered, "Yes, I can tell you now."

I did not spend a comfortable night tied up on Nathaniel's couch. Nathaniel demonstrated the procedure of how he was going to kill me, on himself, putting a plastic bag over his head the way a stewardess demonstrates how to don an oxygen mask. He was of the opinion that familiarizing

me with details such as the fact that I would die within
half an hour or an hour of the bag being closed around
my neck, and that my head might feel stuffy during that
time, would make me less anxious during the death experience; in short, according to him, my knowing what to
expect would make dying less stressful for me.

He said he regretted I would not have the opportunity
to live the rest of my exciting and promising life, but that
he had planned this for so long, even before my life looked
promising.

When I asked him for some explanation as to why he
wanted to kill me, he said it was because he didn't like his
jobs. When I asked him since when had he not liked his
jobs, he said since always. When I remarked that he had
never told me this, and that I had gotten the impression
he *had* liked them, he said: "How is that possible? You
know me. Do I strike you as stupid or boring?"

"No."

"Then how could you think I would enjoy being an
etiquette expert, or a Weight Watchers' counselor, or a
stripper? How could you think that someone like me, with
my mind, my character, would derive any satisfaction
from those things?"

"Then why do you do them?"

"Because I'm not able to perform my true profession."

"What is your true profession?"

"Plastic surgery. Please don't look too surprised, or
you'll hurt my feelings."

I was silent.

"You're thinking about something," remarked
Nathaniel.

"Damon's brother was a plastic surgeon."

"I know him."

"You do?"

"Yes, I'm Ben," he said.

"It's not possible."

"Why not?"

"Because you and I met by chance, in the park, when I was being attacked and you saved me. It would be too much of a coincidence if you turned out to be the enemy of the man I saved two weeks before you saved me."

"Yes, it would be too much of a coincidence. That doesn't mean I'm not Ben. It just means it's not a coincidence. I wanted to meet you, so I arranged your attack."

"Why?"

"Revenge. Against Damon. I have let this simmer, held back, until the perfect moment; the moment in your relationship with him when the feelings have had enough time to grow very strong, but not enough time to settle into boredom or mere contentment. It seems, however, that I may have waited too long. You tell me he tries to *kill* you? I mean, it sounds like he's losing his mind. Or you are. I hope it's you. But if it's him, how is a man supposed to get revenge on an insane mind?"

I said, "So all this time, when you pretended to be my friend, and even to love me, you actually didn't care at all."

He kneeled next to the couch, on which I was lying with my hands tied behind my back, and hugged me. "Goodness, Anna, that's not true! That's why I prefaced all this by telling you how much I cared about you. Don't you remember my preface? It was lengthy. I did love you and still do. More than I've ever loved anyone in my life."

"And yet you want to kill me?" A tear rolled into my ear.

He wiped my eyes and nose with a tissue, and said, "Despite the strength of my love for you, my desire for revenge is stronger. My life has been destroyed by Damon, and yet his life has not been destroyed by me. I can't let that rest."

"But you *have* destroyed his life."

"Not as much as he destroyed mine. Or at least not as directly, or as intentionally. I know he's the one who wrote that anonymous letter. Not his brother."

"How do you know?"

"From an article I read in *Soap Opera* magazine on Philip's life. I'm sure Damon and Philip feared I might come across it. Damon has not only ruined my career, but also my chance at finding love. My plan was to find a beautiful woman and improve her face; alter it in certain ways that would enable me to love her. But then, thanks to Damon, I was no longer allowed to perform plastic surgery. I did try to fulfill my dream anyway, when I met Chriskate, by having *another* surgeon operate on her, following my specifications. But as you know, the results didn't stir strong enough feelings in me. I had sent her to a doctor whose work I had followed and approved of. He and I didn't know each other, but we had a similar style and technique. As I later discovered, he only lacked the vision, the imagination. The work he did on her was good. It was commercial. It was trashy, commercial surgery. It had mass appeal, as was proven by her stellar rise to fame. But it was a little too easy, a little too accessible and light for my taste. I needed more depth and layers within her beauty."

When he had finished his story, Nathaniel asked me if there were any letters I wanted to write to anyone before I died. I tried the usual tactics to make him change his mind: threats, intimidation, begging, pleading, psychological tricks, lying, acting, wise arguments, reproaches, etc.

He said Damon would be notified of my location shortly before the event of my death.

Nathaniel expressed the hope that Damon would show up and witness my end. He then confessed, sheepishly and apologetically, that if this happened, he might decide to torture me (during my half hour of stress-free dying) to make the revenge be of superior quality. "If it does come to that," he added, "let me say in advance that I am very sorry, but also very grateful that you went through the unpleasantness, thereby fulfilling my wildest fantasies of justice."

Damon did show up. He had been warned not to bring the police, or I would be executed on the spot, regardless of the consequences to the executioner. So he came alone. He looked awful: pale, tired, ravaged.

My mouth was covered with masking tape. When Damon entered the room, Nathaniel pointed his gun at me, and with his free hand, pointed to a pair of handcuffs hanging from an iron bar attached to the wall. He told Damon to handcuff himself to the bar or he'd kill me.

"No," said Damon.

"No, what?" said Nathaniel.

"I'm not handcuffing myself."

"But I'll kill her."

"I understand."

"And it will not be painless for her."

"For me either."

"You mean her death?"

Damon nodded.

Nathaniel said, "That's right. That's the whole point. You will suffer."

"I'm counting on it."

"You're *counting* on it?"

"Why do you think I kept taking walks at night even after having been attacked regularly by men whom I assume were sent by you? Including that night in the subway when Anna saved me. It's because for a while now I've been a masochist."

Nathaniel turned his gun against Damon. "Handcuff yourself or I will kill *you and* her."

Damon handcuffed himself.

"That's better," said Nathaniel. A moment later, he added, "I will kill her with a plastic bag."

He took two rubber bands and slid them over my head. They fit snugly around my neck. He tore the masking tape off of my mouth. He slid the plastic bag over my head and tucked its edge under the rubber bands, making sure there were no leaks of air.

"It should take about half an hour for her to die," said Nathaniel. "Maybe a little longer, since it's a large bag."

Through the transparent bag I could see Damon staring at me. He said, "I love you, Anna," and did nothing.

"I love you too, Anna," said Nathaniel. "It won't be painful. I've decided not to use the torture, because this method of dying offers a subtle kind of horror, an exquisite kind of pain to the beholder. He'll see your face and lips turning blue."

Damon and Nathaniel began to talk.

"I'm finally getting what I deserve," said Damon. "It's such a relief, after all these years of torment and agony and guilt."

"It was wrong of you to write that letter, to ruin my career," said Nathaniel.

"No. It was wrong of me to have been the cause of my brother's suffering. So now, finally, justice will be done."

"You're bluffing. It's a ploy to get me to free her."

"No and yes. I'm not bluffing, but it is a ploy. The truth is that my greatest deliverance would come if you killed her, and yet out of love and guilt, I feel I should make an attempt to save her, and the only attempt I can make is to tell you that my greatest deliverance would be if you killed her. That is what would truly put me at peace; I would then have suffered as much as my brother suffered."

"Anna, did you know you were going out with a weirdo? It must be very disappointing to discover this on your deathbed." He paused and turned to Damon, "So you're telling me that the ultimate pain for you would be the pain of not having the pain. But you know, I think I'd rather simply give you the pain of having the pain."

The phone rang. Nathaniel answered, saying, "Etiquette hot line," and then said, "Actually, I'm sorry, that was a slip, I've quit my job and am no longer an etiquette expert." After listening for a moment, he said, "No, please don't insist. It can't be that urgent. No, please." He sighed. "All right. You say you're at your own party and a woman has walked in with dog shit on her shoe, and she's spreading it around your living room carpet, and your question to me is: Can you tell her? The answer is no, or you will forever spoil your relationship with her.

Chances are the damage is not increasing but decreasing with every step. She will eventually notice the problem on her own and clean it off in the bathroom, and she will never reveal that she was the culprit. You're welcome." Nathaniel hung up.

Just then, there was an explosion at the door. Damon's brother, Philip, entered the room in his wheelchair, holding a gun, an antique sword lying across his lap.

"Take that bag off her head," he said to Nathaniel, who happened to be gunless, having placed his weapon aside after Damon handcuffed himself.

Nathaniel hesitated a moment, and obeyed.

"Now untie her," said Philip.

Nathaniel obeyed. Philip tossed me the sword.

"Uncuff Damon," said Philip.

As Nathaniel did so, Damon stabbed him in the arm with a hypodermic needle.

"What are you doing?" asked Philip. "Will it kill him?"

"Eventually," said Damon. "In a few days."

"That's too *long*. I don't want to wait that long. I want to kill him now."

"Okay, but wait a minute. Take off your clothes, Ben," he said to Nathaniel.

Ben just stood there and did nothing, as he became light. "I feel light-headed," he said.

"No, you feel light, period," said Damon.

"Do what he says!" Philip shook the gun at him.

Ben took off his clothes. He hopped up in the air and did not come back down. Damon had overdosed him; he was clearly past zero.

"What is this?" said Ben. "Am I dead?"

"I suppose, in a sense, you are," said Damon.

"One sense is not enough," said Philip. "He must die in all senses of the word."

Philip rolled his wheelchair over to me and grabbed the sword from my hands.

He rolled himself under Nathaniel, who tried to swim away, in air. Philip slashed and poked his sword at him, but Nathaniel was too light to be pierced significantly. Each strike from the sword only caused him to bounce away, escaping with barely a prick.

When he reached a wall, he would push against it with his feet, to propel himself away from Damon, who came to retrieve him. Damon would tap him back, like a balloon, toward Philip's sword. Sometimes he simply tossed him back to Philip, who swung the sword at him like a baseball bat, sending him flying off in another direction, with a shallow wound.

Nathaniel begged me to make them stop. I did nothing.

The phone rang. Damon picked up the receiver and listened. He then hung up, and said to Ben, "The woman of the party said the damage did not decrease but increased and that you can expect to receive her carpet's cleaning bill."

Philip continued trying to stab Ben, but unsuccessfully. So finally, Damon lifted Philip out of his chair and raised him over his head. They were standing under Nathaniel, who was hovering horizontally, face down, near the ceiling. Philip stabbed Nathaniel through the stomach, tacking him to the ceiling.

Nathaniel screamed, and then gurgled, as blood floated out of his mouth. Philip dislodged his sword from the ceiling, and was placed back in his chair by his brother. He shook the Nathaniel-topped sword like a baby shaking a giant rattle. He knocked and banged Nathaniel against the floor, cutting the sword through his stomach further.

It did not take long for Nathaniel to die in every remaining sense of the word.

Philip slid the sword out of his victim, and the bloody corpse was left to float around the room while we fell asleep, exhausted from the turmoil. When the serum wore off, the body gently landed on Damon, who woke up with a low scream.

Chapter Sixteen

We didn't talk about it for three days, but finally Damon brought it up. He could tell I was upset about him having told Nathaniel to go ahead and kill me.

"No, I'm not upset," I said. "There's nothing you could have done, right? It was a ploy."

"What if I'm still tempted to kill you?"

"We'll cope with it. We've coped with it before, we can cope with it again."

"Oh, reckless Anna."

Personally, I knew how I would deal with it. I would make light of it. If I saw him staring at me dreamily in the kitchen while holding the big kitchen knife, I would wave my hand in front of his glazed eyes and say, "Hel-lo!"

And if I woke up in the middle of the night and found him standing over me with a sword raised, I'd say, "Can you please grab me a tissue as long as you're up."

I wasn't sure what I'd say if he pushed me toward an

oncoming subway train. I'd think about it when it happened.

Maybe I could get a whip with which to punish him if
he tried to strangle me again.

Maybe I'd take a class in self-defense.

Maybe I'd keep my pepper spray on me at all times.

But things didn't have a chance to come to that. A few
days after our conversation, exactly a week after Nathaniel's death, I found Damon floating around my living
room, clearly weighing nothing. He had overdosed—I was
certain of it. I knew it the instant I saw him, and I
was overcome with such disgust and horror that I almost
vomited.

Firmly, I said, "I want you to step on the sensitive
scale."

"It's not necessary. What you think is the case, is the
case," he said.

I burst into tears and rushed over to him and grabbed
him and lowered him and said, "What have you done?"

"I OD'd."

"How?"

"I can't live with you, Anna. You must know that. We
have to accept it finally. I'll kill you. We can't have a life
together."

"Damon, how could you do this? I can't live without
you."

"But with me, you won't live."

I was sobbing and hugging him. "You just had a problem. It could have been fixed."

We didn't know how long it would take for him to die.
I wanted him to find a cure. After pressuring him to no

end and convincing him that his murderous impulses could be toned down through psychological counseling, or maybe even through antidepressants, he finally agreed to try to find a cure for having become more cloud than man.

He locked himself in his lab for hours on end, searching, or so I thought. It turned out he *was* searching, but not for what I thought. He emerged a week and a half later with a big solid cloud. He had achieved his life's goal before dying.

I was furious. I shouted at him and my breath blew him away. He grabbed onto my clothing to anchor himself to me. I accused him of being clingy. I told him he killed himself, did it on purpose, so now he had no right to cling to me. What was he doing: being clingy and then leaving me? It wasn't fair. I told him that what he did was the same thing as a person injecting themselves with the AIDS virus on purpose, giving themselves a slow death, and I had never heard of such a thing.

Part of me wanted to detach myself from him emotionally, to diminish my suffering when he died. I marched out of the room, slamming the door, which he later asked me not to do again for it made him flutter around.

I tried to persuade him to spend the remainder of his time looking for a cure. I told him I'd help him, that he could tell me what to do. He refused, confessing that he had only pretended to believe he could be rid of his murderous impulses and masochistic tendencies. He didn't want a cure, and even if he did, he said there wasn't enough time to find one—he could already feel the rain coming. He wanted to spend his remaining time with me. So he did. It turned out to be three days. He spoke about my life, my future. He gave me advice, wished me happiness, told me how much he loved me.

And then he made love to me on the cloud. I retained my full weight, no longer willing to lighten up. I felt the cloud engulfing me, swallowing me, as if out of grief, the way I was swallowing my tears. The cloud felt too wonderful. It clashed with my pain and sadness. Damon and I should have been making love on a hard bare floor. A prison floor, perhaps.

I cried while he made love to me on his cloud. He had invented this heavenly thing, but at what cost? This was perhaps the last time we would ever make love. I held on to him tighter. Even though he had overdosed and therefore was now, technically, more cloud than man, he didn't feel different to me. Except perhaps that he seemed more perfect than ever, more suited to me, made for me. He was my complement.

He pushed me toward the edge of the cloud, so that my head was leaning back, no longer supported by his invention, hair hanging down, swinging. I wanted to fall off on my head, if possible break my neck. But Damon didn't let me. He pushed some of the cloud under me and covered my mouth with a kiss, suffocating me; my nose was filled with tears. I turned my head away to breathe.

I didn't want to come. I couldn't bear the thought of it, knowing he would soon die. But I couldn't help it. It was cruel of my body to play this trick on my heart. Afterward, I lay there, feeling vague. Vaporous.

I wondered if the loss of fluid had brought him closer to death. Each kiss might have taken minutes off his life. His climax: How many hours might that have taken off?

And that mist on his forehead, right now, was it stealing precious seconds from him?

Damon was content—I had come. He was kissing my breasts, my shoulders and neck, aware I was upset, but feeling content. I wished I could just evaporate and see how he'd feel then. I pushed Damon off of me and rolled from the cloud. I went in the bathroom, locked the door. I sat in the empty bathtub, the shower raining over me, my head against my knees. I focused on the hard cold surface I was sitting on, which I had craved.

Damon knocked softly on the door. "Are you okay, Anna?"

I took a deep, angry breath. "Yeah, I'm great."

I heard nothing more from him just then.

It was the next day, when I returned from the kitchen, that Damon was crying.

"Why are you crying?" I asked.

"I'm not crying."

"Yes you are. And why are you perspiring?"

"I'm not."

I said, "Is it the end?"

"Yes, I think I'm raining."

We didn't even know. We had to see it happen to be sure. And we did. And we were.

He took off his clothes and I helped him step into the bathtub. I took off mine and stepped in after him. I didn't want any of my clothing to absorb any of him. I didn't want to lose a drop of him. We lay down, he on top of me. I held him.

"I can't live without you," I said.

"Yes you *will*. You're strong. Do it for me, Anna. My love. Good-bye."

I kissed him, and my mouth got wet; the water dribbled down my chin.

As he rained, he became less opaque, more transparent, like vapor. He was harder to see, his eyes harder to find on the tiled background, his outline harder to make out, his voice harder to distinguish from the distant hum of traffic.

And I had some questions left, that occurred to me when it was almost too late, inevitably. I asked them, but I was no longer sure if the voice that answered me came from him or from my mind.

The last thing I heard was, "I love you, Anna." It was a whisper, like a breeze.

"I love you too," I said loudly, but there was no answer. "Did you hear me? Did you hear me?" But I heard nothing.

My hands were now against my chest, and he was gone. I saw nothing and heard nothing, not even my own mind.

I was lying naked in his shallow water. I laid there a long time, bathing in him, surrounded by him. I was crying.

"I can't live without you," I repeated, hoping it would bring him back.

His water cooled, and I sat there still, shivering.

When I finally got out, I dressed without drying myself and went to the nearest kitchen-wares store. I would waste no time preserving his water. I didn't want to lose any of him in the drain, in case it leaked slightly, or through evaporation.

I was crying as I looked in the store for what I needed.

But I couldn't find it. I knew what I was looking for, but I couldn't remember the name of it, so I went up to the salesman and tried to control my emotion as I said, "I'm looking for that thing that's used when people die, to put their water into a smaller container."

He stared at me blankly, shaking his head. I persisted.

"It's the instrument that is used when people die, when you want to transfer their body into a jar and you don't want to lose any of their water. You would use this instrument for that, for the transference."

He looked at me without answering, stunned. He finally said, "I don't know what you mean."

I drew the outline of a funnel in the air, with my hands. I said, "You pour water in the top, and it goes into a container with a smaller opening."

"A funnel?" he said.

I didn't recognize the word, so just stared at him no less blank than he had stared at me.

He led me to a funnel, and I nodded and sobbed more, and took the funnel and paid for it. I did not like the look of the funnel. I did not like the sight of it.

I stopped by the supermarket and bought four gallons of water. I emptied them on a corner of the sidewalk, and carried home the now much lighter four empty plastic containers.

I scooped Damon's water out of the bathtub with a glass, and poured it in one of the gallons via the funnel. It was a long process, but I continued until the four gallons were full. Then I bought four more gallons at the supermarket and repeated the procedure. Then again four more gallons. I continued until I had filled up twenty gallons with Damon's water. When the water in the bathtub was too shallow for me to scoop, I mopped it up with a sponge and squeezed it over the funnel, filling up two more plastic gallons. Finally I was done. His water took up twenty-two gallons.

I placed the gallons in my bedroom, near my bed, and the days began to pass. Sometimes I left the caps off, sometimes on. I did all sorts of things with the gallons. I tried to listen to the water, in case Damon could speak to me. I peered in and tried to see his eyes.

Before dying, Damon had left me lots of Light Serum (as we came to call it); enough to last me for the rest of my life, in case I wanted to be light a lot. He left me its formula, to do with as I liked—it was up to me to decide if I thought the world needed it, could benefit from it; he said he didn't care about the world. He should have known that I didn't care about the world either.

Anyway, I couldn't get myself to release the formula as long as I was grieving. It would be too frequent and painful a reminder of him if everyone started being light all the time and were everywhere, like Rollerbladers.

He also left me the formula for solid clouds and for small clouds. In addition to these elaborate instructions on paper, he had told me, in simplified form, the solution for solid clouds: it was to take the water by surprise, to abruptly change the speed and pattern of the whipping. It was a sort of trap that tricked the water into a position that was very unnatural for it, a position where it was no longer free, it was a prisoner of itself, it couldn't float apart: each part of it was attached to the other.

I kept the solid cloud in my bedroom, and kept my bedroom locked; I didn't let anybody go in. No friends. No one. At first I kept the solid cloud in my bedroom

closet; I didn't want to see it. I was still angry at Damon
for creating it instead of working on a cure that might
have saved his life. But eventually I started sleeping on the
solid cloud, occasionally. Damon had said solid clouds last
a few years before they rain.

I didn't release the formula for solid clouds either.
Having people riding around on clouds, everywhere,
wouldn't be great for my healing.

And I didn't inject myself with the light serum. I had
no desire to be light; my heart felt too heavy.

I missed Damon unbearably. I continued acting in films,
but I always carried with me at least one of his gallons.
And when I'd go out to dinner, I'd bring a small part of
him along in a very pretty little glass bottle in my bag. I
even had a vial on a chain around my neck, in which I
carried an even smaller part of him, against my breast.
Sometimes I unscrewed the tiny lid and spoke to the water
inside, like talking into a microphone. Sometimes I just
unscrewed the lid to let him in on the conversation, in
case he could hear. I often told his water that I wanted
him to come back to me, that I couldn't take it.

My grief may have endowed my acting with additional
richness and depth, for I was nominated for an Oscar. I
went to the Academy Awards, about nine months after
Damon died. For the ceremony, as a tribute to him, I injected myself into lightness, down to one-twentieth of an
ounce. I wore heavy shoes to compensate. I won the Oscar
for Best Actress. I went on stage to receive the award, and
I made my speech.

"Nine months ago, the man I love died. It is because of
him that I am here tonight, and I wish he were here with
me. Who knows, maybe he is. It *is* a humid night."

I paused.

"He was an extraordinary person," I said, and unveiled my head in Damon's honor, letting people see my hair floating around my face, as if I were underwater. "I'm not being sentimental in saying that. In fact, as I've told him many times in the past, if I could go back in time, I would choose *not* to go through what he made me go through to be here tonight. Being here is nice, but it's not worth it."

There were some chuckles.

"He was gifted not at making the right choices, but at being successful at whatever choice he made. If he found gravity annoying, he would invent a way to be unaffected by it. There was only one thing that had always hurt him. Wherever you are, if anywhere, my love, I hope your choice to end your life has finally allowed you to be un-touched by that pain. I miss you more than I can say."

I refused all interviews afterward and went straight home, which caused my agent to have a temper tantrum with me on the phone, followed by a few others in positions of power. I was finally forced to accept at least phone interviews, which I soon put an end to when I realized I was being asked, obsessively and almost exclusively, who was my hairdresser, and what method or product had he used to make my hair float.

I packed the solid cloud in a crate, loaded it in my car, placed the twenty-two gallons of water in the backseat, and headed for the country. When I reached the deserted area where Damon and I had often flown, I opened the crate, put the gallons on the cloud, mounted the cloud myself, and took off. I had no idea how I'd get back down, and I didn't care. I poured out Damon's water over the woods where we had floated so happily. After I had poured out the last gallon, as well as the pretty glass bottle and the vial I wore around my neck, I sobbed, and in shifting my weight around from grief, I fell off the cloud.

The next thing I remember was waking up in the hospital. I had a broken arm. I had been unconscious for one day. Someone had found me lying in the woods. The doctors informed me that I had fallen from a high distance and asked me how it happened. I told them I didn't want to talk about it. Word leaked out. The media speculated about whether "the mysterious actress had fallen off a tree or jumped out of a plane without a parachute."

I was released from the hospital after two days. I went home. I had no more gallons near my bed and no more solid cloud.

I can't deny that a small part of why I threw out his water was the hope that it would somehow enable him to come back to me. But since I would be a fool to count on this, it was mostly an attempt to put closure to my endless grieving. I hoped I would find it easier to get over him if I didn't have his water around, floating around my consciousness constantly.

What I hadn't predicted was that now that I had released him into the world, all water became precious to me. Damon could be anywhere.

During the week that followed my release from the hospital, I often stood on my balcony and looked up at the clouds and thought of him, and wondered if he was part of any of them. When it rained, I went outdoors and walked without an umbrella, crying, remembering the night when he rained in my arms. He was perhaps raining on me now.

Puddles made my throat constrict, tap water was especially upsetting, not to mention the water in toilet bowls. I could no longer drink water; it was too hard, psychologically. I had to get my fluids from other sources, like fruit juices or sodas. I regretted having thrown out his water; I hadn't anticipated the consequences on my mind.

What was more, I three times imagined I saw him, in crowds, at a distance, the way I had when he came back into my life after my kidnapping. Two of the men I thought were him were not him, and the other I was not able to verify.

I started wondering if I was insane. Why did I catch imaginary glimpses of Damon in crowds when in fact I was certain that if he were alive he would come to me right away? He wouldn't torture me that way. But then again, if anyone would, he would. And maybe it was hard to return to the real world abruptly. Maybe he had to seep back into reality slowly, gradually, or he would get some kind of toxic shock syndrome.

When I came home one day, a week or so after my return from the hospital, I saw a white rose on my balcony.

I took the elevator up and rang the doorbell of my upstairs neighbor, whom I didn't know. A handsome man answered the door.

"How did a rose get on my balcony?" I asked. "You must have thrown it from your balcony."

"I swear to you I did not throw it from my balcony. I didn't put any rose on your balcony."

I then visited my downstairs neighbor, just in case they had had the initiative to stand on their railing to give me a rose. But the tenant was an old woman, and she assured me she hadn't stood on her railing. I believed her.

I pondered the rose. It was very beautiful and of an amazing, almost colorful white. It was not damaged in any way. You'd think if my upstairs neighbor had tossed it down, it might have lost a petal, at the very least.

I remembered a time in my life when objects were left for me, with special messages hidden in the letters of their names.

The next logical thought occurred to me. I knew it was a long shot, but I would try. I went to my computer, opened my dictionary program, and typed in *whiterose*. I asked the computer to search for any anagrams using those letters.

A single word appeared on the screen.

I knew, then, that Damon was back.